Julie was born in Bovey Tracey, Devon and raised in the South Hams on the South Coast. After training as a nurse at the Gloucestershire Royal Hospital she moved to Australia and divided her time between working as a clinical nurse and within the music industry.

This is her first novel and draws on experiences growing up in the spectacular landscapes of South Devon and a passion from an early age to write.

She is a classically trained flautist, proficient horse rider and journalist.

She lives in the Blue Mountains World Heritage Area near Sydney with her husband and two children.

This book is dedicated to my parents Dorothy and Philip
Kemp; a life-time of inspiration.

Julie D. Jones

MOORLAND FORENSICS

BOUND BY POLARIS

AUSTIN MACAULEY
PUBLISHERS LTD.

A CIP catalogue record for this title is available from the British Library.

This book is a work of fiction, and except in the case of historical fact, any resemblance to actual persons, living or dead, is purely coincidental.

ISBN 9781786128829 (Paperback)
ISBN 9781786128836 (Hardback)
ISBN 9781786128843 (E-Book)
www.austinmacauley.com

First Published (2017)
Austin Macauley Publishers Ltd.
25 Canada Square
Canary Wharf
London
E14 5LQ

A huge thank you to my husband Terence for his forensic input, worldly knowledge and support. My children Alexander and Tamsin.

To those who have been on this journey with me: Fiona, Harold, Ian, Máire, Niall and Niki. Friends and family in the U.K. and Australia.
The team at Austin Macauley, for making this possible.

PREFACE

March 25th 2001 – Dartmoor- A place of rugged beauty

Dartmoor was tainted by the remains of a harsh winter. Ponies had perished knee deep in snow and a place known for tranquillity was quickly transformed into ugly peril. Even as Spring tried to creep to the surface there was nothing endearing about the gale force Arctic winds howling relentlessly in off the English Channel. Just as the forensic team brought the first body up from the basement, placing it only metres from the front door, a light flurry of snow drifted in; gradually defining every footprint clearly on the crisp, white mantle.

The first body lay shrouded in mystery with no indication of what had taken place out on the vast moor. She was pretty, estimated to be in her late twenties; at this stage she had no name, just a tag around the wrist and ankle labelling her as victim number one. Twenty-three minutes later the fifth and final victim was above ground as the wind chill factor dropped well below zero.

The forensic team set about their work in silence, trying to unravel the truth behind their gruesome discovery. A quick survey indicated all five women had been killed within the last six months. Their untimely deaths so horrific even the chief forensic officer had to turn away at first glance. So bad were the injuries of one victim, it would take several months to identify her.

At exactly ten twenty-four Ted Cartwright was handcuffed and marched from the house by two plain clothed detectives. Staring straight ahead his unblinking eyes were two small slits of grey granite. If he had emotion he didn't show it.

There was no known motive for the killings and all through the trial Cartwright proclaimed his innocence. He denied ever meeting the victims so how could he possibly have murdered them?

Was there a faint chance Cartwright hadn't been the one to execute these horrific crimes? Had he been erroneously convicted of the heinous acts?

Almost fifteen years to the day the controversial book centred on those murders was published – The Sinner's Daughter.

CHAPTER ONE

There was an urgency in James's voice as he barked instructions through the intercom 'Drop everything sis, grab a lab coat and come through the airlock.'

Looking up, James pointed to a row of labelled Erlenmeyer flasks sitting on racks in the cold-room 'I want those concentrated down and made up to specific volume in labelled 50 ml grad flasks. Use the fume cupboard and be careful when extracting the solvent, it's toxic and highly flammable.'

For the next hour, the siblings worked quietly with little passing between them.

The Western County Foods extortion investigation coupled with the Totnes warehouse fire tests had fallen dangerously behind schedule; the consequence of saturated electrical systems requiring a total new rewire. The rains of February had not been kind.

Both jobs were huge billing items for the company and vital in the year's budget. If Katie could get the results finalised and invoices sent to the Home Office within the week her holiday in the Algarve was safe. She was on a mission.

Katie transferred final solution phials to the automatic sampler attached to the Gas Chromatograph whilst her brother worked with an almost nonchalant confidence and efficiency fine-tuning the magnetic intensity and accelerator voltages on the Mass Spectrometer.

'I need you to warm up the High Performance Liquid Chromatograph' James ordered breaking their code of silence. 'We need secondary back-up confirmation on the GC results'

The exacting, intricate tasks were undertaken with methodical precision; there was no room for error.

'Look at that, just what the initial Infra-Red spectra indicated!' James whistled after hours of toil as they scrutinized a series of peaks emanating elegantly from two chart recorders and analysed the mass spectra of compounds on the computer display. 'Do us a favour Katie and plug the peak areas into the data analyser. It's already calibrated for common pesticides and accelerants.'

'I can't believe how Bristol missed those poisons' Katie commented, 'Probably just sloppy sampling procedures by a junior lab tech.'

'I'd give my right arm to be a fly on the wall at forensics after that stuff up' chuckled James triumphantly 'That guy really had it in for Western County. If those soups had got into the supermarkets just about every emergency department in the country would be overflowing'

'I wouldn't fancy dinner laced with over 1000 times the limit of paraquat and malathion.' Katie winced. 'Interesting he chucked in Copper Arsenate as well. Thank goodness our UV-Vis was working. I almost passed on the technician visit.'

James declined a comment instead suggesting Katie throw in the fire results, 'They'll be grateful we confirmed the detection of kerosene as the accelerant. They can now proceed with arson against the owners. When the shit hits the fan up there tomorrow the media will have a field day. I reckon we can double our fee for this one, no questions asked.'

Katie exhausted by the absorption of work sighed and sank heavily into a chair taking the weight off her aching feet.

James grinned noting the tired expression etched across her fine features, 'We'll make a chemist out of you one day Sis.'

'Not bloody likely.' Katie scoffed. 'It'll take a lot more to convince me to follow a career path in forensic chemistry.'

Whilst James started on the clean-up Katie reflected on her unusual lifestyle. Never in her wildest dreams had she envisaged being part owner of Moorland Forensics with her brother and sister.

Their two storey premises, a converted, non-descript shop front in Bovey Tracey, concealed a fully self-contained operation a short stroll from the old woollen mill. The location was ideal, allowing easy access to the A38 linking the regional centres of Plymouth and Exeter. The building had been cleverly designed for their own needs and specifications. The main office was downstairs; off which was a kitchenette, as well as an extensively kitted out forensic laboratory occupying a dedicated extension outback. The upstairs housed a compact bathroom and double bedroom.

Bovey itself was a smallish, almost 'cosy' town boasting origins to the late Anglo Saxon period before the Norman Invasion. Most of the houses and buildings fronting the narrow, winding high street were built of local granite or painted brick. Due to its pristine location on the edge of Dartmoor National Park it was rightfully known as 'The Gateway to the Moor'. The town and local area were steeped in pottery making and quarrying stretching back to medieval times.

Katie's eyes fell towards the answer machine sitting on her desk. With the light flashing green, she pressed the message retrieval switch.

'Nick here, I've got a potential case for you. Muriel Jennings a sixty-five-year-old widow attacked in her home on the outskirts of Ashburton.'

Katie recognized the voice of Nicholas Shelby, a prominent government forensic practitioner and colleague who referred many cases their way.

Nick's referrals could sometimes be obscure, mostly criminal matters in which the Devon County teams never showed particular interest. Although Katie was not always directly involved in specific lab work she took great interest in the workings and machinations, picking up a lot from being a Clinical Psychologist. Occasionally, like today, she was drafted in to help with testing in the lab or site visits.

The others brought differing expertise to the company; Fiona was a forensic pathologist whilst James had grafted out a doctoral qualification in DNA marking at Exeter University. All of them had established reputations in their respective fields.

In the years prior to setting up the business they'd worked for the government at senior level with involvement in some notable cases; quite remarkable considering they were all well under forty.

Katie and Fiona shared little physical resemblance. Fiona, being on the stocky side didn't possess the same athletic physique as her sister. Her hair was much darker with her eyes set close together giving her a slightly brooding Celtic look. James and Katie displayed similar, classic Anglo-Saxon features: fair hair with striking blue eyes; to an outsider it was easy to tell they were related. Fiona bore the characteristics of her French grandmother and to her chagrin often a subject of mirth within the family.

James was without doubt the most ambitious of the three. Having authored some landmark papers on a variety of forensic subjects he was often asked to guest speak at different venues. His name was a by-word in international forensic circles. The setting up of Moorland Forensic Consultants had been his brainchild and a long cherished goal. James then convinced the others to throw the bulk of their grandfathers' half million pound inheritance into the venture and after five nerve wracking years of hard slog the business had finally moved into the black, helped by an increasing referral of cases, not only from the Home Office but from the defence and other private sources.

The laboratory, although compact, was expertly fitted out in accordance with government standards and procedures and included state of the art temperature control, refrigeration, quarantine, and sample security systems. The siblings were particularly proud of their analytical equipment. A Gas Chromatograph-Mass Spectrometer wangled on the cheap from James' ex Professor at the Exeter University Chemistry Department and a late model German electron microscope with associated probe attachments picked up from a research lab foreclosure in Truro. Completing the line-up were an Infra-Red and UV-Visible spectrometers, an old but top of the range Atomic Absorption Spectrometer and a recently purchased High Performance Liquid Chromatograph.

The main analytical instrumentation was equipped with automatic sampler systems down linked to the latest computer data sorting and analysing black boxes. When coupled with mainstream wet chemistry and chromatography testing the team could demonstrate an impressive analytical capability on a range of DNA, toxicology, microbiological and physical evidence which most cases could throw up.

Katie now relaxed after the morning's roller coaster ride settled comfortably in behind the reception desk to make a start on lab reports. Upstairs James could be heard in the shower singing a rendition of a sixties Bee Gees number.

Shortly after ten o'clock all three siblings had gathered in the office to sit down and discuss the message left by Nicholas Shelby. Fiona sat swinging from side to side in an Ikea chrome swivel chair, James in another whilst Katie positioned herself on the top of a ceramic work bench which the team had recycled from a government lab auction in Bristol.

'I spoke to Nick Shelby this morning on my way in,' James enlightened the others, absentmindedly tapping on the table with his pen. 'He's happy for us to work on this Jennings matter and is going to pop by soon to provide a brief.'

'What have you got so far?' Katie enquired.

'Mrs. Muriel Jennings was struck over the head with a blunt instrument between the hours of four and five yesterday evening. No one claims to have seen the attacker and the update from Torbay Hospital is she remains in a critical condition.'

'Not much to go on,' Fiona remarked catching sight of a silver Mercedes convertible pulling up in the courtyard. 'Here's Nick now. Let's hope he can fill in the gaps.'

Nick Shelby was over six feet and in his early forties. His silver streaked black hair lent a distinguished touch to his refined good looks. Although originally from the deep south of the "Shaky Isles" he'd lived in England over twelve years but a Kiwi twang was still evident. He'd known the Sinclair family for many years so was comfortable letting himself unannounced into the Office through the side door to join them. After grabbing himself a black tea he made a start on information he had to hand. To assist with his brief, he made use of the smart board on the wall. He also produced a stack of photographs which were spread out on a nearby table.

'Muriel took a hefty blow to the left temporal lobe. On impact, she collapsed to the floor in a state of unconsciousness. Her daughter found her at six twenty the same evening when she returned from work, upon which she immediately called an ambulance. Due to the laceration Muriel received to her forehead when the object made impact she lost a lot of blood.'

He paused for a few moments before continuing. 'On arrival to Torbay Hospital she was admitted to the critical care unit where she remains on life support in a serious condition.'

'Were there any witnesses?' Katie asked already guessing the probable answer but seeking clarification.

'None that have come forward,' Nick replied. 'The Jennings's cottage is in a fairly isolated location just on the edge of Ashburton so it could be that until we start making enquiries no one will report anything suspicious.'

'This appears to be a particularly vicious attack,' Katie remarked as she drained her coffee cup and picked up one of the photos taken at the crime scene. It showed Muriel lying in a left lateral position in a pool of dark red blood. 'Do we know much about Mrs. Jennings and why the attack might have occurred?'

'Apparently, she led a relatively quiet life. She was settling well into semi-retirement and a keen gardener according to her daughter Stella. She was living alone until Stella moved in a little over five months ago. No obvious reasons as to why this attack took place.'

Just as he finished his sentence Nick's mobile rang. He took the call. Upon finishing his face held a grim expression.

'That was the Hospital. Muriel had her life support switched off a little over an hour ago. This is now a full blown murder investigation.'

***

Stella Jennings was a small woman in her thirties with mousy brown hair. As she sat opposite Katie her hands visibly shook. Katie was conducting the interview as standard follow up psychological protocol. Stella had already provided a statement to a case detective and undergone preliminary, routine questioning. With the Jennings' home still under police quarantine, the Moorland office had been selected best location for the interview to take place.

'Do you have any objections to me taping our conversation?' Katie enquired placing a full box of tissues on the desk in front of her in case they were needed. She knew how difficult this was for Stella, but absolutely necessary if they were to proceed with the investigation into the death of her mother. Despite years of training and practice in interview technique Katie never found them easy. The victims' families were often a show of mixed emotions; grief, sadness, anger, and regret.

Stella looking drawn and tired gently shook her head. 'If this is going to help in finding my mother's killer I have no objections at all.'

Katie positioned the small metal tape recorder in front of her slightly to the left and pressed the record button hearing it gently hum into life.

'You've probably already answered some of my questions in the police interview, I'm sorry, but firstly I need to ask where you were the day your mother was attacked?'

Stella took a deep breath. 'I left for work at 8:30 in the morning. I have a part-time job as a cashier at a wholesale warehouse just on the outskirts of Bovey Tracey. I work permanent Mondays, Wednesdays, and Fridays – eight hours a day. My boss can confirm I was there that day.'

Katie made a mental note to follow this up.

'Did you notice anything unusual on your way to work? Anyone hanging around outside the house, anything odd or out of place?'

'Everything was the same as usual. Mum was still in bed when I left as she never gets up before nine. I'd taken her up a cup of tea and we talked about what was on the menu for dinner, then I left.'

'Did your mum have any enemies?' Katie enquired softly as she shifted in her chair to a more comfortable position, 'Anyone you can think of at all that may have held a grudge or wanted to harm her?'

'No one springs to mind. Mum was an astute business woman who helped run the family clay business but she made friends not enemies. In fact, my late father used to grumble about her being too soft.'

'Would you say she had a lot of friends?'

'A fair few but mum also enjoyed her own company. Apart from the weekly book club meetings she didn't venture out much socially, mind you at sixty-five that can often be the case.'

'What book club did she belong to?' Katie asked scribbling away in shorthand in case of tape failure. She was determined not to miss any of the conversation.

Stella smiled wistfully. 'They call themselves *The Bookmarkers* and meet every Thursday evening at the Bovey Town Hall between seven and nine. Betty Albright from Elm cottage introduced Mum to the book club and it became a regular part of her life. Mum's been a member for over five years. Some of the books she brought home to read were not for the faint hearted; strong emotional books. They also digested many literary classics. Mum attended every meeting without fail. On occasions if the village hall was being used for other things the members would meet at

21

Mum's. Mum loved hosting. She would spend hours baking cakes and knocking up sandwiches.'

Katie made a mental note to pass this information on to James and Fiona. Any *one* of the book club was now a potential suspect as all of them would be familiar with the layout of Muriel's house.

'What about the weeks leading up to the attack,' Katie asked. 'Did you notice any changes in Muriel either mentally or physically?'

'There were times when she seemed quite vague, almost forgetful, but I put that down to the aging processes,' Stella informed her.

'What about physically, did you notice any changes in her appearance?'

'She'd lost a bit of weight but then she was never a big eater and the weight loss had been going on for some time.'

Stella paused to take a sip of water from the glass in front of her. It was a few moments before she continued. 'Mum had complained of stomach cramps of late. I notified Doctor Ashcroft who was due to come and see her the day after the attack.'

As their conversation seemed to switch to small talk Katie pressed the stop button on the tape recorder before asking, 'Do you have family to help you through this difficult time?'

'My husband and I divorced two years ago and apart from my brother Mark there isn't really any one I can think of.' Stella explained. 'I have friends of course but I don't like to burden them with my problems.'

'I'm sure your real friends would be happy to help,' Katie reassured her. 'What about your brother Mark. Does he live nearby to offer support? This must be a tough time for him as well.'

Stella gave a wry smile as she reached for a tissue to blow her nose.

'He's based in London, but after hearing of mum's death he's moved back to Devon for a few months.' She hesitated for a few moments then added, 'I should be grateful he's around but Mark can be a tad over bearing at times.'

'I can put you in touch with some support groups if you would like?' Katie offered feeling sorry for the woman sitting opposite whose eyes were swollen and red from copious sobbing attacks.

'Thank you, but for now, I think I'd rather deal with this on my own. Not that I don't appreciate all you have done for me Ms Sinclair. Your whole family has shown exceptional kindness.'

'Has anyone explained what happens throughout the investigation?' Katie asked, trying to be as tactful as possible. 'I mean what happens next and when you'll be able to arrange the funeral?'

'Your brother did mention something about an autopsy but to be honest I wasn't really paying much attention.'

'Well as your mother's death is suspicious we need to conduct an autopsy to try and determine the exact cause of death. After completion of the autopsy you can start funeral arrangements.'

'Has a date for the autopsy been arranged?' Stella asked.

'Yes. It is scheduled for next Tuesday. Prior to that date I expect you would like to visit your mother in the chapel of rest.'

Stella mumbled a yes before breaking down; Katie's cue to get to her feet and creep quietly out of the office allowing Stella some privacy. This was part of the job she loathed; dealing with victim's relatives. Words were little comfort at a time like this.

Leaving Stella to her private world Katie checked out Stella's story about being at work the day her mother was attacked. She spoke with a Mr. Butler the duty manager who confirmed Stella was rostered on at nine thirty finishing around six. She also spoke with a young woman Felicity Wood who confirmed she had lunch with Stella that day. They'd wandered over to feed the ducks in the park eating sandwiches in the warm sunshine, no problems there. Stella could now be taken off the list of suspects.

When Katie returned from dropping Stella in Totnes she spotted James in the far recess of the lab hiding behind a row of gas cylinders humming to himself and working on his laptop. Mentally drained she flopped down into a laboratory chair letting the cool air wash over her.

'How did you go with Muriel's daughter?' James enquired, not bothering to look up from his keyboard but continuing to type at a busy pace. His fingers danced, robot-like over the keys.

'I learnt a few things but not a great deal.' Katie replied as she leaned over her brother's shoulder staring blankly at a mass of pathology results being analysed on the screen. Normally the results would mean something but right now everything looked foreign to her. 'According to Stella, Muriel had no enemies to speak of. She kept to herself apart from attending a weekly book club in Bovey.'

'So where do we go from here?' James asked. 'I take it either you or Fiona will investigate this book club she belonged to. That might shed some light on things.'

'Yep it will certainly be worth paying the book club a visit,' Katie agreed. 'How's your side of things going? Has Nick definitely scheduled the autopsy for next Tuesday?'

'I believe so but I'll get clarification when I speak with him later today. He's also working on a preliminary DNA report on crime scene evidence but don't expect anything for a few weeks, maybe longer; you know the difficulties with DNA testing. There's also some physical evidence he wants me to look at.'

'Who's conducting the autopsy?'

'Probably Nick and Fiona but I'd also like to drop into the Exeter mortuary if I can find the time. I have a feeling Nick will want to do as many path tests as possible. I can see it taking the best part of the morning to complete.'

James watched Katie head towards the door, shutting it quietly behind her. He then turned back to his computer screen acknowledging he would most likely be working well into the small hours of the morning. Sleep deprivation was an occupational hazard for most forensic scientists.

***

Liz Palmer was thankful her evening shift had finally come to an end. Normally she loved her position at Torbay Hospital as a Senior Critical Care Sister but losing a dear friend on duty just a few days prior had not been easy. It came as a huge shock to see Muriel Jennings on the list of admitted patients and even more of a jolt to witness her condition. Extreme bruising and facial swelling made her almost unrecognizable. Due to a possible conflict of interest Muriel had not been assigned as Liz's patient, instead she was allocated to Charles Sampson a very experienced Charge Nurse. However, even Charles's skills and expertise could not assist Muriel's recovery. With such horrific injuries and age definitely against her Muriel hadn't really stood a chance. It was a tough family decision to switch off the life support but the only sensible one.

Even knowing everything had been done to save Muriel, Liz felt angry at the end of each day. There were so many questions, yet few answers.

With her thoughts all over the place, Liz headed off the ward to grab her navy blue cardigan from the staff room.

Distracted she didn't notice someone huddled in a corner of the dimly lit room. It was a small muffled sniff that first alerted her to someone's presence. Liz jumped and edged backwards startled by the sound, just making out the slim features of Deirdre Mulligan, a close colleague. Deirdre was sitting on the floor knees bent up to her chest in the foetal position.

'I'm sorry,' Deirdre sniffed. 'I didn't mean to startle you.'

'It's okay,' Liz reassured her kneeling down beside Deirdre so they were on the same level. 'What on earth are you doing here? Your shift finished over five hours ago.'

'I just can't get thoughts of Muriel out of my head,' Deirdre replied between snuffles. 'How someone could deliberately harm her is hard to comprehend.'

'Yes, we're all shocked at losing Muriel,' Liz sympathised wiping away a tear trickling down Deirdre's flushed cheek.

'I just can't understand who would do such a terrible thing,' Deirdre replied glad to no longer be alone with her melancholic thoughts.

'Well I am sure it's only a matter of time before these questions get answered,' Liz reassured. 'Now come on let's get out of here.'

Liz pulled Deirdre gently to her feet and in silence they walked slowly through the bleak hospital corridors.

'Are you ever afraid of dying?' Deirdre asked as they padded quietly along in their flat, soled shoes working their way towards the main exit.

'No not really,' Liz replied thoughtfully. 'Are you?'

'No. Death comes to us all eventually,' Deirdre replied. 'I guess for some it comes quicker than others.'

The north wind filled every void of the vast house which seemed to protest and groan from old age. As she stood by the open window staring into the night she sensed someone touch her gently on the cheek, a soft touch like a feather gliding along in the breeze. Feeling compelled to know the truth she slowly turned around only to realize the fear she knew so well. She was alone; there was no one else in the room. The past was stealing back to haunt her.

CHAPTER TWO

Nick Shelby strolled into the office of Moorland Forensic Consultants to find James and Katie sitting behind their desks working through a large pile of paperwork. A raft of files lay scattered haphazardly over the floor which he expertly side stepped.

'DCI Rose has given us full authority on the forensic side of the Jennings investigation so long as we keep him informed on a regular basis.' he pronounced. 'I'm heading over to the Jennings place now if you'd like to join me?'

James put down his pen, slowly getting to his feet. 'There's nothing like a good crime scene to sink your teeth into first thing of a morning,' he announced.

Katie gave him a gentle shove. 'You're a masochist.' she jibed, before turning to Nick. 'If you don't mind I'll follow in my own car.'

'No problems,' Nick replied. 'Just be careful when you arrive at the property, quite a lot of the house and garden is still sectioned off. I've got a team conducting fingerprinting and a photographer finishing off his assignment.'

'Not a worry,' Katie acknowledged. 'I should only be an hour.'

Katie watched the guys heading out the door before saving a coroner's report she'd been collating. She then grabbed her jacket from behind the door before heading up town.

As usual Bovey was a hive of activity. She stopped on several occasions to chat with people she knew. That was the satisfying thing about living in a small community, the inhabitants were friendly. A total contrast to the frenetic years spent at University when she'd sacrificed a social life for the single minded pursuit of academia.

Passing the newsagents Katie caught an alarming headline on the front of the local paper. *'North Bovey woman battered to death – who will be next?'* Katie seethed inwardly. That was typical of the editor of the Star; Lana Gibbs and most certainly her boss Tom Markham. Lana always felt compelled to put the wind up readers; no doubt this sort of headline would get the results she wanted. People would be demanding answers, looking over their shoulders and not feeling safe to go about their normal existence. It also put added pressure on Moorland Forensics and the Devon Constabulary as the expectation would be for Muriel's killer to be apprehended without delay – no questions asked. Living in fear of the killer striking again would hardly be a boost to local morale.

Katie went inside the newsagents and bought a copy of the Star. Katie now had to notify James to minimize damage control. He would also be pushed into conducting a press conference just to satisfy the media. Passing a bin, she tossed in the newspaper – the right place for badly written garbage.

***

Nick pushed his silver 280 SL into gear, dropped the hood and switched on the period Becker Mexico radio before heading over Mill Bridge towards the picturesque town of Ashburton. Everywhere was green and alive, the imminent onset of summer heralded by a nostalgic mix of intoxicating fragrances and earthy smells. For once James could enjoy being a passenger drinking in the countryside he had grown up in from early childhood. It wasn't often he got to be chauffeured around especially in a classic high-end auto. Although money was not a consideration James preferred his 40 year old Land Rover. Despite the mandatory dents and scratches and a green paint job now looking more like camouflage, Old Bessie got him from place to place without too many hiccups. If the occasional thing went wrong, he could usually fix it himself cheaply and quickly.

Glancing out the window James noticed the hawthorn bushes with blackberries in abundance. A few foolhardy souls stood in the narrow lanes picking berries seemingly oblivious of the cars zipping past centimetres away.

For a while Nick and James drove in silence, eventually striking up a conversation about the Jennings murder by rehashing all the information to date.

As with most investigations the early stages comprised of a lot of information and evidence gathering. You couldn't go on assumptions; you had to gather the facts. No murderer would likely be convicted based on circumstantial or hearsay evidence alone.

Nick drove into the ancient Anglo Saxon town of Ashburton; the largest within Dartmoor, an unspoilt location popular with tourists and walkers. The name was recorded in the Domesday Book (1086) as Essebreton.

On approach to the Jennings property the house was abuzz with crime scene personnel clothed in obligatory white, disposable garb finalising evidence protocols, all assigned by Nick. Modern forensic search and gathering techniques were designed to capture even the smallest of physical and chemical evidence. Wide yellow tape sectioned off the entire cottage perimeter leading from the front pathway and around to the back door. Only authorized personnel were permitted access.

'My team is conducting a final forensic sweep of the house,' Nick remarked, climbing out of the car and lifting

30

up the tape so they could slide under. They were met by the senior officer who proceeded into a progress update:

'We're just about finished here, another hour I guess. Five of the team did another thorough walk round the grounds just in case we missed something. Nothing of any real interest there, we're now concentrating efforts inside the premises. Swabbed all objects and surfaces from front door through to back of the house for any possible DNA and biological.'

'What about physical?' interrupted Nick.

SOCO Heinz continued without looking up from his iPad.

'Well, not much that's suspicious apart from what we already catalogued yesterday in the vicinity of the body. House looks pretty clean generally. Took vacuum samples in hall and living room. UV brought up nothing untoward and no sign of any blood spill clean ups. Also been through the garbage and waste bins. A few stains on carpet and around the place but don't hold your breath; got samples anyway, probably pets. I don't think we need to use luminol spray anywhere. Oh yeah, also lifted fingerprints on just about everything.'

On conclusion of the brief James and Nick went in search of Stella Jennings. Although not permitted to move back into the main part of the house it had been decided Stella could access certain rooms under supervision; provided she didn't interfere with the forensic investigation. James and Nick tracked her down in the Summer House catching a few restful moments. She looked tired and weary from lack of sleep.

'Made any progress?' Stella enquired softly, shielding her eyes from the bright sunlight with the back of her hand as the two men approached.

'Some,' James replied. 'What you need to realise is this is not a straight forward task, it may take months to uncover vital clues.'

'You know I can't help thinking this has all been a terrible mistake,' Stella informed them. 'I'm inclined to believe this was a burglary, one that went terribly wrong.'

'You could be right,' Nick replied. 'Now if you'll please excuse us we're going to take another look at the crime scene.'

As the two men departed for the front of the house James asked the inevitable, 'Do you think it possible Stella is hiding vital information from us?'

'Probably,' Nick remarked.

James hesitated before replying, 'Well we both know a lot of murders are committed by loved ones or near family.'

Nick caught hold of James arm, 'Surely you're not suggesting Stella killed her own mother? She has an alibi for god's sake.'

'Yes but is it steadfast?' James questioned.

Nick kept walking, '…only time coupled with a lot of hard forensic evidence will solve this one. Prepare for a few long hours of half grafting James. The fun starts now.'

***

Katie pulled up outside the large, two-storey, chocolate box cottage with its traditional thatched roof noticing Nick's Mercedes parked up hard on the sloping gravel driveway. There was just enough room for her small Fiat to squeeze in alongside. She reversed into position, grabbed her essentials, handbag and laptop, off the passenger seat and managed to extricate herself carefully from the vehicle without scratching Nick's pride and joy. As she half expected the cottage garden was beautifully maintained, resplendent in a colourful display of spring flowers including bluebells and daffodils. Spring had arrived early this year following an unseasonably mild winter. Curiously, a small wishing well sat half concealed in a far corner, positioned next to a swing seat. The cottage and gardens exuded charm and elegance appropriate enough for the front cover of a glossy country lifestyle magazine.

Katie moved to the well simultaneously taking a coin from her purse. Being a great believer in superstitions she threw the coin into the well and made a wish.

'Superstitious, are we?' Nick laughed as he moved across to where Katie was standing. 'Do you honestly believe your wish will come true?'

'How do you know it just hasn't?' Katie laughed with a twinkle in her eye. She enjoyed seeing the puzzled look on Nick's face. They had been friends for a long time since college when Nick was finishing his MD in forensic pathology in London and yet he was still trying to work her out. James often commented on their suitability as a couple but neither ventured to make the first move. At thirty Katie felt there was a little more time before the need to settle down and start a family. Nick was edging towards forty-five but men didn't have the same constraints or wants as women.

'I think she got one over on you that time,' James grinned walking to join them. 'Stella is out in the Summer House, Katie. She knows we're here and happy for us to poke around.'

'Let's get cracking,' Nick commanded. He showed them through the house commenting along the way on evidence found at the crime scene.

'Definitely no attempt of a break in,' he reconfirmed. 'We can rule out Stella's assumptions. Muriel Jennings opened the door and most probably knew her killer.'

'What makes you say that?' Katie asked out of curiosity.

'Okay, picture this,' Nick used his hands for expression and to point out aspects of interest. 'Her body was found here near the entrance to the living room, a good 20 metres from the front door. This means the suspect was well inside the house before Muriel took a blow to the head. As there was no forced entry or a struggle we can assume Muriel was happy for her visitor to walk the length of the hallway almost up to the living room door.'

'Then she received the blow to the head,' James concluded conjuring up the whole scene in his mind.

'Precisely,' Nick replied pulling open the top drawer of a nearly cabinet. 'The murder weapon appears to be a blue metallic torch, which was usually kept in this drawer by the telephone, and whoever used it knew exactly where to find it. There is no way they could have found it on spec and then used it as a weapon.'

James nodded in agreement. 'Yep, the obligatory blunt object, he or she wouldn't have opened the drawer in the hope to find a weapon; they knew exactly where one was kept.'

'What I found odd about the torch is the batteries were dead,' Nick continued. 'Yet Stella insisted she only placed fresh batteries in the torch two days before her mother was attacked.'

'Could she be mistaken?' Katie enquired taking a closer look at the outlined spot where Muriel Jennings was found, trying to imagine the vicious attack and the angle from where the killer had struck.

'Of course but I very much doubt it,' Nick replied. 'Plus, she has a receipt for the battery purchase and following an extensive search we have yet to locate a new packet of batteries.'

'What's your theory?' James asked, learning back against a two tier buffet.

'I reckon someone, probably the killer, took the new batteries and swapped them with old ones.'

'Why would they bother to do that?' Katie was trying to follow this rather puzzling story. It didn't make sense why someone would go to the trouble of swapping batteries just after they'd clobbered someone over the head and left them for dead.

Nick patiently tried to explain. 'The murder took place when it was beginning to get dark. It's clear the assailant needed the batteries for their own torch to see their way off the property.'

'Why didn't they just take Muriel's torch and then it couldn't be used as evidence,' Katie pressed.

'I would imagine that after you have just whacked someone over the head, leaving them for dead, your adrenaline would be flowing like crazy and logic wouldn't come into play,' Nick replied.

'Wouldn't they just want to get out of here as quickly as possible? Messing around with batteries and torches would surely slow them down,' Katie persisted, wondering if the killer was stupid as well as crazy.

'Not if they knew it was very unlikely anyone would return to the house within the next half hour. If the victim knew her killer, then the killer knew their victim. We can surmise they took the batteries as they didn't want to fumble in the dark exiting the premises. A better option was to take their time and arrange a decent light than risk falling and breaking a leg. They knew no one would be turning up announced at the house. I'd say the killer knew Muriel's routine inside out. I also don't think we are dealing with a straight forward homicide investigation.'

Slightly frustrated by the absence of forensic clues Katie tried to imagine Muriel's last moments before her killer struck.

Katie eventually cornered Nick in the lounge room examining a small drinks cabinet. 'One further question Nick; If you believe the killer needed a torch to get home safely are you suggesting they live within walking distance of the cottage?'

'Possible but not probable, I'd say it's more likely they had a vehicle parked somewhere in the vicinity. It's too early to tell at this stage but we'll certainly have to canvass the neighbours.'

After an hour, Nick decided it was time to leave. An appointment with the case Detective Inspector and leading forensic officers in Exeter beckoned.

As the group were heading towards the front door Stella bustled up to them in the hall way.

'I'm so pleased I caught you before you left,' she panted breathlessly. 'My brother Mark has arrived. I'm sure you'd like a word with him and I know he's very keen to speak with *you* if you have a moment?' She was directing her remark at Katie. 'If you could come along to the living room I'll have a fresh brew waiting.'

Katie pulled a face watching Stella head back down the hallway. She was not looking forward to meeting Muriel's son. From what she'd heard he was a hard-nosed city type who's only real passion in life was money, closely followed by fast cars and women. She anticipated him firing probing questions regarding his mother's death which she wouldn't be able to answer.

'We'll leave this one to you sis,' James whispered in her ear. 'After all you are the psychologist. Talking to people is your forte,' then he turned to Nick and spoke in a cheery tone. 'Time for a beer mate before we head back. There's the Pottery Inn only a mile up the road.'

'Sounds good to me,' Nick replied offering Katie an apologetic smile.

Katie inwardly seethed. This was typical of James to wangle out of an interview and leave her to fend for herself. She reluctantly made her way into the sitting room where Stella was occupying a sofa dunking teabags in a teapot.

'I hope today's been productive,' Stella remarked as she handed Katie a hand painted china cup filled to the brim with piping hot tea.

Katie managed a smile but deliberately didn't answer. She was fighting the onset of exhaustion and wished Mark Jennings would hurry up. It appeared he was deliberately keeping her waiting.

After a second cup and what seemed an eternity Mark entered the small sitting room. Katie was a bit taken a back; she hadn't bargained on someone with movie star looks. She stumbled to her feet.

Mark Jennings made direct eye contact and held out his hand. There was no smile behind those dark brown eyes only a look of contempt bordering on loathing. 'Good afternoon Ms. Sinclair, please sit down, we don't go on ceremony here.'

Katie could detect a hint of derision in his voice which instantly brought annoyance. Good looks he may have but they hid an unpleasant smugness.

'I wouldn't pick you to be in forensics,' Mark commented crisply allowing Stella to pour him a cup of tea. Almost immediately Stella muttered something about leaving the stove on and scurried out of the door like a startled hare leaving Katie alone with the enigmatic Mark Jennings.

'Really what exactly did you have in mind?' Katie retorted. 'I didn't think a science degree instantly typecasts an individual.'

'Let's just say I find you much too pretty to want to get your hands dirty with criminal investigations. Plus, I'm sure the unsociable hours you must keep would play havoc on relationships.'

Katie found herself blushing. She was convinced Mark Jennings would notice the reddening glow and then take pride his remark had created such an adverse effect. She tried to remain allusive offering a steady reply, 'Long and irregular hours are something I've grown accustomed to over the years. Now if we could please press on I'd like to ask you some questions in regards to your mother's murder.'

'Yep, okay. Let's get down to the nitty gritty. After all you don't strike me as the coffee and croissant type who gets involved in idle chit chat. I take it you have someone you think may have committed the crime.' There was no disguising the smug sarcasm in his voice.

'It's really too early to have firm suspects.' Katie wrapped both hands around her cup for warmth. 'However, I do need to ask where you were at the time your mother was attacked.'

'In London with my wife and son.' He looked down at his fingernails whilst making this statement his action indicating he was already bored with proceedings.

Trying not to be put off by his arrogant and complacent demeanour Katie continued the probing questions, 'I take it your wife can verify this?'

'Of course.'

'Did you mother ever mention anyone she was frightened of, anyone who might have wanted to harm her?'

'No.'

'Did she show signs of depression?'

'Do I look like a psychiatrist?' Mark retorted his eyes full of contempt. 'If my mother was depressed she never spoke with me about it. Her Doctor would be the best one to supply that sort of information.'

'I know she was heavily involved with the family clay business. Did she have any money worries?'

Mark suddenly lost patience. He got up from his chair towering over Katie an angry expression etched on his face.

'Look Ms Sinclair this meeting seems pointless. Why don't you take yourself back to your cosy little office and shuffle papers instead of wasting my valuable time?'

Katie tried to remain calm and professional but was fighting a losing battle 'Believe it or not Mr. Jennings these questions are necessary. They give us a basis to work from.'

'Well sorry to disappoint but I am not prepared to hang around answering anymore of your so called 'necessary' questions. You job is to find my mother's killer but so far you seem incapable of doing that. I'm sure you can see yourself out.'

'If I recall you requested this meeting. What exactly do you want to know in relation to your mother's death?'

'I need to know what motivated the killer to act the way they did, are they likely to come after other members of my family? Your job is to find the answers and prevent further murders. Now if you don't think you're capable of this task Ms. Sinclair, I will assign someone who is.'

He walked out of the room leaving Katie alone reluctantly sipping lukewarm tea. With her hands now wrapped around a cold emptiness she put the cup down, quietly rose to her feet and quietly exited the house.

Leaving the Mark Jennings episode behind Katie decided it was time to have a chat with some of the neighbours. The first property she encountered lay about 400 yards further down the road, a clearly dilapidated bungalow buried amongst cypress pines looking badly in need of restoration and fresh paint.

After clambering over debris carelessly scattered along an uneven stone pathway Katie reached the front door knocking firmly on the rotting woodwork. A musty odour lingered strongly in the air making Katie gasp for breath as she listened for a response. With any luck the house was not inhabited so she could move on to the next dwelling. It surprised her that the property was allowed to deteriorate to such an extent in vivid contrast to the Jennings cottage and other neighbouring houses. She imagined the neighbours would not take kindly to such an eye sore in a locale what could otherwise be described as a property market nirvana.

Katie was about to head back down the path when an elderly man appeared introducing himself as Mr. Arthur Fletcher. He seemed harmless enough but from the unpleasant aroma that surrounded him was badly in need of a good soak in a bath. Katie wanted to make the visit brief declining his offer to come inside. The rancid odour outside was bad enough and she could well picture what the inside of the property would be like with no desire to witness it firsthand.

She quickly introduced herself and the reason for the impromptu visit.

'To be honest Maid I didn't notice anything,' he volunteered chirpily in a strong Devonian accent. 'I rarely venture out after 5pm of an evening. 'Twas a terrible thing to happen though, a murder indeed and so close to my own front door.'

'Yes it's certainly not an everyday occurrence,' Katie agreed trying not to breathe too deeply.

'All I can say is if the bugger dares to come near me I'll be quick to grab a big shovel and give 'em a real going over,' Arthur chortled. 'He'd not wanna mess with me.'

Katie smiled at his fierce remarks. His face held such a determined expression she could well imagine him carrying out the threat. The killer wouldn't stand much chance up against him.

'Did you happen to see anyone hanging around during the day?' Katie pressed hoping Mr. Fletcher would have noticed some unusual activity.

'Can't say I did,' he replied with a shake of the head. 'I'm not much help, am I?'

'You've been a great help,' Katie reassured him. 'Thank you.'

Ending the encounter, she turned and practically ran the few yards to the road gasping for fresh air and trying not to throw up. Her initial inclination was to report his unkempt habitat to social services. However, on reflection she decided to mull it over and then make a decision. It would be with regret to see old Arthur carted off and put in a home.

Katie found another neighbour Ruby Smith in her back garden weeding, clad in an old pair of pale green dungarees with a matching scarf tied around her head in a pirate fashion.

'I hope you don't mind me asking a few questions in relation to Muriel's murder?' Katie began careful not to tread on any flower beds after formal introductions were out the way.

'Not at all,' Ruby replied taking off gardening gloves and throwing them into a nearby bucket. 'Dreadful business. Come on into the house. You'll have to forgive my appearance but this is perfect gardening weather after all the rain we've had.'

She managed this sentence without taking a breath. Katie quickly surmised Mrs. Smith was a bit of a talker and probably also a gossip. However, the latter could prove useful in obtaining information.

Seated in Ruby's quaint cottage style kitchen Katie observed the surrounds with interest as Ruby flicked the switch on the old ceramic kettle before searching for mugs on the dresser.

'Poor Muriel,' Ruby remarked with sadness in her voice. 'When my family heard what happened, they wanted to whisk me away to the East coast in case the perpetrator strikes again but I wouldn't dream of it. No one's going to bump me off without a good old fight. I keep a heavy stick in every room of the house. They try anything I'll give them what for.'

Katie couldn't help smiling at Ruby's directness. This was proving to be a very feisty neighbourhood. Ruby didn't have the look or behaviour of a woman in her late seventies which is the age she claimed to be. Ruby's skin was wrinkle free, porcelain white and almost without blemish.

Katie started asking if she had seen anyone around in the immediate area the day Muriel was attacked.

'The only two people I saw all day were young Peter Fleming who's helping the milkman with his rounds and my sister Madge who dropped by,' she answered deftly filling two mugs of hot tea to the brim.

'Milk and sugar?'

'When did you last see Muriel?' Katie enquired taking the brew and placing it on a nearby bench hoping she wouldn't have to drink it.

Ruby screwed up her forehead thinking hard. 'The last time I saw Muriel would have been at one of the book club meetings, just over three weeks ago. Muriel often told me she loved nothing better of an evening than to curl up with a good book. I know she enjoyed attending the meetings to review all the books we were reading. She threw herself into each session. There were often times she could be quite opinionated.'

'In what way was she opinionated?' Katie enquired still not finding the courage to reach for the tea cup.

'Muriel was a highly intelligent lady,' Ruby explained. 'She had a wealth of general knowledge, always willing to part with this information when it came to forming opinions on books we read.'

'Did things ever get heated between the club members?'

'Sometimes, although never in a nasty way, on the whole we all get along extremely well. I vaguely recall an argument of some sorts which involved Muriel; I just can't remember with whom or what it was about.'

Clear frustration was visible on Ruby's face as she desperately tried to remember something that just wouldn't surface.

Katie reached out and touched her gently on the arm. 'Don't worry about that now. I'm sure it will come back to you in time. I'll leave you my card and you can call me if it creeps back into your mind. I'm sure it's nothing too major.'

Katie only said this to reassure Ruby but driving slowly back to Bovey Tracey she kept wondering who the argument could have been with and if there was a slim chance it had any bearing on Muriel's murder.

The silhouette of a man etched an eerie outline against the moonlight. He stood staring out across the open stretch of moorland until he suddenly vanished without a trace. As she reached out she felt his arms embrace her and a tear trickled down the side of her face. She knew he was only a figment of her imagination and wasn't really there to protect her. Why was that? It appeared he no longer wanted to protect her yet she'd done nothing to cause those feelings.

CHAPTER THREE

The large railway clock in the Moorland Office chimed five. Katie was finalising some forensic reports and looking to lock up the office when James walked in. He'd spent a good portion of his day assisting Nick in preparing for Muriel's autopsy and conducting a background search on Mark Jennings. The latter had proved most interesting.

'I've done a bit of delving into Mark's business dealings,' James informed Katie. 'Over the years, he has obviously pissed off quite a few people by cheating them out of the proceeds of legitimate business deals. A couple even tried to sue but Mark was always clever in hiding assets in his wife's name or offshore companies, every time our friend managed to get off scot free.'

'So any number of his ex-business associates had a possible motive to inflict pain on Muriel which in turn would cause grief for Mark,' Katie suggested as she pulled down the blinds in preparation for going home.

'Short term revenge with some twisted satisfaction but what would it really achieve?' James replied. 'Mark would get on with his life after a while so nothing of lasting impact would be gained. Somehow I don't think anyone would kill for those reasons alone.'

Katie could only acquiesce, 'Yes I see your point. Well it was only a thought.'

'Have you had a chance to put together a profile on our killer?' James enquired, his eyes hopeful.

'Without too much to really go on it is proving a tad difficult,' Katie confessed focusing her gaze on the scribbled notes to hand. 'What we do know is the attacker was probably known to Muriel, either male or female. I'd say they are very meticulous by the way they did a pretty good clean-up at the crime scene. This leads me to think the whole thing was carefully constructed and planned over several months, not a spur of the moment attack.'

James raised his eyebrows questioningly, 'If you're right this type of personality may have committed a similar attack before, perhaps even feeling the need to strike again.'

'That's possible but somehow I have the notion it was Muriel they wanted and now that's done they won't strike again.'

'You can't be sure of that though, can you?' James locked eyes with his sister seeking answers.

Katie shook her head, 'No I can't. We're either dealing with an isolated incident or someone who is on the rampage to affect several lives. Until I gather more data I won't be able to determine the probable makeup of our killer. It may take me several weeks to come up with a proper profile construction.'

James sighed, 'I thought as much. I'm organizing to check out the Jennings family clay business over the coming days which could give us a few leads. I've already lined up an appointment with the Company Foreman a Mr. Gregory McIntyre. Initial company searches confirm Jennings Clay is a big money turnover operation with over a hundred employees. I just hope a staff member seeking payback is not the case or we could be months uncovering the truth.'

'It does seem odd as to why Muriel was the target,' Katie confessed pulling on her jacket and zipping it up to her neck. 'Her personality seems quite normal, not you would think someone who would deliberately go out of their way to get people off side.'

Her brother nodded in agreement, secretly hoping further evidence gathered from the crime scene would give them something to work on but deep down he was not convinced. On the surface of it there was not much else from the house, save for the murder weapon and a small blood splatter on the telephone table that pointed to anyone or anything, or gave them any direction to go in. Maybe the swabs might turn up some genetic material, but there was little physical evidence or other obvious alien body fluids one could link to the murder scene apart from fingerprints. And DNA or print evidence was useless without suspects. If they could identify any alien DNA on or near the body, there was a good chance it would be too degraded or contaminated by DNA from the near environment for the newer PCR based STR profiling techniques to copy and replicate accurately. The old RFLP or Southern blot technique could be more specific but was no longer in everyday use and even if available to James an absence of large amounts of DNA sample material and long laboratory lead times made it impractical in this instance. DNA matching was not the panacea everybody assumed it was.

***

It was a sombre group gathered in the Bovey Tracey Town hall that cold, wet Thursday evening. The rain outside streamed down in torrents and the distant sound of thunder only heightened the eeriness of the night. Two small gas fires projected barely adequate warmth as the regular book club members prepared for their weekly meeting. All were in mourning having lost Muriel Jennings,

46

a dear friend and valued member of their small literary community. No one quite knew what to say as they huddled together around the tiny heaters trying to make sense of recent events. Usually the weekly meetings were lively events, but tonight's mood was distinctly subdued.

Bovey Tracey hall was no different to most community meeting facilities with typical worn rustic floor boards and plain white washed walls. A row of fold away chairs were neatly stacked along the back wall. In one corner stood a small kitchenette with a serving hatch; tonight piled high with cakes and sausage rolls. The only thing the hall lacked was a stage.

There was a lingering smell in the air; a rather unpleasant musty stench which would fade the more one grew accustomed to it.

Katie sneaked in at the back of the hall unnoticed, watching keenly the meeting unfold. She was there as an observer to see if she could gain knowledge of those who had perhaps been the last to see Muriel alive.

Cathy Munroe the elected chairperson was a short, plump woman smartly dressed in an expensive looking trouser suit. She stood on a small wooden box and with some trepidation addressed the book club members; 'We're all shocked.' She began fighting back tears. 'Our thoughts and prayers go out to the Jennings family, especially to Muriel's daughter Stella. This is such a sad time. There is no logic behind such a tragedy.'

Sobs echoed throughout the hall mixed with cries of outrage.

'Do the Police know anything?' enquired one lady; her rotund stature enhancing a look of early aging. Short cropped grey hair clung unpleasantly around a face which was tinged an angry red.

47

'Not at this stage,' Cathy replied calmly. 'However, I know the police are doing all they can to find the culprit or culprits. They will be conducting a thorough investigation.'

'Do *you* know anything?' This time the rotund woman directed the question at two young women who were seated behind her. 'You both looked after Muriel when she was admitted to Hospital. Surely *you* know something?'

'No more than anyone else Madge,' Liz Palmer answered with a soft Welsh lilt. 'Neither Deirdre nor I directly cared for Muriel during her time in Intensive Care.'

The group went on to discuss the support they could offer Stella before the meeting came to a premature close. It had already been unanimously decided this would not be a normal meeting. No one felt in the mood to review any books.

The group moved towards the canteen to seek solace in a light supper. Katie decided this would be the perfect opportunity to approach Cathy Munroe for a few quiet words. She introduced herself placing a business card in Cathy's right palm.

'You handled that very well,' Katie smiled warmly. 'It can't have been easy.'

'No it wasn't,' Cathy replied looking weary. Dark circles forming under her eyes accentuated her drawn look, 'We were all extremely fond of Muriel. Did you know it was to be her sixty sixth birthday next week?'

'No I didn't,' Katie replied truthfully.

'We had planned a special dinner. We were going to Mario's, the little Italian Restaurant in Moretonhampstead. I must remember to cancel the booking.'

'Perhaps it would be nice if you went anyway,' Katie suggested. 'You could have a birthday dinner in her honour.'

'Yes I hadn't thought of that,' Cathy replied. 'I'll chat with the members, see what they think.'

'Do you have a list of all the book club members I could have?' Katie asked finding refuge on an empty chair to ease her throbbing feet after another long day.

Cathy opened a manila folder sitting on top of her closed brief case retrieving a piece of paper. She passed it across to Katie. 'There you are. All the names and numbers should be there. Only thirteen of us I'm afraid. We're not a large organization.'

Katie slipped the dog eared sheet into the side pocket of her black leather bag. 'I'm happy to offer counselling if you think it might help,' she volunteered.

Cathy caught hold of Katie's left hand squeezing it tightly. 'That's very kind Ms Sinclair. Everyone copes with grief differently so some of us might like to take you up on your offer.'

A few moments of silence descended between the two women before Katie enquired, 'What can you tell me about Muriel's personality? Would you describe her as being the outgoing type or more on the reserved side?'

'I'm not sure I'll be much help on that one,' Cathy remarked truthfully. 'I only really knew Muriel from our meetings. We never spent time on the social front. If I had to sum her up I would say Muriel was an intelligent woman, widely read so always contributing well to our book reviews. She loved a good laugh. Muriel would often come out with funny anecdotes relating to herself or others.'

Katie scribbled down a few notes as Cathy spoke; a sketchy profile on the victim already forming in her mind.

Katie continued with the line of questioning desperate to block out the banter of conversation drifting from the kitchenette. For a small literary group, they made a fair bit of noise.

'In general terms would you say the group gets along well; I mean is there anyone who doesn't fit in?' Katie asked eyes firmly fixed on Cathy's face trying to detect expressions which might give something away, but she could detect nothing out of the ordinary.

'We're a mixed bunch in age and occupation but on the whole everyone gets along extremely well,' Cathy replied accepting a hot chocolate being handed to her by Liz Palmer. Katie declined the offer of refreshments.

'Could you tell me about the book or books you were reviewing prior to Muriel's attack?' Katie asked as Liz returned to her colleagues.

'We've just finished reviewing *The Sinner's Daughter* by Lillian Webster. It's truly an amazing book, a real tragedy. Are you familiar with it?'

'Sorry I can't say I am. However, I'd be keen to borrow a copy if you happen to have a spare.'

'Most certainly.'

Cathy reached into her handbag for a medium sized paperback. The picture on the cover depicted a single white rose.

'It's the story of Ted Cartwright who murdered five women in his remote home on Dartmoor a little over fifteen years ago,' Cathy informed Katie passing over the book. 'He's now serving a life sentence in Dartmoor prison. One of the reasons these murders are fascinating, apart from the local aspect, is the fact Cartwright's ten year old daughter was apparently also living in the house when these murders took place. To this day, Cartwright declares his innocence but refuses to suggest who might have been responsible.'

Katie found herself spellbound by all this information.

'Do you think his daughter could have committed the murders?' she asked lowering her voice to barely a whisper.

'I very much doubt it. The victims' injuries were quite horrific, beyond the capabilities of a ten year old child.'

'What conclusion did the book club members come to?'

'There were mixed opinions,' Cathy continued. 'On the whole people felt sorry for Abby, Cartwright's daughter. However, one or two critics felt she could have done more to prevent the murders.'

'Do you happen to remember who these individuals were; the ones who felt Abby could have done more?' Katie's asked both cheeks burning with intrigue. She was curious to hear more about Cartwright and the five women he'd allegedly murdered. There were certain elements that would elevate her psychological mind.

'I'm afraid I don't. However, I'd be interested to know your thoughts on the book Ms. Sinclair, especially in your capacity as a forensic psychologist. I am sure you will find it quite a fascinating read.'

'I'm sure I will,' Katie replied. 'Thank you for your time Ms. Monroe. If it's alright with you I'd like to pop by next week and chat with some of your members.'

'That'll be fine. We meet again next Thursday at seven. Good night Ms Sinclair. Thankfully the rain has stopped so you won't get wet returning to your car.'

'Good night.'

Katie walked out of the hall with the paperback tucked firmly under her right arm. This was shaping up as a fascinating read. Knowing it was probably the very last book Muriel Jennings read made it even more intriguing.

***

Stella pondered over the quarterly accounts trying to work out why the figures didn't balance. She was normally good with numbers but today her mathematical brain wasn't up to scratch. According to her estimates they were out by almost thirty-one thousand pounds. This was a worrying discrepancy.

After several reconciliations and a good two hours checking and rechecking she finally picked up the phone. 'Katie, its Stella Jennings here. I've found something of interest. Are you able to drop by the house when you have some free time?'

Kate was about to immerse into a hot bath when she received the call from Stella. There was a hint of urgency in Stella's voice which Katie couldn't ignore. Leaving the water to get cold she threw on a light grey tracksuit and jumped into her car. It only took twenty-two minutes from receiving the call and getting dressed to arrive at the Jennings home.

Stella was standing by the front door to greet her. She led Katie through to a large, separate, self-contained annex at the back of the cottage; the rooms predictably decorated in the Laura Ashley style. The drawing room in particular was crammed with expensive antique furniture and a smattering of valuable decorative pieces, the sumptuous, overall affect not lost on Katie. She'd not had a chance to see this part of the house before as it had still been under police quarantine.

'I came across this whilst sorting through Mum's things in the study,' Stella informed Katie sounding a little out of breath from all the excitement. 'It struck me as a bit odd that's all,' she continued anxiously, picking up a wad of papers in a leather binder.

'I'm no accountant,' Stella confessed, handing over the contents, 'But these figures can't be correct.'

At a quick glance Katie noticed the discrepancies Stella was on about. It really didn't need a mathematical genius to work out these sums weren't adding up.

'I'll have to take them away for scrutiny by a professional accountant,' she advised Stella, not for one moment wanting to comment on the apparent anomalies. In any murder investigation, it was important to keep things close to your chest. Although liking Stella, Katie learnt from bitter experience over the years to trust no one.

'I also found this,' Stella continued as she opened the drawer of an antiquarian desk removing a half used cheque book. 'More than five cheques from this book were made out to cash and each cheque for between five and ten thousand pounds.'

'Can I also take this for analysis?' Katie asked as the book was handed to her. 'I don't suppose you have any idea who the cheques might have been for?'

'I can take a guess,' Stella muttered lowering her voice and taking a quick glance over her shoulder as if afraid someone might overhear. 'I think Mark may be behind all this. He has a bit of a gambling habit. To what extent I don't really know; he always reacts aggressively when the subject comes up. My guess is mum must have bailed him out on more than one occasion if this cheque book is any indication.'

So deep in conversation were the two women neither noticed Mark Jennings entering the small study. Both jumped in surprise as his booming voice echoed around the room, his broad frame filling the doorway.

'If you're implying I took money from my own mother to pay off gambling debts you're way off course,' he shouted.

Stella looked frightened at the sudden appearance of her brother. Katie tried not to show any fear, determined to remain calm and appear unruffled as Mark continued to rant. 'My gambling habits have *made* me money. I'm not your typical sorry loser. In fact, if you don't believe me why don't you get in contact with my accountant? I'm sure he'd be happy to provide you with some healthy looking numbers. If my mother was handing money out to someone it certainly wasn't *me.*'

His voice carried so much conviction in this last statement Katie realized he might be telling the truth. Yet if Muriel had not been supplying money to Mark then who had been the beneficiary? A beguiling question with no obvious answer; her killer perhaps?

***

The BBC 9am news had just concluded on the 'Landie' radio when James arrived at Jennings Clay Company. He had taken the road through Kingsteignton, turning off onto a dirt track, driving approximately half a mile before coming to a wrought iron security gate mounted with barbed wire. Off to the right was a small square intercom button for intending visitors. Looking beyond the gates James observed several loaders noisily dumping aggregate into large underground storage bins amidst clouds of dust. He waited patiently for the automatic gates to swing open allowing him access into a car park surfaced with crushed stone. Parking the Land Rover, he headed to the main office which resembled little more than an oversized caravan sat on concrete blocks. Setting foot inside he realized it was more than adequate as a site office cum general meeting place.

Having arranged to meet the company foreman Greg McIntyre at nine thirty his watch indicated he was early. Choosing to ignore this fact he strolled up to the reception desk announcing his arrival and who he was seeing. The receptionist was a mere wisp of a girl probably no more than eighteen with a mass of curly blonde hair swept to one side in a rather unruly style.

Her fingers flicked through a well-thumbed diary searching for the appointment. 'I'm sorry sir I don't seem to have you in here,' she declared seeming a little flustered. 'Perhaps you arranged to meet Mr. McIntyre on another day.'

'No definitely today,' James reassured her with his best winning smile.

Returning with a noticeable frown she mumbled that she would ring Mr. McIntyre's extension as he was probably already in his office.

James knew full well the reason the appointment was not scheduled in the receptionist's diary. Greg McIntyre wanted to keep the meeting a secret from his boss; Mark Jennings – a very wise move. If Mark knew McIntyre had agreed to chat with James, there was the distinct possibility he would try to sabotage any talks that were scheduled to take place.

James loafed about the office a further ten minutes killing time before Greg came bustling up. He was an affable chap in his early sixties with thinning grey hair and a neat moustache which curled at the ends. He greeted James warmly shaking his hand firmly and grinning like a Cheshire cat. *Obviously ex-RAF* James mused.

'You don't sound local,' James commented after hearing Greg's accent. 'Further up north I'd hazard a guess, but I can't quite pick where.'

'Lancashire born and bred,' Greg replied proudly showing James into a small but neat looking office. 'My father was originally from Scotland, The Isle of Skye.'

'Beautiful place,' James replied taking up residence in one of the vacant office chairs. 'I was there for business once.'

'Now, what do you know about the ball clay industry,' McIntyre enquired, changing the subject.

'Not a lot,' James answered truthfully. 'Although I've driven past the pits on numerous occasions.'

'Its big business, always has been,' Greg informed. 'About 200 million euros a year being dug out, most goes to export, essentially into paper, porcelain, tyres as a filler, but it also has hi-tech uses, especially Devon clay. Being a chemist you'd know what I'm talking about. Now what was it you're after again?'

'I'd like to know if it *is* the family who owns Jennings Clay?' James asked.

'It is,' Greg replied. 'Muriel, god rest her soul, was the primary stake holder with sixty percent, Mark and Stella both have a twenty percent share each.'

'So do we know if Muriel's shares now get divided equally between Mark and Stella?'

'That I'm unsure of until the reading of the will takes place,' Greg confessed. 'I imagine the family lawyer Marshall Davidson would know all about that but unfortunately he's in Australia at the moment, not due back for another two weeks.'

James made a mental note to get in contact with Marshall when he returned.

James continued his questioning. 'So with Muriel being the primary owner was she in control of the financial side of things?'

'Ah now that question I *can* answer.' Greg grinned appearing pleased he was able to be of some assistance. 'Muriel was the self-appointed Finance Director and had total control over all the company cash. No one could sign off on cheques or remove money from company accounts without Muriel's signature. You might like a word with the Chief Financial Officer, Peter Swift. He's in his office and I'm happy to see if he has a few minutes to spare? These sorts of questions are more up his alley.'

James seized this opportunity. Talking with the CFO would be handy. 'That sounds like a good idea if you wouldn't mind.'

Greg went out of the room appearing a few minutes later with Swift. He then excused himself so the two men could talk. Just prior to leaving he passed James one of his cards 'If you think of any more questions Mr. Sinclair please feel free to call.'

'Thank you.' James then turned to Peter Swift quickly sizing him up. A short, stocky individual with a pale complexion and overall unhealthy aura, he was probably mid-forties but looked older, clearly showing the signs of heavy nicotine abuse and a liking for hard liquor. Obviously professional appearance was paramount betrayed by highly polished shoes and an expensive Italian suit.

Officious would best describe the answers he supplied to the questions James asked, which could easily have been interpreted as rudeness. James being thick skinned continued to fire a barrage of questions not in the least perturbed by Peter's brisk manner.

'I understand Muriel Jennings controlled all the company financial transactions? Would this be normal practice for a business this size?'

Peter shuffled uneasily in his seat, pondered the questions for a few seconds before scratching his head and answering, 'Probably not, although there is good reason behind this system.'

'Being?' James prompted Peter as the conversation paused. It was a good half minute before he deigned to reply.

'Muriel never had a lot of trust in her son Mark. He's into fast cars, leads a perversely extravagant lifestyle and has a penchant for risky property deals. I know Muriel felt it would be a bad move to allow him access to the company finances.'

James's estimation of Muriel Jennings began to soar. She had certainly made a very wise decision. If Mark had been allowed unbridled access to money the company could easily have slipped into receivership very quickly.

'Did Muriel actually say this was her decision for keeping control of the money?' James pressed.

Peter laughed, easing up a little, 'She didn't have to Mr. Sinclair. Most people know what Mark is like with money and Muriel was certainly no fool.'

'Can I safely assume that Mark and Stella receive a reasonable income for their involvement in the firm?'

'They do,' Peter replied, his voice a little wistful as he unconsciously played with papers on the desk. 'Mark being Managing Director receives a bigger income, however they both receive a substantial share of the profits. Their share gets distributed equally at the beginning of each new financial year in April. Last year they each netted over three hundred thousand pounds extra income tax free alone.'

James raised his eyebrows, 'I think we can safely assume that business is doing well then?'

Peter merely nodded his head.

'Mr. Swift, I am aware that Muriel had written some cash cheques over the past twelve months. Our preliminary research indicates a totalling sum of over one hundred and eighty-five thousand pounds. Would you happen to know what that money was used for?'

Peter shook his head. 'My role is not to ask questions but to ensure the company ticks along at a profit. I did try and find out once but Muriel brushed me aside by laughing and saying, 'Can't an old woman indulge herself every now and again.' I never dared to bring up the subject again, just wrote if all off on expenses at her request.'

'I see. Would *anyone* know what the money was used for?'

'I know Muriel confided in Marshall Davidson a fair bit. As well as being the company lawyer he was an old friend of the late Mr. Jennings. He's been the family lawyer ever since I can remember. You could try speaking with Marshall when he returns to England.'

Before James could dig further the door flew open; Mark Jennings stood threateningly in the doorway.

'What the hell do you think you're doing?' he demanded of James. 'You have no right to come around here questioning my staff. Get out before I have you thrown out.'

Peter Swift was clearly ruffled by Mark's unexpected appearance.

Not wanting a full blown confrontation James decided it would be best to make a hasty exit. He could always arrange further meetings with Jennings employees another time if need be, preferably at a different location too. It was just his luck Mark had shown up. He'd nearly got through the interrogation.

It took a lot of willpower for James to keep his temper under control as Mark continued a rant liberally sprinkled with obscenities. There was something about Mark Jennings that was markedly disagreeable.

James turned to Peter who obviously looked uncomfortable, probably wishing he was anywhere else but standing facing an angry boss. 'Thank you for your time Mr. Swift. I'll be in touch if I require any additional information.'

'Like hell you will,' Mark spat back as he took a menacing step forward. 'Get out of here before I call security.'

***

James sat with his feet up on the desk flicking idly through the Guardian. With his phone persistently ringing, Fiona reached out to answer it.

'It's Superintendent Izzy Bax,' she advised. 'He'd like us to head up to Haytor where a young lad has fallen to his death. Half his guys are tied up with a major fire investigation at Dartington.'

'You go,' James instructed. 'Tell him I'm busy.'

'Yes but you're not are you.'

'He doesn't need to know that,' James snapped. 'Go on, tell him I'm busy.'

Fiona hesitated before continuing her phone conversation, '*I'll* be able to make it but unfortunately James is otherwise engaged.'

After ending the call Fiona turned on her brother. 'What the hell is wrong with you? I could have used your help.'

'I don't do Tors,' James reiterated not bothering to look up.

Fiona swore loudly as she grabbed her forensic kit. On the way out she slammed the door with a bang.

Arriving at the incident scene Fiona noticed there was already a gathering of people trying to get a glimpse of the body. The Super greeted her with a wry smile. 'Hi Fiona thanks for coming. You'll find the lad round the East facing side of the Tor. He's a bit of a mess, probably been dead several hours.'

Fiona's stomach did a quick somersault as she digested this information.

'Quite a rock,' Izzy commented glancing up at Haytor with its impressive formation. He was fairly new to Devon with limited knowledge of the local area and its history.

'As children, we nicknamed it "Death's Tor." My grandmother believed anyone who visited after the sun went down would be cursed by the devil.'

'Nice.'

'She also told us that on nights when there's a full moon you can see a solitary figure standing on the highest stone staring out across the open Moor. Did you know the monolith stands around 120 feet? Quite a long way from the ground.'

History lesson over Fiona strolled around the rock to take a look at the body screened off from public view, Izzy close on her heels. She placed her forensic case on the trampled heather edging in close to the young victim.

'I'd say he died on impact,' she informed Izzy. 'Although I'm not certain it was the fall that killed him. Definitely need an autopsy.'

Fiona began jotting down anything relevant while two forensic officers worked to document all site details including measurements and photographs.

'Do we have a name?' she asked the duty policeman standing a few metres away.

'Barlow. Tony Barlow,' came the reply.

Fiona noticed the officer looking a bit green, 'You okay?'

'My first death.'

'You get used to it.'

Tony Barlow's body lay a few yards from the craggy granite. It appeared he'd speared into the ground head first. A large pool of blood lay in a 20cm wide band around the crown of his head.

'He wouldn't have felt much,' Fiona muttered to herself *'Poor kid.'*

'So what's the verdict?'

Fiona remained kneeling by the body as Izzy fired this question at her.

'Don't know but it looks like he slipped or overbalanced.'

'So he wasn't pushed?'

'Not really sure. From what I've been overhearing the lad was up on the rock by himself last night. I'll schedule routine toxicology drug screens but we'll wait till your people collate all the evidence.'

Heading away from Haytor Fiona sensed a sinister presence surrounding her. She pressed hard on the accelerator keen to get off the Moor as quickly as possible.

***

Going onto Haytor at midnight seemed a bit of a lark. The balmy night beckoned. They were bored teenagers, had consumed too many drinks and were looking for adventure. James had managed to get his hand on some good quality 'ice' so the party was in full swing. Being the designated driver and not even considering he was over the limit James negotiated the sharp bend exiting Yelverton heading onto open Moorland. Crossing Cadover Bridge he accelerated and shifted into top gear momentarily taking his eye off the road. Switching vision back to the darkened road he realised the ponies were directly in the firing line. To avoid a collision, he swerved losing control of the kombi van. Fighting for survival James managed to direct the vehicle towards a steep embankment where it plunged through the safety barrier smashing into a tree.

As James lunged forward in slow motion his head slammed hard into the steering wheel. The windscreen shattered and warm liquid ran down his face. Then his world descended into the abyss.

Rubbing his forehead James could no longer concentrate on the tabloid. Opening the top drawer, he found the bottle of vodka still wrapped in its Christmas cellophane and proceeded to help himself to a double nip and two strong analgesics to ease the pain of an old shoulder injury. Fiona's unexpected visit to Haytor revived vivid memories of the fatal car crash. A journey he desperately tried to forget. His head throbbed from the persistent nightmares which took him back to the accident 18 years earlier, culminating in the death of his best friend Timothy Hall. With the shot of vodka downed and desperate to get the fatal accident out of his mind James opened an invoice sitting on the desk.

Perhaps purchasing a new ICP/MS analytical system had not been the best idea. He was about to file the bill away when another envelope caught his attention; the scrawny writing on the envelope all too familiar. James tore it open retrieving the letter stowed inside. Yep, he was right, another request for money from Tim's father.

James tossed the letter in the bin. Right now he had more important things to think about. Later however, he would need to open his cheque book and send off another five thousand pounds: The yearly sum agreed upon to ensure no one ever found out James had been under the influence of amphetamines at the time of the fatal crash.

***

'Any leads on the Jennings case?'

Fiona turned to see Tom Markham the egotistical owner and self-appointed chief journalist of the Newton Abbot Star standing on the footpath, grinning and blocking access to her car. He had the annoying habit of cropping up and asking inquisitive questions, often catching people off guard.

'You're asking the wrong person,' Fiona replied curtly, who had never been a Markham fan. 'You of all people should know Tom that Forensics never give that sort of information away.' Then she added as an afterthought, 'Especially to people like you.'

'Ouch! I never can pull one over on you can I Fi?'

'Nope, now run along, there's a good little copy writer. Go concoct some story on a homeless puppy. I'm in a hurry.' Fiona brushed a strand of hair from her face before heading to her car. Not one to be put off, Markham hurried along beside breathing heavily. 'I take it that means you're heading to the press conference at the town hall?' he pressed for detail.

'See you know what's going on already,' Fiona jibed with sarcasm. 'You don't need my help to mind everyone else's business.'

With that off the cuff remark she triumphantly brushed aside her nemesis, got into her car and drove off without a backwards glance knowing full well she would bump into Tom Markham only a matter of minutes later at the press conference.

A noisy, expectant crowd of around seventy gathered in the Bovey Tracey Hall comprising journalists, assorted forensic types, members of the general public with nothing better to do and a smattering of police officers. Also present were a crew from Television South West and several media representatives.

As Fiona slid into a seat next to Katie she spotted Tom Markham two rows in front giving her a sly wink. Choosing to ignore him totally she turned to speak with Katie.

'I'm glad James is the one addressing this little group. Markham's bound to throw a few sticky questions his way.'

Katie nodded. 'Yeah, he's a ruthless bastard.'

James made his way to the microphone stand, switched it on and tapped a number of times to silence the throng. Public speaking never fazed him in the slightest in fact he rather enjoyed playing to an audience. D.C.I Rose the officer leading the investigation stood behind James ready to add support with any questions.

James cleared his throat before beginning his introduction, scanning the room for familiar faces. He recognized one or two members of the press, a few local well known identities and some policemen and women he'd worked with over the years. Mark Jennings was seated next to Stella in the front row, a few seats along was Peter Swift and other Jennings employees, easily distinguishable by blue polo shirts with the company logo 'JC' embroidered in navy thread.

'Good afternoon ladies and gentlemen. Thank you all for coming today. As you may or may not be aware my name is James Sinclair and I'm one of the consulting case Forensic Scientists investigating the recent tragic death of Mrs. Muriel Jennings. I would like to give you a brief update on findings to date and then allow for ten minutes of question time. If we're all here I'll begin.'

He waited a few moments while some stragglers made their way to vacant seats and then launched in.

'We can confirm the death of Muriel Jennings was suspicious and that she did not die from natural causes. We also know the object used in the attack was a heavy duty torch which is being tested for fingerprints. We have reason to believe the torch was owned by Mrs. Jennings.

It is too early in this investigation to have a definite suspect or suspects; however, we do feel that Mrs. Jennings most likely knew her attacker. Over the coming weeks my forensic team will be involved in gathering evidence and conducting scientific examinations jointly with County forensics, which hopefully will bring the police closer to finding the person or persons responsible. We will give the media and general public updates as often as possible. Thank you, any questions?'

An elderly woman in the back row stood up. Katie recognized her as Ruby Smith one of Muriel's neighbours who she'd questioned not long after the attack. 'Do you think this was a random attack Mr. Sinclair or are you looking for a serial attacker?'

'It is too early to rule out if this person might strike again. However, as we believe Mrs. Jennings knew her assailant we are not under the impression they will strike randomly. We believe they had a motive for the murder but as yet we do not know what that motive was.'

Ruby sat down and a youth in his early twenties quickly stood up. 'What makes you so sure she knew her killer?'

James smothered a grin at this naive question. The lad obviously craved a few minutes in the lime light. Knowing the television cameras were rolling he wanted to go home tonight and be able to brag to friends about being on the evening news. This was his five minutes of fame.

'Good question,' James replied wanting to give the youth a boost. 'There were no signs of forced entry into Mrs. Jennings' house which clearly indicates she willingly opened the door to her assailant. The attack also took place several yards from the front door which means the person gained complete access into the house. There was no evidence of a struggle so it would appear Mrs. Jennings spent some time chatting with her attacker before they dealt the fatal blow to the left temporal lobe.'

The youth seeming suitably satisfied with this reply, grinned and resumed his seat.

Next to direct a question at James was a man in an expensively tailored business suit with a loud tie. He was somewhere in his mid to late fifties and spoke with a strong

Glaswegian accent. James had to train his ear carefully to pick out the sentences.

'Are you confident this case will be solved within a reasonable amount of time Mr. Sinclair? Surely you must be aware that the general public in the local area are becoming more nervous by the day as the perpetrator remains at large?'

'I would like to reiterate that we do not feel this incident was random, therefore the person who committed this crime is not likely to go for members of the general public.'

'But you can't be certain of that?' he added.

James took a deep breath before replying. 'No we can't but it's highly unlikely.'

Out of the corner of his left eye James saw Tom Markham get to his feet, a sardonic smile etched on his face as if he was holding a loaded shot gun.

'Is it not fair to say that your little lab tests can sometimes be hit and miss when trying to accurately uncover the facts?' Markham fired at him. 'We often hear of evidence getting contaminated or lost and not being conclusive.'

James paused momentarily to take a sip of water from the glass on an adjacent table.

'I appreciate your concern Mr. Markham but I can assure you there are dedicated, highly professional forensic personnel with access to the latest facilities working on this case.'

'I see,' he barbed in a patronizing snarl. James remained calm as Markham piped up again.

'Would you like to advise everyone here today exactly how many police investigations your organization, what is it again, 'Moorland Forensics', has been involved in to date?'

'Happy to,' James replied. 'In total fifteen other cases for the Crown, that is.'

'Big or small?'

'I've always been told size doesn't matter,' James smiled confidently.

The hall collapsed into laughter. James decided this was his cue to finish and let DCI Rose handle the final proceedings.

Mick Rose took three more questions, thanked James for the technical updates and concluded the presentation with usual formalities.

The cameras stopped rolling and James exited the hall like a celebrity.

***

James was putting the finishing touches on his updated analysis of the Jennings case to date when the phone intruded into his senses. Reaching across the desk he picked up on the fourth ring.

'James, Chief Inspector Saville from Exeter. I've received a rather serious complaint from Mark Jennings the son of the late Mrs. Muriel Jennings.'

'Really…' James tried not to sound bored realising he was in for a lecture.

'He claims he's being harassed by Moorland Forensics.'

James nearly over balanced off the stool he was perched on. 'You're kidding me right?'

'Wish I was. However, the guy turned up at Exeter Police HQ less than an hour ago and lodged a formal solicitor's letter. It's all here in black and white.' James could hear the Inspector rustling papers. No doubt Mark's formal complaint!

'I'd hardly call a few lines of questioning a form of harassment,' James fought back in defence. 'After all, Chief Inspector we *are* investigating a murder, the victim being his mother.'

'I'm well aware of that but he is still within his rights to file a complaint James. All I'm asking is for you to channel your investigations elsewhere for the time being. If you don't have any good reasons you need to go easy with the man.'

James bit his tongue, making a huge effort to keep his growing temper in check.

'No problem,' he managed at last. 'I'll see what I can do.'

'Good man. That's all I ask.'

The Inspector hung up leaving James muttering a stream of curses before slamming down the receiver.

Mark Jennings really knew how to push his buttons. Sadly, James realised they would have to back off. The worst case scenario would be pissing off the Deputy Chief Constable and getting them kicked off the case.

It was a balmy night. The same thoughts were spinning around in her head. Scary, dark thoughts on a merry go round with loud music thumping in time to the beat of a steal drum. Suddenly waking from a deep sleep she sat up and screamed.

CHAPTER FOUR

Tucked up in bed Katie became captivated by the book; reading for hours, unable to put it down. The shocking reality of the Cartwright murders became increasingly apparent as she turned each new page. Cartwright had lured all five women into his home over a six-month period strangling them all. Prior to strangulation they were subjected to violent torture. His sixth victim had survived through a lucky escape; aided by Abigail Cartwright the so-called 'Sinner's Daughter' – a name bestowed on her by the media. According to the book, Abby had put herself at risk by helping the woman escape. Later as the trial begun she also played a big part in assisting with the conviction of her father, although after the trial she refused to say anything more about the murders.

Katie skipped over any gory details, amazed that for nearly seven weeks the sixth victim remained captive in a dark dank cellar desperately trying to escape. There had been no lighting, no toilet facilities, no furniture and very little food or water provided. Survival was purely based on sheer will power with the desire to live.

Katie read passages written by the last victim known as 'the survivor'. The accounts she recalled so real, Katie was able to picture herself inside that ghastly basement. She shivered at the thought of what that poor woman had been through.

At 3am she finally placed the book onto the bedside table simultaneously flicking off the bedside light. For ages her mind remained within a whirl of sinister thoughts keeping sleep at bay. It was a good hour before she started to drift into a restless slumber, but the subconscious remained focused on the victims of Ted Cartwright. Their faces emerged in front of her; sad lost little souls who were desperately crying out for help. One victim was so pretty, she looked like an angel.

'I'm okay now,' she whispered to Katie. 'Tell my family I love them and I'm okay.'

With perspiration forming on her forehead Katie woke from the fitful slumber. Her senses told her she was not alone in the room, the pretty angel was there watching over her, a guardian protecting her from all the evil things in the world.

***

The death of Muriel Jennings was a real puzzle. No one claimed to have seen or heard anything and despite constant pleas from the police no witnesses had come forward. There she lay on a cold slab in the mortuary yet someone had to be responsible for her death.

Nothing productive had eventuated from forensic tests on materials from the house undertaken thus far and no anomalies with the physical evidence had surfaced. A lot was resting on the autopsy. Nick was determined to leave no stone unturned arranging a thorough examination to analyse all major organs.

Muriel's blood had already been screened for drugs both licit and illicit and tested for microbiological pathogens. These had come back negative. A medical pathology lab was also running a routine check on blood sugar, lipid and protein levels. Toxicological testing for heavy metals, common and obscure poisons was scheduled with Moorland sharing some of the case load.

Several days following the death of Muriel Jennings Katie officially arranged attendance of the next book club meeting in Bovey, the intention being to interview members. The small group had played a major role in Muriel's social life, perhaps they had valuable information to offer. All were duly advised, interviews would take place kicking off around seven.

The evening was pleasantly warm as Katie strode purposefully up the Bovey high street negotiating the traffic across the road to the town hall. A stark contrast to the storm that was raging the first night she'd ventured there; tonight was clear with a half crescent moon. The first stars sparkled in the charcoal sky, the streetscape bathed in a soft, shimmering light. Katie looked around; the small town was momentarily devoid of souls. She searched the heavens for the Pole Star; easily spotted in the North Sky by tracing a hand's breadth from the two 'pointers', Dubhe and Merak, at the end of the Plough. Always a guiding beacon.

Entering the hall Katie was greeted by friendly chatter. The members either sat or leaned against the walls deep in conversation.

Cathy Munroe was there to welcome Katie and introduce her to the members before a makeshift interview room was erected in the small kitchenette creating a relaxed atmosphere. Katie sought permission to tape all conversations placing her trusty pocket recorder centre stage on the small wooden table. First scheduled meeting was with Liz Palmer a tall spindly woman in her mid-thirties; with a fashion sense dated and dowdy. Liz sat opposite Katie, legs crossed. If she was nervous there was no outward sign, her demeanour relaxed and confident, not seeming to mind being in the lime light.

Katie began with idle chit chat before asking her first formal question. 'Do you manage to attend the book club meetings every week?'

'There are odd weeks when I get rostered on to work but most weeks I attend,' Liz replied, shifting slightly in her seat.

'That's right you're a nurse, aren't you?' Katie prophesised.

'Yes.'

'How well did you know Muriel?'

'Fairly well, I've been a member of the book club a little over two years, Muriel a lot longer than that.'

'I understand you've all been reading *The Sinner's Daughter* by Lillian Webster. What exactly did you think of the book?'

'It was okay, nothing special.' Again, Liz marginally shifted her position.

'Apparently, a lot of people found it quite disturbing, upsetting even.'

'Let's just say I prefer to read more classical literature such as Jane Austen,' Liz laughed softly. 'Being a nurse I see a lot of death. Reading about such horrific murders is not a form of relaxation for me.'

'Do you remember Muriel's thoughts on the book?'

'It was not uncommon for Muriel to form strong opinions regarding our reading material but for some reason this particular book seemed to tip her over the edge. Why, I have no idea.'

Katie thanked Liz for her time moving on to the second interview which took place with Deirdre Mulligan another nurse who worked alongside Liz at Torbay Hospital.

'I didn't read the whole book,' Deirdre confessed. 'I probably got a quarter of the way through and gave it back.'

'Why was that?'

'I found it too disturbing. I don't usually sleep well at night and didn't want to add to my insomnia problems.'

'Did you feel sorry for Abby, Ted Cartwright's daughter?'

'Absolutely.'

'Do you think she could have done more to prevent the murders?'

'Only Abby would be capable of answering that question. I don't feel anyone else has the capacity to comment unless they were actually there.'

'Thank you for your time.'

'You're welcome.'

Jane Anderson was the next interviewee sitting poised on the edge of a chair adapting the pose of a professional model. Although immaculate in appearance everything about Jane seemed false; from long glossy acrylic nails to a contrived laugh with its irritating edge. She wore excessive amounts of makeup while her wispy bottle blonde hair was neatly styled in a French roll. Even in a force nine gale, it had no chance of being blown about. Jane was reasonably attractive in a pretentious sort of way, someone who obviously spent time and money to achieve her glamorous looks. She claimed to be in her forties, which was very plausible but, in Katie's view, she still resembled mutton dressed as lamb. What didn't help were the aging lines just above her upper lip, a result of years exposed to nicotine consumption.

'Do you mind if I smoke?' Jane enquired wistfully, taking a fresh packet from a large handbag and removing the cellophane wrapping. 'My nerves are shot at the moment, what with one thing and another.' Her diction betrayed a mediocre education, probably not straying far from the wrong side of the tracks. Someone who wanted to be high on the social ladder yet in reality only got to the second rung.

'Actually, I'd prefer if you didn't,' Katie replied curtly. 'We won't be too long so if you could wait a while before lighting up it would be appreciated.'

Jane gave her irritating laugh popping the cigarettes back in her bag. 'I guess it's a bad habit,' she chided unconvincingly. 'Now what can I help you with Ms. Sinclair. I'm assuming you're here to talk about Muriel Jennings?'

'Yes, I was hoping you could begin by telling me how well you knew Muriel and if you have any idea who may have taken a dislike to her?'

'I'd say I knew her as well as anyone else belonging to the book club. I do a bit of admin work for Jennings Clay so naturally I come across Muriel from time to time. She liked to keep company employees strictly on a professional level so our brief encounters were always work related. Twice a month I would go to Muriel's house to work on marketing campaigns.'

'I see. I've been learning a bit about the book you were all analysing at the time *The Sinner's Daughter*. What did you think of the book?'

'Too graphic for my liking,' Jane replied screwing up her face in disgust. 'Also, I found the book to have been written with one view point in mind which was odd.'

'Would you mind elaborating on that statement?'

Jane paused for a brief moment giving the question careful consideration before replying. 'The author leads us to believe Cartwright's daughter was as much a victim as the murdered women, which is utter nonsense. In my opinion she could have done a lot more to assist those poor girls, yet she came out of it almost a heroine. I have no sympathy for Abigail Cartwright, none what so ever. I strongly feel it should have been more subjective, similar to other books I've read. I once had an experience not dissimilar to... '

Katie began to switch off as Jane lost herself in waffle, forming set opinions on how someone should write a book. It was all too apparent *her* literary skills were limited. Katie forced herself into a more upright position in an attempt to remain focused. If she wasn't careful she'd nod off listening to Jane's high pitched droning voice.

'You're not from Devon?' Katie remarked when Jane finally came up for air. 'I can't quite pick your accent but it's not Devonian.'

Jane's expression turned slightly hostile. 'I've spent a number of years in different parts of the country and several years in France,' she replied curtly. 'The past four years have been in Devon so I'm hardly a foreigner now, am I?'

'I guess not,' Katie replied sounding non-committal. 'Well thank you for your time Ms Anderson. That's all for now but I may have further questions to ask later on.'

'Let's hope you catch the person who committed this atrocity,' Jane remarked candidly. 'You can't be too careful nowadays. I even lock my car door when I drive. You hear of people being car jacked when stopping at traffic lights. That's exactly what happened to a friend of mine. It's hard to trust anyone. I also prefer not to use public toilets in case someone is lurking behind the door. I heard once...'

Katie stifled a yawn. Jane seemed to have opinions for everything. No doubt she'd talk her way through sex given half a chance causing the poor bastard to die of boredom.

Jane, realizing the interview was officially over, leapt to her feet heading for the nearest exit. The way she scuttled across the room was almost manic. She'd barely set foot outside before lighting up and engaging in conversation with anyone prepared to listen.

Katie lent back in her chair sighing heavily. She'd come across Jane's type on several occasions throughout her career as a psychologist. One minute they seemed to be on an extreme high, bubbling with enthusiasm, yet almost immediately their mood would change; they'd seep into chronic depression. People like Jane could never be trusted; one minute they would be your best friend then if something didn't quite go their way they blamed everyone but themselves. She showed signs of anxiety; linking her with an obsessive compulsive disorder.

Ruby Smith came bustling up to Katie greeting her like a long lost friend. 'I am a lucky lass aren't I,' she jibed digging Katie in the ribs and almost winding her. 'Being interviewed twice in one week, now where shall we start?'

She parked her rather large posterior onto a vacant chair looking more like the one who was going to be asking questions than answering them.

Katie smiled warily. This had the makings of being a long drawn out interview.

'As neighbours, would you say you and Muriel were particularly close?' Katie began a little hesitantly.

'I'd like to think so. We were both widows. That alone gave us common ground. We would pop over to each other's place for a cuppa at least once a week.'

'Did you notice if Muriel had many visitors?'

'Her daughter in law would sometimes drop by. Well I think it must have been Mark's wife. Fairly tall, blondish hair, although without my glasses me eye sight's pretty poor.'

Katie made a mental note to check out details of Mark's wife. So far they had not encountered the woman whom they understood resided in London.

'Do you remember what Muriel thought of the book *The Sinner's Daughter*?'

'Well I know Muriel had quite a strong opinion of Ted Cartwright. To put it bluntly she had nothing nice to say about the man. The way she spoke about him Ms Sinclair you'd almost think she harboured a personal grudge.'

Finally, with all the relevant interviews over Katie thankfully called it a day and headed off home. It had been an interesting evening but not really eventful.

***

Anger took over as James reluctantly wrote out a cheque for five thousand pounds. Graham Hall was persistent James had to give him that. With the cheque written and tucked into an envelope James reached for his mobile punching in Nick's number. 'Hi mate. Got much on next week? If not, I could do with your assistance.'

James ended the call at the same time Katie strolled in looking dishevelled from a torrential down pour.

'I only ventured out to the Post Office,' she grumbled peeling off her wet jacket. Seated behind her desk she pondered her next move. 'Don't suppose you can help me put together a one-page speech on "the physical effects of Ecstasy" she enquired of James. 'I'm guest speaking at a Plymouth University seminar next week and haven't got a clue where to begin.'

'I'll see what I can do,' James replied. 'I'm away the next two days at a science fair in Southampton so am a bit pressed for time.'

The shadows from the moonlight were tormenting. The trees resembled menacing wraiths with twisted body parts reaching forward ready to grab at any moment. Sobbing with grief she threw herself under the covers not willing to immerge until morning. No one told her it would be this bad. Why didn't it all just go away and leave her alone? She'd done nothing wrong. She was the victim in all of this.

CHAPTER FIVE

Nick Shelby entered the mortuary nice and early at six sharp intending to get started on what he envisaged would take most of the daylight hours. He was sporting a three-day growth, his hair unruly in need of grooming. The heavy bags under his eyes betrayed the need for a solid uninterrupted sleep. A back log of autopsies had built up and there was mounting pressure from the county coroner to get things moving. The last thing he had time to worry about was his appearance, after all the patients were hardly likely to complain.

Nick scrubbed up and went in search of Tony Partridge his assistant pathologist for the day.

Unfortunately, James and Fiona had sent their apologies late last night; something urgent had cropped up preventing them from attending; they would have to wait for Nick's detailed report.

Tony Partridge was a waif of a man a characteristic accentuated even more by his tall figure and wore thick, dark rimmed glasses balanced precariously on a razor sharp, elongated nose. Hardly a flattering appearance, yet to Nick he was a real treasure. Tony was one of those rare individuals who knew a lot about everything and was currently working through a part time Masters' thesis in nuclear chemistry at Bristol University. Certainly, the right man for the job when it came to autopsies; Tony often unearthed things others missed.

When both men were scrubbed up and ready they brought the body of Muriel Jennings out from the freezer on a gurney.

Due to Muriel's maturing years the first thing to determine would be evidence associated with foul play not just the aging process. For inexperienced pathologists, it was easy to merge the two together with the result an inaccurate picture. Before starting Nick and Tony once more went over file notes and examined pictures of Muriel's body lying in the hallway of her Ashburton home.

Switching on the tape recorder Nick recited today's date, the exact time, full name of the deceased, and who would be carrying out the autopsy. With this out of the way he set to work on a full autopsy for Muriel Elizabeth Jennings, who died at approximately 5pm on Tuesday 4th March 2016 aged Sixty-five.

***

'The Coroner has released the body for burial,' Nick informed James, bowling unannounced into the Moorland office, two days following the completion of Muriel's autopsy. 'I've put through a call to Mark Jennings to advise the family can now go ahead with funeral arrangements.'

'So autopsy complete and report upstairs I take it?' James quizzed.

'Yep, bloody thing took me forever to put together,' Nick complained helping himself to water from the machine.

'Do you have time for a bite?' James offered. 'The Coffee Bean is open and I could monster a big breakfast.'

'You must be kidding,' Nick laughed draining the cup. 'I've a meeting at the Coroners' office in two hours. I can't stop now but suggest you all drop by my lab on Thursday

81

so I can give you the full autopsy results. By the way is that shoulder still giving you grief?'

'Occasionally,' James confessed. 'Perhaps I'll drop by later in the week for some of the good stuff.'

Nick disappeared leaving James knowing exactly why *he* hadn't pursued a career path in government medical forensics. The volume of paper work coupled with long hours dissecting cadavers was not on James's occupation A list. He much preferred the clean, efficient world of the scientific laboratory.

***

'So how was the science fair?' Fiona enquired, as James entered the office with his small overnight bag.

'Yeah okay, nothing special.'

Fiona noticed a bandage supporting his left wrist. 'What happened to you?'

'Got jammed in the car door, only a bruise, not broken.'

Her watch indicating a minute after one Fiona switched on the radio tuning in to Radio South West to get the local news:

We have a report just in that prominent South Hams business man Graham Hall was attacked last night leaving the Tavistock Conservative Club. He is recovering in Torbay Hospital with broken ribs and concussion. Devon police are urging anyone with information to please come forward.

***

'OK, what do you guys have?' James enquired walking into Nick Shelby's office with Katie and Fiona early Thursday afternoon. It was crunch time. The Moorland Forensic team were on edge anticipating the autopsy results Nick and Tony had put together. Also attending, Matt Taylor, a Home Office and part time freelance IT expert sometimes assigned by Moorland Forensics to unravel the inner secrets of computer hard drives taken as evidence from crime scenes. The data collected often invaluable in cracking cases. Matt and Katie first met in London at a seminar on "The Psychology of the Terrorist" and had remained good friends. Associates conjectured it was only a matter of time before they became romantically involved, the chemistry between them plainly obvious. Matt was a likeable guy, his best assets a mass of dark wavy hair framing striking, emerald eyes; and a well-toned physique developed from endless hours in the gym an instant turn on for the ladies.

'Ah you may well ask my friend,' Nick grinned as he put his arm around James and led them into a compact annex off the lecture theatre. 'Come see for yourself.'

Katie was permanently fascinated by what she had christened 'Nick's Sanctuary'. Copious scientific volumes filled shelves on the walls. Obscure and bizarre medical instruments mostly of an antiquarian nature were interspersed haphazardly amongst the publications. Katie could only guess at the grizzly function of some of the implements sending a cold shiver down her spine. She sat herself down on one of the wooden stools eagerly waiting for Nick to enlighten them with his dissection discoveries.

He wasted no time in getting to the point, standing at the white computer board and addressing the small group as a teacher would his pupils.

'The autopsy indicated a blow to Mrs Jennings' head with a small blunt object tying in nicely with the torch found at the crime scene. The other interesting fact was the autopsy showed an inflamed stomach with trace quantities of arsenic in the digestive tract.'

'Umm, that's interesting,' James interrupted.

'There were also indications of arsenic in the liver, fingernails, kidneys and hair,' Nick informed them as he began writing on the board to reinforce his comments. He also drew diagrams.

'This fits in with what Stella was saying,' Katie broke in. 'She said her Mother had complained of stomach cramps and vomiting. She'd also noticed considerable weight loss over a series of weeks.'

'It certainly points to a classic case of heavy metal poisoning,' James evaluated.

'To sum up,' Nick concluded. 'It looks as if initially someone was trying to poison Mrs. Jennings, however, when realizing this method of homicide was going to be drawn out they opted for a blow to the head.'

'From a psychologist's position, I think perhaps there's a bit more to this,' Katie piped up once more. 'I believe it wasn't the fact the poison was taking so long to work but more that the killer felt they weren't being listened to. The slow act of poisoning wasn't enough for them to get their point across. Poison as the method of choice didn't give the killer that sense of control.'

'Interesting theory,' Nick remarked, always willing to listen to Katie's viewpoint. 'There is one other fascinating fact. We discovered a tiny burn mark on Muriel's left thumb. The shape and size indicates being from a cigarette.'

'I can't recall if Muriel was a smoker but I don't believe she was,' Katie said, trying to think back to her past conversations with Stella.

'Just for the record she wasn't,' Nick enlightened them. 'The lungs showed no tar build up or toxicity from cigarettes. However, that doesn't fit the equation anyway as it appears the burn occurred after the attack took place. Our killer took it upon themselves to inflict the burn, most likely out of anger. There are no other signs of ill treatment.'

'Then our killer is a smoker,' Fiona supposed.

'Perhaps,' Nick suggested casually. 'But that's not a certainty. It could have been a deliberate rouse on their behalf to make us think that. I've prepared a paper for the coroner's court which I'll copy you in on. Now if we're all done I'm heading back over to the Jennings house. Perhaps you'd like to accompany me James? The DNA fingerprint analysis will probably be fairly inconclusive so I want to try luminol spray. There may be some things we've overlooked.'

James stood up to leave with Nick. 'Anyone else care to join us?'

Matt, Katie and Fiona shook their heads as one.

'I might drop into the county library to do a bit of research.' Katie announced as James and Nick departed. 'I want to find out more about the Cartwright murders to see if anything can be linked to Muriel's death. I'm keen to learn if *The Sinner's Daughter* can offer any insight.'

Fiona let out a small sigh, 'It'll be like looking for a needle in a haystack Katie.'

'Maybe, but it's worth a shot.'

***

Katie strolled into the Devon County Library in Exeter greeting Sarah, the librarian, with a warm smile before handing over a cappuccino donned in a white polystyrene takeaway cup. The women had met at Yoga classes a few years back where they'd build up a firm friendship. Sarah was very easy going with a bubbly personality. Not your typical bookish stereotype. She was accustomed to either Katie or Fiona dropping into the library at least once a week for research purposes. Most of the time they would head straight to the computerized newspaper section tucked away in a separate room at the back of the building. Katie usually visited on a Thursday afternoon; the library's half day closing. It was easier to carry out research when the general public weren't added to the equation. Sarah was also happy with this arrangement as it meant she could head home early leaving Katie to lock up. She was just rounding up the last of the public, ushering them out the door, when Katie turned up that afternoon.

'Can I use the research office?' Katie asked taking a sip of her cappuccino. It was more a polite formality not actually thinking Sarah would say no.

'Be my guest,' Sarah replied. 'The key's in the usual spot. Just make sure you lock up for me when you're done. I want to leave in about half an hour. Stan my assistant is around somewhere but he'll leave via the back door when he's ready, you probably won't even see him. The cleaning lady is also pottering around but don't worry about her. She'll vanish out the back door when done. They both know to ensure they lock the door behind them.'

'No problems. By the way, have you read this book?'

Katie held up a copy of *The Sinner's Daughter.*

Sarah nodded. 'Yep. I finished it about two months ago.'

'What did you think?' Katie enquired interested to gauge Sarah's opinion.

'All up a good read but not for the faint hearted,' Sarah remarked dropping a couple of returned library books onto the wooden trolley behind her. 'How one man can destroy the lives of so many people is beyond comprehension. It's the victims' families I feel sorry for. How would they ever come to terms with what happened to their loved ones? Cartwright was a monster.'

'Yes it's a terrible waste of lives and the book doesn't really state why he committed these crimes,' Katie said, 'not from a psychological perspective anyway.'

'Yes but according to Cartwright they've locked up the wrong person,' Sarah continued, 'and who knows he could be innocent. If the forensics conducted back then were not up to scratch, perhaps they did send down the wrong man. We're talking fifteen years ago. Perhaps the tests carried out at the time weren't as thorough as they should have been.'

'There are certainly a lot of ifs and buts,' Katie agreed. 'I'd be interested to find out who the forensic team were on the Cartwright murders and pay them a visit. You never know you could be right Sarah. How would that be if at the end of the day I discovered Cartwright was not guilty after all?'

'You'd either be a real hero or a bloody nuisance,' Sarah laughed. 'OK spill the beans, what are you looking for today?' Sarah was always interested in Katie's work. It added spark to an often mundane life.

'I'd like to get some details on Abigail Cartwright, Ted's daughter. It's alleged she lived in the house while the murders took place. I find that very strange. How could a ten-year-old not be aware of her surroundings and what was going on?'

'Anything's possible Katie,' Sarah replied, lowering her voice a touch. 'The Cartwright's house was hardly a two up two down. Have you seen it?'

Katie shook her head.

'It's huge,' Sarah informed her, 'you should drive onto the moor and take a look one day. The only reason I know about the place is I drop library books up to Millie Sandhurst. Her property is the neighbouring farm to

Cartwright's. It's a lonely, rundown proposition now, not the impressive house it once was.'

As Sarah resumed the task of herding the remaining stragglers out the main door Katie made straight for the computerized newspaper section balancing the coffee with a pile of papers she'd brought along. Knowing exactly what to look for she hoped to be rewarded.

All local papers were archived in the years they were printed then they were subdivided into weeks. The year and months of direct interest Katie was searching for was March to September 2001. Placing the drink on a nearby window sill she switched on one of the computers and waited for it to hum to life. Then she began punching in relevant data keen to find information on Abigail Cartwright and the subsequent murders of all five women by Abigail's father Ted Cartwright. The local gazette at the time had reported quite heavily on the story and pending court case. One article focused solely on Ted's life championing him as a pillar of the community. Another spoke of a man almost godlike who'd suddenly turned evil. It was hard to figure out the real Ted Cartwright. He'd built up a successful upholstery business over a number of years until a fall from a horse resulted in a severe back injury. One psychiatrist predicted it was Ted's disability that made him turn to murder; sheer frustration his affluent life had vanished almost overnight. The murders had been a distorted way of seeking revenge on a world that had caused him pain and suffering.

Katie was disappointed to find limited information pertaining to Abigail Cartwright. She'd hoped for a picture but was out of luck. As Abigail was only young when the murders took place she would have been protected by the Crown.

Reading on, Katie discovered more background history on Ted and his wife Jessica but only occasional snippets about Abigail. One particular article threw up Cartwright's defence lawyer, Dexter Sims, listing his law firm, 'Sims and Co', based in Princetown on the edge of Dartmoor. Katie jotted down this information with intentions of paying Sims a visit sooner than later. If anyone could shed more light on the Cartwright murders it would be him. There was also a picture of the family home, 'Heather Lea', situated four miles out of Princetown, described as an elaborately appointed late 19th century manor house, sympathetically restored over several years during the Cartwright's occupation. Looking at the photograph it was clear the property was potential front cover material for "The Weekly Realtor".

After two hours of scanning articles, computer eye strain was taking its toll. It had been a worthwhile exercise as Katie managed to gain useful insight into the Cartwright family with some promising leads to work on.

The temperature inside the library seemed to have dropped several degrees. Katie glad of her cashmere coat wrapped it firmly around her body fastening the top buttons. Perhaps it was the fact she'd been reading up on a serial killer or the realization everybody had left the building but instantly she felt a sense of foreboding. Without people around the library always felt a bit eerie but tonight seemed more so than usual. Without sound or movement, it became apparent Stan and the cleaning lady had already left.

A dim light in the main section of the library gave little comfort as Katie headed out of the research room making for the main entrance. She shot a quick, nervous glance over her right shoulder, half expecting to see someone standing in the shadows behind a reference shelf lined with volumes.

An instant or two later the main light alarmingly began to flicker on and off, before going out completely. Katie trying not to panic fished anxiously in her handbag for the small led torch carried for emergencies. After several frustrating seconds the compact torch was located and switched on, the powerful beam cutting through the gloom, lighting the way to the main exit. Hurrying across the main foyer Katie didn't notice an object centre stage. Her right leg caught the full impact of the obstacle causing her to trip and lunge forward. Simultaneously a pile of books crashed noisily to the floor near the main counter. For a brief moment, Katie froze unable to move. This unexpected and frightening event made her rudely aware she was *not* alone in the library; now she fought to get out as quickly as possible.

Limping slightly and rubbing her sore leg Katie scrambled for the exit her heart skipping several beats along the way. Not for one second did she now think the flickering light or the sudden crashing of books to be part of her imagination. Most certainly there was an intruder in the building and for all she knew they could be armed and dangerous.

Almost stumbling through the door, she managed to lock it behind her before cascading down the stone steps and onto the pavement. Low, heavy cloud enveloped the streetscape blocking out any moonlight. Desperate to put as much distance as possible between herself and the library and convinced she was now being followed Katie's pace quickened, high heel shoes pressing hard against the pavement. Her leg was throbbing from the fall, but it was imperative not to stop to take a look at the damage. Adrenalin was taking over and she had no immediate recollection of where the Punto was parked. She pushed herself onward looking for the sanctuary of a shop or group of commuters hurrying home. Entering an unfamiliar part of town Katie ducked into a poorly lit alley her main focus now to lose her stalker as quickly as possible. Seizing an opportunity to hide she ducked behind a parked delivery van hardly daring to draw breath. Peering out from around the side of the vehicle she glimpsed a figure standing near a poorly illuminated shop front but could not make out any discernible features, male or female.

How long Katie crouched behind the van she had no idea but her fingers were starting to numb from the cold and cramp was creeping into her right calf muscle. Finally, she could remain in the uncomfortable position no more and gingerly stretched up into a standing position, moving slowly on the spot to try and restore circulation. Carefully looking around she saw no sign of her pursuer and let out a huge sigh which turned into a sob of relief. A look at her watch indicated she'd been behind the van for a good twenty minutes.

Remembering the aching leg, she assessed the damage. Her faded jeans were covered in deep red blood stains. Carefully, rolling up the leg revealed a three-inch gash with a large chunk of flesh torn away. Fighting a wave of nausea, Katie grabbed a scarf from her bag tying it securely around the gaping wound. Although no medic swift observation indicated the urgent need for stitches. More than likely she'd lost a fair amount of blood, no surprise she felt faint. She must have fallen heavily onto a sharp object when she tripped in the library not realizing it at the time. Something she now believed was deliberately put there to cause injury.

Limping across town Katie made a conscious attempt to breathe deeply fearful of the onset of one of her unpredictable asthma attacks. Recognition of the surroundings brought with it another gasp of relief.

Katie wasn't expecting a sudden and violent lunge from behind, propelling her forwards. She felt her trusty brief case being torn from her shoulder. Too weak to fight off the determined assailant her legs buckled. Katie momentarily glimpsing the pavement shooting up, a wave of blackness washed over her…

***

'Been in the wars I see.'

Katie recognized the comforting face of Doctor Mike Armstrong from Newton Abbot Hospital. 'Quite a nasty cut you've got there, young lady,' he was taking a look at the gash on her thigh as he spoke. 'You'll require a number of stitches. I'll get one of the nurses to bring you into the clinical room and we'll make a start on fixing you up.'

Katie feebly muttered her thanks as she hobbled along the corridor to the clinical room aided by a young female casualty nurse.

The effects of delayed shock ruled as her head and knee were competing with each other to inflict maximum pain.

Watching as the young nurse gathered the suturing equipment Katie experienced sudden flashbacks of the eventful night but couldn't remember much detail, any recall was a puzzling blur.

The patient looked away as Mike began his handy work. She abhorred the sight of blood, especially her own. First, he numbed the area with lignocaine and cleaned the wound before commencing the deft suturing task.

After twenty minutes, he looked up and smiled, 'Thirty-three neat little stitches. You'll feel quite a bit of pain for a few days and rest is a priority; it'll heal nicely.'

Katie groaned. 'I've too much to do. I can't possible put my feet up.'

'I'm not asking you to rest, I'm telling you to rest; antibiotics and painkillers' he firmly reiterated placing two small plastic containers in her hand.

Katie's head pounded like the clappers of hell above the right temple but she was not about to mention this to any of the medical staff. If they thought for one moment there was possible concussion they'd be keeping her in for observations and right now Katie was desperate to get out of the wretched place – although well looked after, being fatalistic, Katie had a loathing for hospitals reinforced by the smell of solvents and antiseptics. Then a thought struck her. How did she happen to arrive at the hospital in the first place? The last thing she remembered was passing out and heading at 100 mph towards the asphalt. She enquired at the nurses' station on the way out.

The nurse in charge couldn't shed any light on events. She hadn't spotted anyone drop her off. Apparently, Katie had wandered into reception looking pale and weak and was assessed almost straight away by the emergency Doctor who happened to be Mike, an old family friend.

Katie puzzled over this as she found her way into an almost empty reception area where Fiona patiently sat waiting.

With no time to immediately revisit events Katie took the arm Fiona held out to her.

'Ready to go,' Fiona managed a watery smile. 'My goodness Katie you certainly don't do things by half. We've been worried sick. James is bringing the car around.'

Katie forced a weak smile hobbling along as fast as her sore leg would permit. Instant tears blurred her vision as she welcomed the cool night air. It had been one hell of a day and she just longed to get home and crawl into bed.

Over the coming weeks, Katie kept having recurring nightmares and flashbacks of the assault. She abhorred walking anywhere at night alone and always insisted on the company of a sibling if she did have to venture out of an evening. Infuriatingly the briefcase and shoulder bag were now in the attacker's possession. Gone was the garnered data relating to the Cartwright murders. It was back to square one.

Making headway on the Jennings murder was proving difficult, it was now clear to the Moorland group the attack on Katie was premeditated. She had been watched and the assailant had a good idea what she was doing at the Library. Further aggressive assaults on Katie or the team could be on the cards.

James had questioned Sarah at the library but nothing useful resulted. Stan, the library assistant, had been a fixture there for a number of years and came with impeccable references. Grilling the cleaning lady revealed she'd left five minutes after Sarah due to the onset of a migraine. No one could shed any light on a possible suspect. Furthermore, the sharp object causing Katie to trip and secure her injury was nowhere to be found. It has mysteriously disappeared.

Her mind was a blur. Before everything had seemed so easy but now things were different. She shouldn't really care, yet she did. Why couldn't they go away and leave her alone. She hadn't done anything to them. Not really. She'd not done anything as bad as before. Perhaps they already knew too much and if that was the case they needed to be silenced.

CHAPTER SIX

Her heart racing and between heavy breaths Fiona drained the last mouthfuls from her water bottle and bent over forwards, hands on knees. Her lips felt dry and cracked and a misty perspiration lingered on her face and neck as she thankfully flopped onto the couch. It's one thing to try and keep fit but another to nearly kill yourself Fiona mused ruefully as her breathing slowly edged back to normality.

First cab off the rank this morning she intended to quiz the senior consulting pathologist working on the Jennings case in Plymouth. Nick Shelby had carried out the preliminary examinations and autopsy passing the results on to the Home Office Coroner. Coincidently, she vaguely recalled that this medico had also worked on the Cartwright murders.

It was an easy forty-minute drive along the A38 into the outskirts of the city. Fiona picked the travel time carefully to slot in between peak hour traffic. Plymouth, an important naval base, had been almost raised to the ground during the Blitz. Reconstruction in the 50's and 60's using Portland stone and concrete combined with government architecture of the day had been all encompassing; the result once seen by many as grim and imposing, now recognised as representative of the times and worthy of heritage protection. Fiona, who once looked forward to trips to the city, now detested the soulless, overpowering facade of the modernist architecture overtaking the retail district with its glitzy shopping malls.

It was easy to locate the Pathologist's offices just off Union Street, above one of the major department stores and accessible by a flight of steep stairs leading up from a glass door directly off the main street. The etched sign on the door read 'Rubble & Co Forensic Pathologists.'

Reaching the top of the stairs Fiona wondered if she had got the dates wrong as the front reception desk was deserted. A buzzer sat on top of the desk return. As Fiona reached forward to press the button a middle aged woman in a lab coat appeared rubbing her eyes like she'd just woken from a mid-morning siesta.

'If you're selling we're not buying,' she grumbled stretching her back. 'Ain't got time for such nonsense.'

'No I'm not selling anything,' Fiona informed her politely. 'I've an appointment with the pathologist, Mr. Rubble.'

'Oh I see,' she chortled. 'Well Mr. R is out the back working in the lab. Go on through and don't leave the airlock open, and watch where you're treading. He's been dissecting an eye ball and the damn thing flew right off the bench and landed somewhere on the floor.'

Fiona smothered a grin. Mr. Rubble's offsider assistant was quite a character; no doubt ideally suited to the job of lab assistant which demanded a good sense of humour coupled with a strong stomach for blood and guts. Following the assistant's instructions Fiona headed out the back to the lab where she found Rubble washing his hands at a row of obligatory stainless steel sinks.

He glanced up as Fiona approached, simultaneously grabbing at a roll of paper towelling and proceeding to dry both hands vigorously.

'Welcome, welcome my dear,' he beamed remembering he had an appointment with her. 'I'm Barney Rubble. Pleased to meet you.'

Fiona stifled a laugh, surely, he couldn't be serious. She had watched the Flintstones as a child and was all too familiar with Barney Rubble and Fred.

He saw the look in her eyes and laughed, 'Don't worry I get this all the time,' he reassured her as he scrutinised her card. "Dr Fiona Sinclair F.P." 'I was about to reward myself a ten-minute break with a cuppa and the sandwiches Mrs. Rubble packed for me. Can I offer you anything for a fellow colleague?'

'Coffee would be nice,' Fiona replied following him into a room just off the lab, which doubled as a storeroom-cum-kitchen.

Barney reached up to a cluttered shelf and retrieved a couple of ancient looking mugs; he then proceeded to give them a good rinse under running water. From all the empty take away cups scattered around the room it looked like Barney rarely *made* himself coffee relying heavily on the local takeaway places to get his daily caffeine fix.

'How long have you been sited here?' Fiona enquired, intrigued that a seemingly antiquated operation was still functioning.

'They've wanted to move me for years to more contemporary premises,' Barney remarked as he flicked on the kettle. 'I took over the premises in the late eighties when old Doc Prendergast finally chucked it in.'

Fiona, glancing across, hoped the kettle contained fresh water. He hadn't bothered filling it up.

Instantly dismissing these thoughts, she continued her questioning. 'So I take it you're not keen on moving?'

'No I'm not,' Barney retorted going on the attack. 'Who needs a state of the art abattoir with the latest mod cons. If you're a forensic pathologist worth your salt you

97

can work with the most basic equipment. Wouldn't you agree Miss?'

Fiona wasn't sure she entirely agreed with his remark so refrained from commenting. One could only imagine the frustration of the authorities stuck with a path room in the middle of the retail sector – they must have been tearing their hair out for years trying to evict him. One could only assume he had friends in high places.

Fiona glanced around the messy office – rubble by name and rubble by nature. How anyone could work in such confusion was hard to fathom. Personally, Fiona liked efficiency and organization; with everything in its place. However, despite the semblance of utter chaos Barney easily located everything needed. He even managed to unearth a packet of digestive biscuits tucked away behind some old jars.

'I understand you were the Senior Pathologist who worked on the Cartwright murders back in 2001?' Fiona remarked as she watched Barney put a generous tea spoon of coffee into each cup then pour in boiling water. He indicated milk and sugar before leading the way back to the lab to answer Fiona's question.

'Yes that's right. I worked like a man possessed to bring that show to a close and see justice for those poor women. Great Caesar's Ghost, we're going back over fifteen years now. You must have still been at school when that case hit the spot light miss.'

'Indeed I was.' Fiona laughed placing her hands around the warm mug and taking a generous sip trying not to baulk at the taste. The strength of the coffee would most probably see her up all night. 'Do you happen to have all the file notes and evidence from the Cartwright case Mr. Rubble?'

'Yep it's still all in here and please call me Barney,' he patted the side of a metallic four drawer filing cabinet next to him. 'By the way, we're not allowed to ditch anything for a minimum 10 years. Of course copies of these files are also stored at the Home Office in London anyway. I'm partial to these docs. Many late nights were spent working on the Cartwright matter. I was extremely pleased with the outcome. A great justice was done when that man was found guilty and locked away up at Princetown.'

'Would you mind if I took a look at some of the files?' Fiona continued. 'I'm very interested in the case and the testing which led to Cartwright's conviction.'

'I really shouldn't allow you access,' Barney replied dubiously. 'I'd be shot if the Constabulary got wind.'

Fiona resorted to her best pleading expression which usually worked on most males. It had the desired effect on Barney who quickly opened the top drawer of the filing cabinet and produced a large folder placing it on the desk in front of her. 'Perhaps just this once wouldn't hurt, seeing that we're both in the same game,' he remarked. 'I'll make Mrs. Simms a cuppa while you scan over the file. Anything you learn you didn't get it from me.'

With Rubble gone Fiona began opening the file, handling it with care as some of the binding had worked loose from frequent use. She didn't need the embarrassment and chaos of the pages spilling onto the floor.

The folder was easy enough to navigate through. There was an index at the front listing all the contents. She went straight to the section listing names of all Cartwright's victims. The first victim listed as twenty-one-year-old Tracy Liddle, a third year student nurse from Bristol University, noted as being on holiday in Devon during her semester-break when she'd encountered Cartwright. According to the report she and a group of friends were hiking across Dartmoor when Tracy had strayed off the designated track losing her way on open moorland. Looking for assistance she'd stumbled upon Heather Lea – the rest was history. The forensic evidence indicated she'd been dead for almost six months by the time her body had been discovered along with the other four victims. Turning the page Fiona came across a photograph of Tracy's partially decomposed body. Both hands were placed across her chest and lying diagonally in the centre of her middle was a withered flower.

'A single white rose was found on all his victims,' Barney informed Fiona as he stood looking over her shoulder at the photo she was studying.

Fiona bizarrely fascinated stared closely at the image taking in all the details. It seemed a very odd thing to do. Why would you bother going to the trouble of placing a flower on each victim?

'Cartwright physically tortured all his victims before murdering them,' Barney went on to explain. 'Charming fella, wasn't he?'

'So it seems,' Fiona replied softly a little choked by these horrific murders so close to her own family home.

'The interesting thing was that although all evidence pointed to Cartwright as the culprit he did a good job trying to cover his tracks,' Barney informed her, 'he hid all the items used to torture and kill his victims deep on the moor so it ended up being a lengthy process bringing him to justice. Have you visited Heather Lea; the scene of the murders?'

'Ah, not yet,' Fiona replied. 'I've heard it's a very intriguing place.'

'You'll see what I mean when you do,' Barney said softly, 'could get yourself lost for hours in that old place and still not find what you're looking for. Now can we make a start on some of the Jennings tissue preps? There'll be plenty of time to take another look at the Cartwright file later.'

Fiona reluctantly handed him back the file which was immediately placed back in the filing cabinet under lock and key. Barney was not about to risk damage to his prized possession and quite rightly so. Forensic medicos were passionate about their work.

Fiona followed Barney to the working area of the lab and after donning a gown, mask and gloves she watched and assisted Rubble with extraction and preparation of several sterile frozen tissue samples. These were labelled and systematically examined on slides under a powerful conventional microscope, any abnormal cell formations being noted.

Barney Rubble was certainly a character. He possessed a wealth of interesting, quirky stories, some work related, others not. He was also a first rate pathologist performing his tasks like a strong heartbeat.

'I also conducted the autopsy on young Sasha Williams,' Barney informed Fiona with his eyes glued to a high-tech microscope. 'She was the only person to escape from Cartwright but sadly she committed suicide a few years later. I believe her family reside in the vicinity not far from Dartmoor prison. Odd if you ask me. Why anyone would want to remain in close proximity to the man who was partially responsible for their daughter's death baffles me.'

Fiona took all this in like a sponge. 'Would I be able to see Sasha's file?' she asked.

Barney looked a bit sceptical. 'I'm not meant to allow anyone access to that file either.'

'This really could help my current investigation,' Fiona urged. 'It could help immensely with the case.'

Barney moved over to another filing cabinet, this one was a lot smaller than the one that housed the files of the other women. He retrieved a blue folder and passed it to Fiona who skimmed through the first few pages. It appeared the death and autopsy of Sasha Williams was quite straight forward. The sad part was the fact she had taken her own life. In theory, this meant she was actually another of Cartwright's victims, bringing the total to six.

'We should have today's test results within a couple of days, but the blood tests and DNA preliminaries could be a while,' Barney informed Fiona bringing her thoughts back to the present. 'I'll give you a call when they come through from histology and the path labs in Bristol.'

'Can I ask you more questions in relation to the Cartwright murders?' Fiona asked as they sat in the lab drinking more strong coffee.

'Fire away,' Barney said smiling. 'It's been a while since anyone's shown such interest in Ted Cartwright.'

Barney rambled on for another hour with reminiscences and background facts relating to the murders and court case but Fiona gleaned no real value from the banter.

On leaving the premises she left Barney rummaging around on all fours searching for the missing eyeball he'd been dissecting earlier. It had been a good day. Barney was a bit eccentric and an obvious anachronism, but she could put up with that. She could relate to him and he had responded with help. A friendship had been forged.

Fiona was yawning repeatedly by the time she reached the haven of her small flat. It was only eight-thirty but it had been a long tiring day. Putting a jazz LP on the Hi-Fi from her prized collection she lay down on the sofa hoping to drift off slowly into welcoming sleep. Her much needed rest became fretful as pictures of Cartwright's victims bounced into her head, images of their corpses lying on the dank cellar floor like sleeping beauties all with a single white rose across their midriffs. Never would a white rose mean quite the same again. It was amazing how to the human mind something so beautiful in appearance could suddenly become ugly and sinister.

***

Before Fiona even got to the office the following day she took a call in her car from Barney with pathology and blood DNA results; a lot earlier than expected. The news he brought was most interesting and saw Fiona hopping around the office impatiently waiting for her siblings to arrive, anxious to share the information.

'I've just received some initial path results back from the consulting F. P. Barney Rubble in Plymouth and some interesting conclusions.' Fiona began as they took off their jackets and headed to the lab.

'Such as?' James enquired, throwing his over the back of a chair and easing himself onto a stool.

'Such as the blood found at the house was definitely that of Muriel Jennings but there was also a splatter of blood at the crime scene belonging to another person. At a guess, it would appear the mystery blood came from a small hand cut. The unknown blood had a pattern indicating a similarity to Muriel's offspring; however, the fascinating thing is the DNA typing although only preliminary at that stage does not match that of Stella or Mark. This now begs the question that Muriel must have another child we don't know about. We are running further pathology tests for clarification but the plot certainly thickens.'

James gave a sharp intake of breath. 'By Christ, you have to be kidding me?' he replied looking stunned. 'As far as we are aware Muriel only had two children. This really is a turn up for the books.'

'I wonder if Mark or Stella is aware of another sibling,' Katie chimed in. 'If not I'd hate to be the one to break the news. Could you imagine the look on Mark Jennings face if this was thrown at him?'

'I'd rather not,' James remarked truthfully. 'Besides this is something we really need to investigate before we speak with any of the Jennings clan. If neither Mark nor Stella has knowledge of another sibling, we are sure to be opening a can of worms.'

'One person who may be able to shed light on things would be the Jennings family Doctor,' Katie suggested. 'Surely Muriel's medical records would have to indicate if there was a third pregnancy.'

'Ah there's a job for you sis,' Fiona shot at Katie. 'Good luck with that one. Doctors are sworn by the Hippocratic Oath keeping all patient information confidential.'

'Once more like a lamb to the slaughter,' Katie grinned with good humour.

'Here's another fascinating thing,' Fiona informed her siblings. 'I took a look at photos of all five Cartwright victims and each one was found with a single white rose lying on their stomachs.'

'That explains the cover of the book,' Katie remarked. 'I wondered why a rose was depicted on the cover, now I know.'

'Why would Ted Cartwright place a single white rose on each of his victims?' James asked. 'Seems a bloody strange thing to do.'

'I don't believe Ted did place the roses on each of his victims,' Katie replied frankly, her psychological mind in overdrive. 'It's not something that matches his profile.'

'He must have,' James argued forcefully. 'Photos don't lie – they provide proof. We all know Cartwright murdered those women.'

'Do we?' Katie replied softly. 'Think about it James, suppose Ted isn't the one who murdered those women. For years, Ted could have been put away for a crime he didn't commit. Perhaps the focus should have been on Abigail Cartwright, his daughter.'

***

Fiona greeted her ex-husband warmly, planting a friendly kiss on the side of his cheek. He reciprocated with an affectionate hug. There was no animosity between them at all; it had been a reasonably amicable split. Twin seven-year-old boys had resulted from the union but both parents shared the responsibility well and there had been little to feud about in recent times.

Angus was a Detective Sergeant with the Devon Police based in Crediton. He took his job very seriously but always made sure he betrothed quality time to be with his sons.

'Hi Angus.' James greeted his ex-brother-in-law with a healthy handshake as Angus entered the Moorland office. 'You should bring the boys over for dinner next Saturday to watch the big rugby test. Young Ben's already showing signs of playing for England.'

This was all said with good humour, Angus was from Motherwell in Scotland and proud of his northern heritage.

He laughed good naturedly giving James a firm slap on the back. 'He'll be playing for Scotland not the Sassenachs, James my boy. Got a beer in that fridge of yours?'

James extracted a cold beer from the fridge tossing it to Angus who caught it deftly. 'So what brings you to these parts? I take it if the boys aren't with you, this must be a business call?'

'Ay 'tiss that Lad,' Angus replied, opening the beer and taking a swig. 'I have some information you might find interesting in relation to the recent murder of Muriel Jennings.'

James sat bolt upright in his seat. 'Bring it on. We're at a standstill. I'd welcome any new information you have to hand.'

Angus placed a hard cover book on the desk in front of James titled *Breathing in time with Forensic Science.*

James picked it up examining the front piece which depicted an over embellished coffin and some nails. 'Can't say I've heard of this one before,' he remarked. 'Is it one I should be reading?'

'Perhaps you've heard of the author?' Angus enquired.

James shook his head as he read the name on the glossy cover, 'Doctor P Thornton-Jones. 'Nope can't say I have.' he remarked truthfully.

He was intrigued with where this little game was leading. He'd never heard of the author and never read the book. What made this tome any different from all the others written on the subject of forensic science and what link could it possibly have to the late Muriel Jennings?

Angus moved across to James and flicked open the book to the back inside cover. There were a few short paragraphs followed by a picture of the author; a man early fifties about, dressed in a lab coat standing next to an elaborate array of laboratory glassware filled with bubbling liquids. James was still none the wiser.

'Okay I give up,' he chided, putting his hands up to show defeat. 'You'll have to put me out of my misery D.S. Martyn.'

'Read the start of the second paragraph,' Angus instructed, a bemused expression etched on his craggy face.

James did as he was told, reading aloud, 'Doctor Peter Thornton-Jones has spent the last five years lecturing at the University of Cardiff in Wales. He lives with his wife Stella Jennings and their two black Labradors in the Welsh valleys.'

As he read the name Stella Jennings his mouth drifted open. 'Well I'm blessed. She certainly never led on she was married to an expert scientist.'

'Probably means nothing but I thought you should know,' Angus replied casually. 'You can keep the book if you like. I have no use for it.'

The men chatted for a while, finishing their beers before Angus bid his farewell.

Once alone in the office James picked up the book again. Well, well, well. Stella was a dark horse. She probably knew a fair bit about forensics yet never let on. It was a slim possibility she could have had some involvement in her mother's attack, being au fait with the technical tricks to cover one's tracks. James now needed to undergo a further background check on Stella before she could be completely taken off the list of suspects. God this case was becoming frustrating. All leads led to nowhere.

The basement was cold and damp. Five bodies were lined up on the cement floor. Young, pretty faces lined up like porcelain dolls. Suddenly before her eyes they began to move, each one coming to life and dancing to the lively tune being played on the violin. She put her hand to her head begging them to stop but they kept dancing, tormenting her with every new beat. The one with large blue eyes began twirling in circles until they all joined in. Round and round they went; five pretty maids all in a row.

CHAPTER SEVEN

It was the morning of Muriel's funeral and a cooler morning than would be expected for the time of year. Katie dressed in a pair of black loose fitting trousers with pale grey shirt, not wishing to look too much like a businesswoman. A waterproof bandage covered the stitches in her leg which required the wearing of loose fitting clothes. A taxi had been pre-booked; driving was definitely off the menu with the amount of painkillers in her system. Falling asleep at the wheel was a highly likely prospect.

Katie never liked attending funerals as part of her work, feeling these occasions should really be reserved for family and friends. Arranging to meet James and Fiona at the church a little before eleven most domestic matters were taken care of early to ensure she arrived on time. It was not a good look to arrive late to a funeral.

Katie left the house as a light drizzle began to descend from the edge of the moor. At St Andrew's church in Ashburton a few small groups of mourners had already gathered in the churchyard. The taxi driver manoeuvred to pull up on the grass verge directly opposite the thirteenth century church so Katie only needed to hobble a few yards across the road.

She waved, catching sight of James and Fiona waiting by the church gate, heading over to them when the road was clear.

A sizeable crowd had turned up. As to be expected all the book club members were present with about eighty others comprising of family and close friends.

Fiona and Katie made small talk with Cathy Munroe and Liz Palmer from the book club. With the service about to start they made their way inside to claim a pew.

The church was tastefully decorated with copious bunches of freshly cut spring flowers. The fragrant scents of freesias, daffodils, foxgloves, and roses wafted through the air. A slight breeze drifting through the open doors held the inside of the church at a comfortable temperature.

They watched as Stella arrived supported by Marshall Davidson the Jennings family lawyer. Katie recognised him from a recent article in the Newton Abbot Star. James spotted Greg McIntyre, Peter Swift and a few others from Jennings Clay. Again, they all sported the company shirt with the J C logo as a mark of respect. After all, Muriel had been their boss. However, it was Laura Jennings who attracted the most attention. Katie pointed her out to her siblings recognizing Laura from a photograph hanging on a wall in Muriel's living room.

As Laura Jennings entered the church on the arm of her husband Mark all heads turned. Dressed in a Giorgio Armani suit her slim porcelain figure reflected classic elegance.

'You know, I wouldn't mind betting Muriel's killer is here right now,' James whispered to his siblings as they waited for the proceedings to begin. 'It's a well-known fact most killers enjoy attending their victim's funeral.'

A hush descended as the vicar moved to the altar to start the ceremony.

A simplistic, straightforward service followed. Stella deliberately kept it mostly upbeat in an attempt to celebrate her mother's life rather than focus solely on her death. The eulogy was read out by Marshall Davidson at Mark's request. Public speaking was not really his forte and although usually projecting a tough exterior the pain he was suffering today didn't go unnoticed.

Marshall's prepared little speech reflected on Muriel's role as a mother and grandmother capturing her love of books and the great outdoors. Towards the end, he spoke of her position as MD of Jennings Clay. The congregation learnt she'd taken up the reins when her husband died unexpectedly in 1994. She had put a lot into the business rescuing it from receivership not long after her loss.

As the eulogy ended the first hymn followed almost seamlessly. The organist's fingers moved effortlessly over the keyboard playing a traditional but uplifting standard selection gleaned from the English Hymnal, very stirring with an enthusiastic chorus, unmistakably Vaughan Williams with its Tudor undertones. Stella had flatly refused to have anything dour and depressing.

'That was such an inspirational service,' Cathy commented joining the Sinclair's sheltering under some large oak trees by the main doorway. 'Muriel would have certainly approved, god rest her soul.'

'Yes it was nice,' Fiona agreed. 'Are you joining the family in the village hall for the wake?'

Cathy gave a brief nod. 'I feel I must pay my respects although I shan't stay too long. I've never been one to intrude on families in their time of grief.'

'True, these moments can be quite difficult,' Fiona acknowledged. 'We'll be heading straight home but I'll have a few words with Stella before we leave.'

'You lot still hanging around?' Mark chided almost knocking into the small group as he came bounding up. 'Just can't keep away can you?'

Choosing to ignore these remarks James led his sisters along the church path towards the wrought iron gates. Not liking the fact he was being ignored Mark followed closely behind letting forth with a barrage of invectives loud enough for several people close by to hear.

Those feeling uncomfortable dodged around the graves in order to escape. If it hadn't been such a tactless act on Mark's behalf the sight of people falling over headstones might have raised a few laughs.

Katie spotted Laura Jennings standing alone near the church steps. On the spur of the moment she decided to go across for a quick word. Advising the others she wouldn't be long, she caught up with Laura and introduced herself.

Laura seemed pleased to have someone to talk to and they chatted for almost ten minutes. The bulk of their conversation focused on Laura's aspiring music career but they also discussed other things before the conversation came back to Laura's role as Muriel's daughter in law. According to Laura they had got along fairly well.

'So are you heading back to London tonight or will you be sticking around for a while?' Katie asked with interest.

Laura shrugged her shoulders. 'I'd like to stay but things are a bit strained between Mark and myself at the moment. My staying would only cause greater friction. I'll most likely head back shortly before five so I can get Mitchell settled into his usual routine.'

Katie wished Laura a safe trip back before re-joining her siblings who were patiently waiting by the car.

***

It was just after seven when the last person vacated the village hall enabling Stella to quietly make her way home. She flatly refused company insisting her preference was to be alone. Having just buried her mother she was in no mood for idle chit chat.

111

Punching the remote to open the double garage doors Stella drove straight in parking at a slight angle. She then approached the internal door, which lead directly into the house; a convenient entrance in inclement weather. The key in the lock turned smoothly enabling her to step into the hallway as she simultaneously let out a long sigh. Finally, she could relax from what had been one of the worst days of her life.

Deciding to spend time soaking in a warm bubble bath Stella climbed the stairs to the landing checking the thermos on the way to ensure there was enough hot water. As she slipped into oblivion, her head slightly emerged above the water, time drifted slowly. She bathed for a good hour before hopping out and drying vigorously all over with a towel until her skin became red raw. A freshly folded pink night dress was retrieved from her dresser before reaching into a French Empire wardrobe for dressing gown and slippers. Back downstairs in the kitchen she placed some chamomile tea leaves into a china tea pot.

The tea made, she sunk into a chair taking a welcoming sip, glad the night was drawing in. Later she could look forward to climbing into her comfortable bed and putting the strenuous day behind her. With the curtains in the sitting room drawn, she felt completely shut off from the outside world. In a few minutes her eyelids grew heavy and peaceful slumber beckoned.

The shrill sound of the phone suddenly made her jump. She wasn't expecting any calls and felt annoyed. People had no respect for privacy during her time of grief. Easing haltingly onto her feet and in a semi-dazed state Stella entered the hallway where the phone kept up its persistent ring. About to lift the receiver and without warning the sound of breaking glass shattered the silence and a large flying object ricocheted off the wall narrowly missing her head. The shock forced Stella to her knees cowering in fear. Still in a half trance she reached out and picked up the phone. For several moments, there was nothing then a jarring click as the party at the other end put down the receiver. Unable to move Stella sensed someone very nearby was watching. She slowly curled up into a ball and sobbed.

***

'What a day,' Fiona commented to James and Katie kicking off her two inch heels.

'You bet, funerals are not my favourite happenings,' Katie remarked, as she made her way to an art deco drinks cabinet and proceeded to pour everybody a large port from a crystal decanter.

'At least it went off without too much theatrics,' James smiled, reminiscing on a funeral they'd attended back in January when a disgruntled mistress of the deceased had stripped down to her underwear to make some sort of statement. She'd then taken to running up and down the aisle screaming for the murderer to come forward. Rather embarrassing for all those in attendance. Having said that all the males present had felt their blood pressure soar as the woman in question was endowed with a sizeable pair of breasts and an impressive figure. It was one funeral James wasn't likely to forget in a hurry.

'I suppose Mark could have behaved a lot worse,' Katie reflected thoughtfully. 'We got off lightly with a few sarcastic comments.'

James laughed reaching for his smart phone which had starting buzzing. He wasn't expecting any calls and there was no caller ID.

After a few minutes of reassuring the person on the other end of the phone and suggesting they sit tight until he get there he turned to his sisters.

'That was Stella Jennings. Someone has just thrown a brick through the glass panel of her front door. I'm heading straight over there if anybody wants to come?'

'I'll grab my jacket,' Katie said, getting to her feet 'No need for you to venture out again tonight Fi, we'll see you tomorrow.'

When James and Katie pulled up outside Stella's cottage she was waiting for them on the doorstep. She looked pale and drawn clad in her pink dressing gown and slippers.

'You did the right thing calling me,' James reassured her. 'I've notified the police.'

Katie headed straight for the drinks cabinet in the living room in search of some brandy. James meanwhile was studying the brick lying in the hallway.

'Do you think the person who threw this could have been the one who made the phone call?' Stella asked, her voice starting to crack from the pressure.

'Quite likely,' James replied, carefully picking up the brick with his gloved hand and placing it in a clear plastic bag for later examination.

When the police arrived some thirty minutes later Stella seemed calmer and able to assist with giving a statement. Not that she could provide them with much information. She'd not witnessed anyone lurking about outside the house nor did she hear a voice on the other end of the phone.

Whilst Stella was chatting to the young police constable James pulled Katie aside. 'I think it would be best to try and get Stella police protection. If she declines she should at least spend the night with friends.'

'We're done here for now,' a young policewoman remarked joining James and her fellow officer. 'We'll file a report but there's not much more we can do for the time being.'

'No problem, and thanks anyway,' James replied, easing open the door and walking with them to their patrol car.

Katie stayed behind joining Stella in the drawing room where she sat staring into space.

'We think it would be best if you stay with friends tonight,' Katie advised Stella sitting beside her. 'It's been one hell of a day and after what happened here it wouldn't be wise to spend the night alone.'

Stella nodded an approval, opting for the least path of resistance. She was exhausted and craved sleep.

Early next morning James and Katie, alerted by a police phone message, hurried back to the Jennings's residence. Walking through the front door they were shocked to find the place had been turned upside down. 'The SO discovered it about an hour ago.' informed the attendant constable.

James gave a low whistle as he surveyed the chaotic scene. 'I don't think our brick thrower had any intentions of harming Stella after all,' he declared. 'It looks like the objective was to get Stella out of the house. With this accomplished it paved the way for them to return and search for something of obvious importance.'

Katie shook her head in disbelief. 'It certainly appears plausible. I must admit they've done an excellent job of ransacking the place. Good God, even the contents of the fridge have been scattered all over the floor. I wouldn't like to be cleaning up this mess.'

James entered the sitting room and carefully stepped over broken furniture, smashed ornaments and a mass of strewn papers until he found a clear space to stand. As they had no idea what the intruder had been searching for there was no point even trying to figure it out.

'Whatever they came back to collect must be of vital significance,' Katie sighed. 'It would appear they went to great lengths in an attempt to get it.'

'Too right sis and we have no idea if they succeeded in their mission,' James concurred.

'This is interesting,' Katie remarked glancing upwards. 'We didn't spot this before.'

'Good grief, how did we miss that?' James uttered, noticing what had caught her attention. 'Must be a switch or something around, see anything?'

"Over here,' Katie exclaimed, motioning to a small button situated on the wall near the light switch. With a deft press, and hey presto, the ceiling opened and articulated stairs glided silently downward.

'I'll let you venture up there,' James said, as he turned to Katie, 'I'll continue to nose around down here in case there's anything else we've missed. I don't think those stairs will take my weight.'

'Gee thanks for that,' Katie replied sarcastically. 'I always get the exciting jobs don't I?'

'Yep, I'm generous to a fault,' James chuckled. 'Sing out if you find anything interesting.'

With mixed feelings of apprehension and curiosity Katie made her way upwards, stepping warily into a small, cramped attic room at the very top of the house. Turning on a light in the tight space she looked around. The only thing of note appeared to be a decidedly worse for wear antique trunk which she prized open with her Swiss army knife.

Peering inside the trunk Katie reached in extricating a bundle of dog eared black and white photographs consisting primarily of what she assumed to be pictures of members of the Jennings family intermixed with a few of the obligatory rural and beach scenes. One photo stood out amongst the rest; a snap of a young woman standing with three children against a rose garden backdrop: a girl and a boy of about four and six and an older girl who looked about fifteen. The two girls wore long white dresses the boy was dressed in a suit and tie. The older girl's face was blacked out with crayon.

Then there was a more recent colour shot of Stella and Mark standing with a third person, whose face was also blacked out with crayon. The photo could only be a year or two old. Intrigued, Katie removed both photographs and stuffed them into the inside of her jacket for closer examination later.

Finding nothing else of interest Katie closed the lid of the trunk and started to work her way backwards down the stairs. She was startled nearing the last few treads, discovering Mark Jennings waiting at the bottom almost hidden by a coat stand. She let out an involuntary cry, stumbled losing her footing and slid embarrassingly down the last few treads wrenching an ankle in the process.

'Not you again,' Mark raged. 'This house is not a public right of way, you can't pop round every five bloody minutes.'

'I can do what the hell I like,' Katie fired back at him, her temper flaring up as she rubbed her ankle, simultaneously trying to gain some composure. 'This is a murder investigation Mr. Jennings. I am only doing my job.'

He stood only inches away, well inside her territorial comfort zone with powerful arms folded, blocking any escape. He was enjoying empowering her, having the upper hand.

Katie was about to shout to James for assistance when thankfully he materialised standing close behind Mark.

'Please move Mr. Jennings. I'm sure you don't want to see yourself arrested.'

'You lot can't take a joke, that's your problem,' Mark smirked. 'I was larking around, which for your information is not illegal Sinclair.'

'Obviously, I don't share your wonderful sense of humour,' James smiled sardonically. 'Now get out of my sight.'

James turned to Katie. 'Come on let's get out of here. We'll leave this filthy rat to clean up the mess.'

***

Professor Bradbury waited quietly behind his desk for the patient to arrive watching the clock on the wall with anticipation. He was half expecting her not to turn up. He was therefore slightly taken aback when she strolled into the office moving unerringly towards the vacant chair opposite.

'Sorry if I'm a bit late,' she apologized, taking the glass of water he was offering. 'Some sort of road works on the A38.'

'No problem; Take a seat and we'll get started.' He knew she didn't drive but she often commented on the traffic and how her old MG needed a kick-start every now and again.

She obliged flopping down into a heavily patterned leather chair. Her hair was messy and it looked like she'd only just crawled out of bed; a look the Professor has grown accustomed to. The unkempt appearance never fazed. It was her mind he was interested in.

'So how have you been since we last met?' he asked casually, a hand resting on his chin.

'Much the same,' came the reply, in barely more than a whisper. 'I just need more time to digest everything that has happened over the past few weeks. It's not been easy coming to terms with the death of all those women. God knows what Ted was thinking about at the time.'

Professor Bradbury realized she was digressing with this statement. It had been years not weeks since it all happened. Careful not to mention this fact for fear of repercussions he offered his usual support.

'It won't be easy. We've often spoken about thought processes in an attempt to move on and focusing on the future. Now tell me what troubles you the most?'

'Being like him. I don't want to be like him.' She looked beseechingly at Professor Bradbury for reassurance.

'Come now you're nothing like him.' he replied, offering that assurance.

A frown appeared deep on her forehead, a zigzag line running the whole depth. 'Of course I'm like him,' she snapped crossly. 'What makes me different?'

'Well apart from the fact......'

He was in mid-sentence when she stood up and put her hands over her ears in protest indicating she'd had enough. She started pulling at her hair babbling unintelligibly.

'We can work through this.' Professor Bradbury remarked, switching to a positive approach. He noted familiar signs of extreme anxiety. Observing his patient's agitation increasing with each second passed he reached into his coat pocket for a tiny bottle of pills. He took out one small white tablet placing it into her outstretched hand.

'Here you go. This will help.'

The pill was grabbed and swallowed swiftly with the water she still had. Hands shaking a little she sat back down.

'Good afternoon Doctor Bradbury. Not late am I? The traffic was a bit heavier than usual.'

He realized she had no recollection of the past five or so minutes. Her condition was a lot worse than he'd first thought.

'So how have you been since we last met?' he asked casually.

The voices kept calling out her name over and over again. They wouldn't stop. Over and over again they whispered through the darkness until in the end there were over twenty voices echoing in unison. All through the night they kept calling out her name, softly whispering the name...

CHAPTER EIGHT

Katie walking into the office just before noon placed a pile of papers onto her desk and set about fixing a strong cappuccino. The previous night had been spent sorting through forensic reports and signing off on findings for the Coroner's Office; not hitting the sack until well after one.

James entrenched at his desk looked up as his younger sister sidled into her chair ready to begin work. Although her eyes were slightly red and puffy, Katie still managed to radiate glamour.

'I've just received a call from Laura Jennings advising Mark was not in London the night Muriel was attacked,' James informed his sister. 'She sounded notably upset so I'm guessing they'd had a row.' He smiled contemptuously as he relayed this information leaning back heavily in his chair, hands relaxed behind his head. 'It appears Laura's been covering for Mark but now she wants to come clean. Perhaps she's finally realizing what a rat he can be.'

'It looks that way,' Katie agreed stifling a yawn. 'Assisting Mark to lie about his whereabouts won't do either of them any favours. It could bring with it unwanted publicity; that won't help her music career.'

James nodded his agreement. 'You do realize this now means we need to thoroughly check out Mark's whereabouts the night his mother was murdered, don't you? Although highly unlikely he's our killer we can't leave anything to chance.'

Katie brushed a long strand of blonde hair away from her blue eyes. 'How do you suggest we quiz Mark on his whereabouts without getting our heads ripped from our shoulders dear brother?' Her gaze meeting his.

'I had hoped you'd volunteer sister dear,' James replied, with a lopsided grin.

Katie shot him a murderous stare. 'Oh no, you're not suggesting I interrogate him on this one surely?'

'Well I'm behind on some crucial DNA tests,' James answered; real conviction etched in his voice. 'They were meant to be handed into the Coroner three days ago. If I don't get them finished pretty quickly we could all be in trouble and even find ourselves with the referrals drying up.'

Katie groaned. It appeared there was no opting out of this one. James wouldn't pass something like this on to her if he wasn't under real pressure. Okay so she'd pay a visit to Mark Jennings. What was the worst that could happen? He could get cranky and throw his weight about, maybe even have her collapse on the floor in a blithering mess but even from that she would recover. Katie stood up, pushed back the desk chair and quietly exited the room wondering why she'd ever opted for a career in forensic psychology; her second choice, horticulture, now seemed much more appealing.

Scarcely allowing time to digest lunch Katie carried the empty plate into the kitchen where it was dropped into the sink with a mass of other dirty dishes to keep it company. Psyching herself up she decided it was time to tackle Mark Jennings; the encounter couldn't be put off any longer. Butterflies crept into the pit of her stomach fluttering around precariously. If drinking and driving were permitted she'd welcome a glass to steady decidedly wobbly nerves. She resisted the temptation – maybe on the way home at the local.

After phoning Jennings Clay and speaking with Claudia Dunnridge, Mark's personal assistant, Katie finally tracked him down in the gym at Ferngrove, a holiday resort on the outskirts of Newton Abbot. She arrived at the upmarket studio to find him pumping weights looking sweaty albeit in very good shape.

Katie felt her face tinting pink studying his well firmed abs with matching washboard stomach. Trying to focus on the task at hand she cleared her throat to announce her presence.

'What the hell are you doing here?' he barked, replacing the weight he'd been lifting onto its stand with almost consummate ease. He moved into a sitting position, grabbing a nearby towel and wiping it over his moist face.

'I have a few more questions I'd like to ask you Mr. Jennings,' Katie replied trying to sound matter of fact vainly keeping her eyes from his well-sculptured torso. 'I need to know exactly where you were the night your mother was murdered?'

'I've already told you,' he snarled, standing up and heading for the nearest exit, Katie close on his heels.

'Yes and I know your statement about being in London was incorrect,' Katie retaliated, in a slightly raised voice, not caring who heard the declaration. 'You were not in London the night your mother was attacked so how about we start again and this time you tell me the truth.'

Mark swung around cursing his PA for disclosing his whereabouts. Katie not expecting him to turn so suddenly, losing her balance, falling backwards. She was saved by Mark's arm reaching out to steady her. This small act of kindness one of complete surprise.

'Oh great, so now I'm a suspect, am I?' He threw at her. 'Quite charming.'

'Mr. Jennings in order to complete a thorough investigation into your mother's murder it is necessary for me to ask you a series of questions and I need accuracy with your answers.' Katie stuck out her chin in a determined fashion holding onto the wall for support. She wasn't going to make a habit of losing her balance in front of this man.

'Ok so I admit I was not in London the night my mother was attacked, but that still doesn't point the finger at me,' he conceded.

'No it doesn't,' Katie replied truthfully, 'but I need to know where you were that night.'

A few clients working out nearby on various apparatus suddenly stopped their exertions appearing to listen with interest at the unfolding conversation. Mark increasingly aware he was the focus of unwanted attention lowered his voice and gently urged Katie to move with him through the exit doors out of ear shot. She dutifully obliged also not keen for others to be privy to their conversation.

'A drink?' he suggested, another unexpected gesture.

Katie stuttered a yes, following him into the cafe where he ordered two lattes from the bar. He then led her to a secluded booth where they could talk, away from eavesdroppers.

As he slid into the booth Mark held up his hands in mock surrender. 'I have no intention of misleading you or interfering with your investigation Ms Sinclair. The truth is I was at an AA meeting in Reading. The core truth Miss Know-it-all is I'm a chronic alcoholic trying to dry out. There. Confession over.'

Katie found herself stumbling over the next sentence. 'Why couldn't you have told me this in the first place? It would have made things so much easier.'

'It would have been easier for you.' Mark replied, his eyes boring into hers.

'Surely you must have realized we would uncover the truth of your whereabouts sooner or later? After all this is a murder enquiry and unearthing the truth is my job.'

'So am I meant to congratulate you for this latest bit of detective work?' Mark jibed.

Katie declined an answer. 'I'm merely trying to determine a possible motive for your mother's murder and any useful information you can give me would be appreciated.'

'You're wasting your time sweetheart,' Mark chortled. 'I have no idea who killed my mother. Correct me if I'm wrong but I actually thought it was your bloody job to find out, not mine.'

'Let me try rephrasing this; do you have any idea who might have wanted to harm Muriel?'

Mark took a sip of his coffee brought to their table by a pert young waitress. He gave her an admiring look and a hefty tip before she departed. He then turned his attention back to Katie trying to be as amicable as possible.

'It could easily have been one of my old business associates,' he confessed. 'Any one of them could be guilty of such an horrific act.'

'What makes you say that?' Katie enquired stunned. 'Surely there's not that much animosity towards you and your family.'

Mark grinned well naturedly as he tried to explain. 'Jennings Clay is a profitable company Ms Sinclair. I daresay quite a few people are jealous of what my family has achieved. Any number of past employees could easily have decided to demonstrate their frustration. Not all employees leave on good terms and there are any number of competitors who feel they have been cheated out of a share of the business.'

'Yes but frustration alone is not usually enough motive to commit murder,' Katie informed him curtly. 'We deal with evidence Mr. Jennings, not mere speculation.'

'Then clearly, we're wasting each other's time,' Mark replied, getting up from the table and throwing a ten pound note next to his empty coffee cup. He strolled off without a backwards glance leaving Katie subconsciously playing with the sugar bowl. The meeting had proved fruitless. The only insight Katie had gained was exactly where Mark had been the night his mother was killed and once his story checked out Mark could then be taken off the suspect list. Reality as it was she *had* achieved what she'd come for but she wanted more, much more. Muriel's life had been cut short so viciously and Katie was desperate for answers.

***

After her meeting with Mark Jennings, Katie went in search of Nick Shelby. She spotted him exiting the autopsy room clad in gown, mask and gloves. He deftly removed mask and gown throwing them into a nearby bin, before peeling off his gloves and proceeding to scrub his hands.

'That little dissection exercise took me nearly three hours,' he remarked, acknowledging Katie's presence. 'Young Asian man found dead in his Exeter apartment. The evidence so far definitely indicates foul play, although not without complications.'

'Do you have suspects?' a fatigued Katie enquired, leaning against a nearby bench.

Nick shook his head. 'Nope, the police are doing a thorough investigation but my theory is the killer's done a runner and is already overseas. All I know is our suspect is likely to be male as the injuries bear the signs of considerable force. Most women wouldn't have the strength to inflict these sorts of injuries.'

'I thought you might fancy going for a drink?' Katie remarked, as Nick finished drying his hands. 'I have a few things I want to toss around with you in relation to the Jennings case.'

'Sounds like a plan,' Nick replied. 'Let me shower and change. I'll only be about ten minutes if you want to wait in my office,' then added as an afterthought; 'Have you eaten?'

Katie shook her head. 'Not since lunchtime.' As if right on cue her stomach gave a small groan.

'Then I suggest we head into North Bovey,' Nick said. 'There's a new Thai restaurant just opened which serves the best crispy fish you'll ever taste.'

Within an hour, Katie and Nick were seated by the window in a secluded booth at The Tasty Thai restaurant devouring spring rolls and sharing a bottle of merlot. It was a cosy place with authentic Thai cuisine and décor to match.

'I can't help feeling we're just going around in circles with the Jennings case,' Katie sighed raising the glass of red to her lips. 'There seems to be no reason at all why Muriel Jennings was murdered and all evidence so far draws a blank.'

Nick studied her frustrated countenance. 'I admit it doesn't appear straight forward my dear but there has to be a reason why Muriel was attacked. The problem is we've not yet cracked that motive. What about the photographs you found up in the Jennings attic; the ones you showed me the other day. What puzzles me is why someone deliberately blanked out the face of the third woman in the picture.'

'I guess you're right,' Katie said softly. 'Perhaps Stella Jennings knows something about the photographs.'

On completion of their meal Nick invited Katie back to his place for a nightcap. It was a little before nine – the night was still young.

Whilst Nick headed to his office to check emails Katie excused herself to use the bathroom. A bit tipsy she staggered up the stairs almost tripping over the laundry basket positioned by the sinks. Bending down to retrieve the lid of the basket which had rolled onto the floor Katie's sharp eyes spotted a small fluffy white residue near the toilet bowl. Instinctively she took a couple of tissues from her handbag and scooped up the powder placing it into her lipstick holder. Adjacent to the spilt powder she noticed a used razor blade not the usual disposable type Nick used.

Her mind in overdrive, Katie slowly descended the stairs completely forgetting the reason for heading to the bathroom in the first place.

'You okay?' Nick enquired, as Katie joined him in the lounge where he sat lazing on the settee.

'Actually, if you don't mind, I think I'll phone for a cab and call it a night. I'm a bit done in,' she lied, grabbing her jacket and reaching for her mobile.

'No worries. Thanks for a great evening. We must do it again sometime.'

***

'Can you take a look at this?' Katie said the following morning as she approached James in the lab. She was holding out the ceramic lipstick case. 'I'm interested to learn what this powder is.'

James reached out and took the case. 'Sure. Where did you get it from?'

'The lipstick case is mine but I can assure you the contents aren't. Just something Andy Michaels gave me yesterday down at police liaison. I think its redundant evidence or something unlabelled from the seizures vault he wants checked; might be a narcotic.'

Katie lent on the bench close to James so she could watch him perform the necessary tests. 'How many are you doing?' she enquired.

'Only one. An I.R.'

'You always tell me at least two definitive tests are required for confirmation,' a puzzled Katie replied.

'You want a positive colour test or thin layer chromatogram, plus an irrefutable spectroscopic match, say infra-red or mass spec. But that's if we were going to court or charges are pending. With this sample, I already have a good idea what it is just by examining the powder closely,' James informed. 'Infra-red is pretty conclusive and quick.'

The powder residue was rinsed into a beaker with 30 mls of water and placed on a magnetic stirrer for 5 minutes. He filtered the contents, made the resulting clear solution alkaline and extracted it in a flask by shaking it with 20 mls of chloroform. The organic solvent layer was decanted off and evaporated down in the fume cupboard leaving behind a small amount of oily, pale brown liquid. With deftness James removed the sample and smeared a thin film onto a clear spectrographic grade sodium chloride disc. He then placed the disc in the beam of the infra-red spectrophotometer which was reset to zero and switched to scan. Katie watched intently as a complex peak pattern emerged seamlessly from the chart recorder, mimicked by a similar pattern on the computer display.

'Flick through the data base spectra and see what it matches,' James instructed.

'Those three peaks at 1275, 1700, and 1106 cm-1; are they characteristic?' Katie asked.

'Yeah, what does the computer match come up with? Cocaine base,' James remarked looking over her shoulder. 'Looks about 90-95% purity.'

Katie stared at the readout in disbelief. Was Nick mucking around with Cocaine?

***

Rounding a hairpin bend Mark Jennings glanced for the fifth time at the silver Jaguar saloon now filling his rear vision mirror. It had been following at some distance on the deserted B Road for almost 10 miles since Dartington and was now creeping uncomfortably closer. It aped his every move, accelerating when he accelerated, slowing when he slowed.

Briefly tempted to lead the big cat on a wild goose chase but with the fuel warning light flashing intermittently Mark wisely decided against it. A better option would be to try and lose his stalker as quickly as possible, not encourage them to take an extended high speed jaunt through the Devon countryside.

Being only 10 minutes off Jennings Clay Mark decided to head there. Swearing out loud to himself and spearing into the next turnoff at breakneck speed he floored the accelerator in an attempt to put distance between himself and the persistent Jag. As the clay company loomed rapidly into sight Mark momentarily took one hand off the steering wheel groping in the glove compartment for his remote control. Grasping the little black device, he pressed the red button watching thankfully as the gates swung open. With timing and luck Mark just squeezed through the entrance causing the rapidly approaching pursuer to brake and swerve violently as the gates closed behind.

Slowing to a more reasonable pace and heart racing he guided his BMW to the rear of the building ensuring he was out of sight of the main entrance, unnerved by the chase. For all he knew the assailant could be armed. With a shaking hand and adrenaline still coursing through his arteries Mark switched off the security alarm after three attempts before reaching the sanctum of his perennially untidy office. Once inside he flicked on the overhead fluorescent lights simultaneously flinging open the second drawer of his desk to retrieve a full bottle of malt whisky. He then poured himself a double shot upending the contents in one gulp savouring the burning jolt as it scorched its way down his throat. Then he poured another and another until the contents were drained. With the empty bottle in hand he forcefully hurled it at the wall watching it smash.

How long he was out for Mark was unsure. The phone ringing on his desk roused his intoxicated consciousness enough to pick up the receiver. He could barely string a sentence together so waited for the caller to speak first.

'You think you're so smart, don't you?' the female voice echoed down the line. 'You sit there in your fancy office, not giving a damn about anyone else.'

'Who is this and what do you want?' Mark stammered, unable to recognize the voice.

'I want what is rightfully mine.' the voice continued. At first, she was calm but her tone soon changed to anger. 'You're nothing but a stinking drunk. You think you're such a big shot, don't you? You're the bastard who destroyed the Sinner's Daughter, that's who you are.'

***

A light frost on the grass and a sharp bite in the air welcomed Katie as she ventured out just before seven. An early start was in order if she was to make it to Bristol by midday to meet Jessica Cartwright, or Jessica Fisher as she now preferred to be known. The meeting had been agreed upon in order for Katie to put together a more accurate profile on Ted Cartwright. She desperately hoped that could lead to a possible connection between the Cartwright murders and that of Muriel Jennings.

Heading East towards Exeter, Katie merged onto the A38 expecting the usual morning rush hour chaos, however to her surprise she encountered only light traffic which continued well into the M5. Within a two-hour frame of leaving home punctuated by a short stop to devour chocolate croissants washed down with flask coffee Katie turned her little Fiat off the motorway heading into Bristol, a city she was very familiar with having spent a large chunk of her University clinical placement at The Avon Coroner's office in Old Western Road. Now returning after a few short years not much had changed with the city infrastructure. Time permitting after her visit with Jessica Fisher, Katie even planned to drop in on a few old friends.

Why did the wind have to blow so unforgivingly? Didn't it know she wouldn't be able to sleep with the loud crashing noises and the creak of the old rustic gate? Although the house was scary she knew she had to be here. This was where she belonged. Besides where else was she to go. The bodies needed protection and it was her job to do that. They weren't just bodies though, were they? All five women were beautiful. At least as a mark of respect each one deserved a single white rose. Yes, that's what they needed; a beautiful flower for a beautiful woman.

CHAPTER NINE

A light drizzle was drifting in off the Severn Estuary and slowly enveloping the city when Katie pulled up outside number forty-three Brighton Avenue finding herself staring up at an imposing three storey Edwardian edifice situated in quiet leafy surrounds in Clifton, one of Bristol's most affluent suburbs. Residential prices in Bristol had sky rocketed well above the national average in recent years and Clifton had recently featured in a new television series, 'Aim High and Buy'. The presenter, Ashley Mortimer, was a debonair ex RAF helicopter pilot who flew to different locations around Britain each week to view a new property. Definitely a bit quirky but Katie was hooked catching the show each Tuesday night at seven thirty. It was interesting to see where Ashley would land his helicopter and under what conditions. Often landing and getting the chopper out from difficult locations in gardens or backyards was the highlight of the series.

Katie stood on the pavement for a few moments casting wary eyes over the old house. She winced slightly at the pain shooting down her right leg and reached in her bag for codeine tablets. For some reason, she felt a little nervous at the prospect of meeting Jessica. She wasn't sure what sort of welcome awaited. Taking a while to gather some composure she finally found the courage to ascend the dozen or so steps which led to the front door.

At first, Jessica had flatly refused to meet with Katie stating she had nothing to say to reporters, police or any other individual involved in murders or detective work. It had taken a lot of gentle coaxing on Katie's behalf to bring her around.

After ringing the doorbell twice and getting no response Katie wondered if Jessica had gotten cold feet. About to turn around and head back down the steps the door suddenly opened and a smart looking woman about late fifties beckoned her to come in.

'Faulty doorbell,' she apologized. 'Been meaning to replace it with a knocker. You only hear it from certain parts of the house. You caught me just coming down from the attic.'

'Jessica Fisher?' Katie enquired, holding out her hand.

The woman nodded, returning the handshake. 'Yes, and you're Katie Sinclair. Do come in. I thought you might be hungry after your drive from Devon so I've fixed us a light snack. Nothing fancy, just a fruit and cheese platter.'

The greeting was more welcoming than Katie had anticipated. She gladly followed Jessica along a dimly lit hallway before entering a reception room situated at the back of the house.

Jessica was not at all as Katie imagined, appearing more placid in nature than the impression gained over the phone. She was strikingly attractive for her age with good natural features requiring minimal makeup.

Katie reiterated a heartfelt thanks to Jessica for agreeing to meet. It had taken a lot of gentle persuasion and she wanted her to know the visit was much appreciated. Katie then tried to shed some light on recent events explaining what she thought could be gained from the meeting. She talked about the book club and in particular how the members were reading *The Sinner's Daughter* around the time of Muriel's death.

'So you see,' she concluded. 'We are trying to see if the book holds any links to Muriel's murder.'

'I cannot imagine how there could be any link,' Jessica remarked candidly. 'These murders happened over fifteen years ago, Ms Sinclair. As you will surely be aware Ted has been in prison the bulk of those fifteen years.'

'All the same I am trying to see if there could be any possible connection,' Katie pressed. 'Tell me how did *you* feel when the book was published? It couldn't have been easy to read about the murders in print.'

'To be honest I have never read the book, nor do I ever have any intention of doing so,' Jessica replied.

Katie was taken aback. She obviously assumed Jessica had read the book. It never occurred to her that she hadn't.

Jessica went on to explain, astutely picking up on Katie's open confusion. 'I am aware my ex-husband murdered five women Ms Sinclair. However, I do not see the point in reading how or why he did so.'

On reflection Katie had to agree this made perfect sense. Why would anyone need reminding of such dreadful events especially when the murders were committed by someone so close? Certain things were best forgotten, put to the very back of the subconscious. It couldn't have been easy for Jessica to come to terms with her ex-husband being a serial killer.

'Trying to make a fresh start must have been difficult? Especially after all the publicity the trial attracted,' Katie continued.

'Yes it was difficult. I reverted to using my maiden name in an attempt to avoid any controversy. It's amazing how cruel humans can be to each other. I knew if people associated me in any way with Ted Cartwright they would think me to be just as guilty.'

'When exactly did you and Ted split up?' Katie asked, helping herself to a piece of brie from the plate on the table, pangs of hunger intruding.

'Approximately two years before he killed his first victim,' Jessica replied. 'When Abby was seven our marriage started to fall apart. I started receiving anonymous letters from someone claiming to be Ted's former lover. It put a great strain on our marriage and eventually I decided to call it quits. I always suspected Ted to be suffering from depression, he was becoming increasingly difficult to live with and that magical spark had disappeared from our relationship.'

'How did Abby cope with everything, in particular to the murders? It can't have been easy for her when the bodies were discovered in the basement.'

'How would any young child cope on learning their father is a murderer?' Jessica replied rhetorically.

Katie didn't reply, she already knew the answer.

'Abby spent quite a bit of time receiving counselling.' Jessica volunteered, after a moment of silence. 'It helped a lot but she'll bear the scars for life.'

'I don't suppose you have any photographs of Abby?' Katie asked. Even after extensive research she'd never been able to locate any pictures.

'Not to hand. It was recommended that I destroy all photographs of Abby when she was put into the police protection program. I did keep a few but they are securely locked away in a safety deposit box. I could not and would not put my daughter at risk Ms Sinclair by leaving a few images lying around.'

Katie helped herself to some fruit, realizing she was ravenous.

'Talking does that to you,' Jessica smiled, as she poured a glass of orange juice passing it to Katie. 'During the months leading up to Ted's trial I must have lost over ten kilos. Just from all the stress I endured.'

'I can imagine. It must have been a horrific thing to have gone through.'

'I am sure you can picture what it was like from a professional view point Ms. Sinclair but from a personal view point that would be impossible. Unless you have actually been through such hell you can only surmise on such a thing.'

'Have you ever been back to the house where the murders took place?' Katie asked.

'No never. Heather Lea is such a beautiful house. I have many happy memories of growing up there as a child. Sadly, those memories are now filled with grief from those horrific murders. My great, great grandfather bought the house in 1880 when he moved the family from the Welsh valleys. I was sorry to leave the place initially. When I split from Ted I agreed to him remaining in the house with Abby. I didn't want Abby moved from the family home. Have you seen Heather Lea, Ms. Sinclair? It is truly a remarkable place.'

Katie shook her head. 'I hope to arrange a visit over the coming weeks. I believe the house is still up for sale with a local Devon estate agent.'

Jessica nodded, 'I've been trying to sell the house for years but local gossip is very powerful. As soon as potential buyers learn about the murders they change their minds and how can you blame them? Would *you* want to live in a house where five women were brutally murdered?'

Katie shivered at the thought, shaking her head, 'No I don't suppose I would,' she replied truthfully. 'Jessica why did Abby stay with Ted when you separated? Quite often daughters opt to go with their mothers.'

Jessica gave a sigh. 'Ted and Abby were always close. Ted doted on Abby. You see Ted had a daughter from a previous relationship. Sadly, Lilly died just before her fourth birthday. Her death was a tragic drowning accident in one of Dartmoor's Reservoirs. Looking back on things now I believe that's when Ted started to display problems. But you see when I walked out on Ted I didn't feel it was right to take Abby away from him as well.'

All this was news to Katie. It was the first she heard of Ted having another daughter.

Jessica continued with her explanation as if she needed to justify what could have looked like abandonment.

'At the time, I was also finishing my law degree and it seemed the best solution for Abby to remain in Devon. Would I have left Ted knowing what he was going to do? The answer is no. I would have sacrificed my own happiness to save those poor women.'

At that moment, the phone on the table next to them rang. Jessica seemed a little startled looking around before picking up the receiver. 'Hello. No, I'm afraid she's not here at the moment. Perhaps try again this afternoon. Yes, that should be fine. Thank you.'

She hung up.

'This is certainly a beautiful house,' Katie remarked, taking in the room's features. 'I love the ornate ceilings and light fittings. You do such a wonderful job keeping it immaculate both inside and out. It must be a challenge keeping it clean?'

'Clean?' Jessica seemed pre-occupied as if the phone call had troubled her somewhat.

'I should think it would take a good few hours each week to keep the dust at bay?' Katie continued.

Jessica laughed. 'Yes but I'm fortunate to have a cleaning lady who comes in twice a week to help out. Mind you, Heather Lea was much bigger than this and took two full-time housekeepers to keep it in order.'

Katie couldn't quite decide if the expression covering her face was boredom or frustration. For some reason, Jessica also kept glancing at the clock above the fireplace, then across at the door.

Katie decided to hurry things up, concerned her visit was now turning into an inconvenience for Jessica.

'I'd just like to ask you about Abby, her personality, likes and dislikes?'

Jessica once more glancing at the door replied softly. 'Abby is a sweet girl. Even after everything she went through she has managed to remain a normal individual, which is quite remarkable.'

'Do you still have any contact with Abby?' Katie enquired.

'I have not heard from Abby for a number of years now. We had an agreement she would only contact me if she felt I could be of assistance.'

Inwardly Katie found this hard to fathom but refrained from commenting. How a mother could sever all ties with a child was astonishing.

Katie calculated there was little more to be gained from the meeting with Jessica; time to call it a day. As she stood up to leave Jessica clutched hold of Katie's hand. 'I love my daughter Ms. Sinclair. I never stopped loving her. I'd do anything to see her again but I know if I did her life would be in peril. I'm prepared to keep her at bay if it means she will never be harmed.'

Unsure of what to make of Jessica's remark, Katie offered to find her own way out, navigating down the hallway to the front door.

Stepping outside into a brisk afternoon she encountered an elderly lady heading up the front path having just exited a community minibus carrying a couple of TESCO shopping bags, for an elderly person she walked quite sprightly.

'Can I help you with anything my dear?' she stopped to enquire politely, giving Katie a toothless smile. 'It's taken me all morning to buy a couple of items from the supermarket. Cost a tidy penny as well.'

'No I'm fine thank you,' Katie answered, continuing to her car. She reflected on her visit with Jessica, not giving the old lady a second thought.

***

Two days later James scheduled a meeting with Marshall Davidson, the Jennings family Lawyer in the hope of extracting inside information on the company finances. In particular, he sought details on withdrawals Muriel had made from the company bank accounts over the past few months. Peter Swift the CFO had gone over the balance sheets at James' request but was reasonably happy with the current accounts, even allowing for the cash withdrawals.

As majority owner of Jennings Clay, Muriel was within her rights to make withdrawals as often as the need or whim dictated, however all the accounts required mandatory reconciling at the end of each month, which meant the slightest discrepancies, needed signing off.

What Muriel had done with the cash Peter had no idea.

Still determined for answers James gunned his Land Rover southwards to West Charleton, a post card village just outside the Anglo Saxon estuary holiday town of Kingsbridge. Making good time for his 11am meeting he drove over New Bridge still known to many as Bowcombe Bridge, heading east along the coast towards Dartmouth.

Round the next bend, he sighted Marshall Davidson's property set on a private road overlooking the Salcombe-Kingsbridge estuary. *Not much change from two big ones for that* he whistled softly.

Pulling the 4WD to a halt on the circular driveway James couldn't help but notice a brand new Aston Martin in the garage parked next to a vintage Rolls Royce, total value about quarter of a million. Both sported personalised number plates, Marsh 3 and Marsh 4. James guessing there were probably a Marsh 1 and 2 around doubtless equally as impressive.

'Do come in,' Marshall beamed, flinging open the large, bespoke oak door dressed in a designer t-shirt and cream chinos. 'If you don't mind I'll ask you to take your shoes off. My wife is extremely fussy when it comes to carpets and footwear.'

James dutifully obliged, taking off his well-worn topsiders and placing them on the welcome mat. Luckily, he'd put on clean socks before heading out this morning, one of the few pairs that didn't have gaping holes.

Marshall led the way to a large sitting room expensively decorated in the art deco style with a mix of modern retro furniture and period decorative artefacts, money obviously no object. James fancied himself a bit of an expert on 20th century design and quickly picked out several rare and valuable items including an elegant Tiffany vase circa 1910 displayed in a French fruitwood vitrine along with other glassware. From a reference book at home he knew this piece to be worth at least twenty thousand. However, it was the panoramic view of this part of the estuary looking south towards Salcombe which riveted his gaze. Further out it would empty into the English Channel.

'This magnificent view is the main reason we bought the house,' Marshall stated, as he joined James by the window. 'You never get tired of scenery like this. Even when the tide is out there's plenty to keep you interested with all the wildlife around.'

Being nearly dead low tide the mudflats were clearly visible. Several boats rested in an upright position, their bilge keels preventing them from toppling over. A lonely grey heron stood on one leg in a small pool of water searching for titbits. As James watched it deftly caught a fish, swallowing it whole within a split second.

'Yep, lots of seabirds around here,' Marshall informed. 'Herons are in abundance, along with curlews and egrets.'

'You're certainly in an enviable spot for watching wildlife,' James replied.

'You sail Mr. Sinclair?' Marshall asked switching the subject.

'I've been out a few times but I'd hardly call myself an expert,' James replied. 'I take it you do?'

'My oath I do. I'm the fortunate owner of a 1930's West Solent One Design, not strictly a blue water boat mind you, more of a harbour racer. You can just see it out in the Eastern channel, last boat on the mooring pontoon.'

Squinting through the glare rising off the estuary James could just make out the unmistakable white hull form of a classic yacht shimmering in the late morning heat.

'Made a quick dash two handed across the Channel last year when we got a favourable weather window. Tide race around Cherbourg was tricky but got it there and back in 15 hours; wind on the beam all the way. There's nothing like classic cars and wooden yachts to keep a fella happy.'

Great if you've got the money, James mused wistfully but refrained from commenting. Few folk could afford the lifestyle Marshall Davidson was accustomed to. Marshall noticed his visitor enviously eyeing an antique baby grand piano, exquisitely crafted from the finest woods in the adjacent sunroom.

'My wife's, I can't play a note. She's touring with the Bournemouth Symphony. Sorry I forget my manners can I offer you a drink? I've got a super Aussie sauv blanc chilling in the fridge.'

With both men seated and glass in hand James tactfully broached the subject of Jennings Clay and the errant funds.

'So you see, with information volunteered by Peter Swift it happens that Muriel withdrew large sums as cash cheques from the company accounts over an eight month period. Would you happen to know what the money was used for?'

'I can only hazard a guess Mr. Sinclair,' Marshall replied. 'Muriel often discussed her concern having all the family cash tied up in the company. I suggested because of the perilous economic climate she move some out into other liquid and portable assets such as gold bullion, bearer certificates or other precious metals. Hopefully she took my advice and did just that.'

'I take it you didn't actually see any metal or assist her with the purchasing?'

'No I didn't. Muriel disclosed many things to me but she was not one to lay all her cards on the table. She trusted very few people where money was concerned.'

'Were you also aware Mr. Davidson that a significant lump sum of eighty thousand pounds was withdrawn from the company account at the Nat West Newton Abbot in three tranches the week before her attack?'

Marshall's perplexed expression immediately gave the game away indicating he was completely in the dark as to the withdrawals. 'Certainly that's news to me, although I can say something had been troubling Muriel for a while. You know, certain things she said, the way she was acting, you pick up on it. I came to the conclusion someone may have been blackmailing her.'

James sat bolt upright. 'Can you be more specific? Did she mention any names?'

'No names, but she did make odd remarks such as "I always knew the past would come back to haunt me". To come to the point Mr. Sinclair money was not an issue for

Muriel. Jennings Clay has a current market value around 800 million pounds. If Muriel *was* being blackmailed the reason would be more devastating to her than the fact she had to part with any sizable cash amounts. I still feel Peter Swift is the man to talk to; he should be au fait with all the day to day transactions. He'll give you the answers.'

On that note, Marshall put down his glass, rose from his chair and suggested they head out onto the beach thus cutting short any further discussion down that particular avenue.

Two hours had passed and the tide was now in full flood. Both men strolled casually along the shore carefully stepping over occasional clumps of seaweed and watching boats begin to rise off the mud and bob earnestly at their moorings to a strengthening sou'easter.

James impulsively picked up a small piece of slate stone and skimmed it across the water. He managed about 5 skims and threw his arms triumphantly up in the air.

'I've still got the knack,' he jibed.

Marshall laughed, before adopting a more serious tone. 'I don't see how I can be of help with your enquiry into Muriel's death James. Do you have any idea who the killer could be? I was devastated when Mark phoned me in Australia to break the news of Muriel's death.'

'It's too early to have any definite leads,' James said. 'Do you know if Muriel had any enemies? I understand you've known Muriel and her late husband for a number of years.'

Marshall turned and addressed James earnestly. 'Muriel didn't have any enemies,' he said with conviction. 'She was a beautiful person. Sure she could speak her own mind but I for one admire that in a woman. When Bill was alive you could see the affection in his eyes whenever he spoke about his wife. Muriel had a very big heart.'

'Would there be anything unexpected in her will?'

Marshall shook his head. 'Nope. It's pretty standard.'

'Did you ever hear her argue with her children?' James asked.

'No more than most mothers,' Marshall replied. 'Mark could be a bit of a handful at times but Muriel knew how to keep him in line. You should also take note that Mark absolutely adored his mother. If you ever had him down as a suspect, you can cross him off.'

'So, you definitely can't think of a single person who had it in for Muriel?'

Marshall shook his head. 'Nope can't help you on that score. Anyway, the afternoon's getting on. If you have the inclination, I'll take you for a spin in my 300S Maserati. I want to give it a work out on the Slapton Beach road. Come on, I'll even let you get behind the wheel.'

James walked back to the house with Marshall. No more would be gained today from questioning him about Muriel Jennings. The warmth of the sun was seductive, perhaps it was about time he let his hair down to enjoy the rest of the day.

***

'You off again?' Katie quizzed James.

'Yep I need to get the Clifford water pollution results to their head office in Torquay. I'll catch you tomorrow.'

After James left Katie spoke to her sister. 'I thought those documents were sent yesterday via courier?'

'They were.'

'Am I missing something?' Katie asked, looking perplexed.

'Only a five foot six brunette named Cindy.'

Katie still looked puzzled. 'He certainly hasn't mentioned her before.'

'That's because she's married,' Fiona answered. 'James knows you don't approve of his relationships with married women.'

Katie's soft features hardened. She thought James was cured of this habit – obviously not.

***

Katie was responding to a call from Jane Anderson, a member of the Bovey Book Club. She'd phoned to notify Moorland Forensics her car had been vandalized in the driveway of her home. Although technically a police matter Katie decided to drop by and take a look. It would also act as an excuse to ask a few more questions relating to Muriel Jennings.

It was a more subdued Jane who greeted Katie when she arrived. Not the woman of bravado she'd interviewed a few weeks back in the Bovey Town Hall. This time Jane appeared more humble, not quite so full of her own opinions. To Katie this Jane was more likeable.

'So when do you believe the vandalism occurred?' Katie enquired. 'Can you estimate a time it could have happened?'

Jane screwed up her face thinking hard. 'I returned home from Paington around one and fixed lunch. At around four o'clock I went outside to grab my coat from the back seat of the car, that's when I noticed the scratches and broken mirrors.'

'So we're looking at a window of about three hours?' Katie surmised.

'Yes, no more than three,' Jane advised.

'Did you hear or see anyone lurking around outside?' Katie enquired, as she took a small note pad from her jacket pocket scribbling down some comments.

'Nope. I spent most of the afternoon in the kitchen, which is down at the back of the house. It would have been easy for someone to damage the car without being seen or heard.'

'Would you have heard a car's engine from where you were?'

Jane smiled wistfully. 'That's highly improbable with Pink Floyd blaring out from my CD player.'

'And you didn't notice anyone hanging around during the day before you headed into Paington?'

'No one.'

Katie carefully examined the scratches and dangling mirrors taking photos with a pocket digital camera. Whoever vandalized the Ford Focus did a thorough job. The repair bill wouldn't come cheap.

'Do you think whoever did this will be back again?' Jane asked, in a voice beginning to crack. 'Are they the ones who murdered Muriel?'

'I don't see any connection,' Katie replied calmly. 'You *will* need to file a formal report with the local police. I can give the station a call on your behalf and get them to send someone over if you'd like me to?'

'I'd appreciate that. Can I drop the car off to the repair shop or will they need to obtain more evidence such as finger prints?'

'That question I can't answer,' Katie replied truthfully. 'I doubt the police will uncover any prints and trying to match them with a data base of known criminals would be very arduous. Anyway, the police force probably wouldn't be interested due to time and cost.'

'I see,' Jane sounded disappointed. 'There's no point us hanging around outside, why don't you come into the house.'

Katie nodded her acceptance.

'I understand you work part-time for Jennings Clay. Is it a job you like?'

Jane looked surprised by Katie's question. 'It pays the bills.'

'How would you say your relationship was with Muriel?'

'Extremely good, it's that bastard son of hers I loathe, he should have been the one done in not her.'

Now it was Katie's turn to look surprised. 'What makes you say that?'

'He's always big noting himself and throwing his weight around.'

So there's no love lost between those two, Katie thought, but was that enough for Jane to have murdered his mother. She very much doubted it.

'From what I hear the clay mining game is really on the up,' Katie said, helping herself to a custard cream from a plate on the coffee table. 'I mean high demand, limited suppliers, low extraction costs, no real marketing effort required – just dig it out and ship it.'

'That's where I strongly disagree,' Jane replied. 'The likes of Mark Jennings would drink a fair share of the profits. Someone needs to protect the venture.'

The remainder of their conversation was about the book club with nothing much to be gained. Finally, Katie made her escape, promising to ring the police on the way home so they could take a look at the damaged car. She found Jane a touch incongruous but couldn't quite put her finger on the reason why.

The owl hooted in the dead of night, its screech penetrating right inside her head like metal grinding on concrete. Her hands reached up to cover her ears as she closed her eyes tight. Everything became dark, not a sound could be heard. What had happened to the owl? It was only a matter of minutes before she opened her eyes again realizing there was no owl. How could it vanish without a trace? Yet again her mind was playing tricks with her imagination.

CHAPTER TEN

'Where are the bloody files I've asked for?' Mark snapped into the intercom system. 'If you value your job you'll get them for me now.'

Jane Anderson pulled a face, grabbed the two files in question and headed into Mark's office.

He was already on the phone when she walked in but still managed to give her a dirty look as she placed the documents onto his desk.

'Well what are you waiting for?' he barked, looking towards the door indicating she was required to leave, at the same time covering the phone mouth piece so the person at the other end couldn't hear his wrath. 'Go on, leave.'

It was obvious from his behaviour Mark was suffering the effects of a hangover. He looked like death and the smell of stale booze combined with rancid body odour almost made Jane gag as she made a hasty exit.

Temptation was to slam the door behind her but common sense prevailing she decided against it. Mouthing a few obscenities she bumped into James Sinclair on his way to try and find Peter Swift. When James had arrived, the front desk was vacant so he'd taken it upon himself to explore the office.

'I wouldn't waltz in there if I were you,' Jane instructed briskly, indicating to Mark's office. 'Not unless you want your head bitten off. Our lordship is in an extremely bad mood.'

Heeding the advice James headed back to reception where young Polly now sat typing at a computer. He enquired if she knew where Peter Swift could be located. After several phone calls and enquiries Polly could only shrug her shoulders.

'He may be at lunch,' she volunteered at last. 'In which case, he'll be in the courtyard fagging away or possibly in the canteen.'

James finally found Peter in the canteen attacking a bacon roll and a carton of chocolate milk. He glanced up and grimaced when he saw James approaching.

'You being here is going to land me in hot water again,' he complained, shaking his milk carton vigorously. 'The mood Mark's in today I'm likely to be fired.'

Ignoring this statement James pulled up a seat. 'How long have you worked for Jennings Clay?'

'A little over five years,' he replied, sipping his drink.

'Were you ever instructed to fiddle the accounts?'

Peter visibly shifted uneasily in his chair deliberately avoiding eye contact. 'No.'

'Can you be sure about that?' James pushed.

'What is this, the Spanish Inquisition?' Peter mocked.

'No. Just a murder enquiry,' James answered, as he casually leaned back in his chair resting his arms behind his head. 'There's no need to look so scared Peter. I'm not working for Inland Revenue if that's what you're worried about.'

Peter looked furtively at his watch as if he had somewhere more pressing to be. 'I really can't stop and chat. I have an urgent meeting with auditors in Exeter.'

'No problem,' James responded coolly. 'I can make this brief so long as you're prepared to cooperate. Please just answer the question. Were you ever instructed to hide monies exiting the company accounts?'

Swift scanned the room to see who was in earshot then lowered his voice to barely a whisper. 'Muriel approached me asking if I would organize school fees to be paid for a young girl attending Moor View Boarding School. She refused to tell me anything about it. All I was told was the bank details, the amount to be deposited and the frequency. The remittance advice was merely to show JC Holdings.'

'Did you not think to volunteer this information before when I was enquiring about the company finances?' James shot at him.

'I'm an accountant, Mr. Sinclair, not an informant,' Peter answered defensively. 'How the hell would I know what was important to you people.'

James let out a sigh. 'Thank you Mr. Swift that's all. I won't detain you any longer from your pending meeting.'

James stood up from the table heading for the exit. His meeting with the CFO had borne fruit. The unexplained school fees were certainly a good lead. It seemed implausible for Muriel to be paying school fees. Perhaps this was linked to a possible blackmail. In which case; trace the school child and everything might just fall into place. Bingo.

***

'Seen the Star?' Fiona shot at James as he walked through the office door. His pale and hang dog features betrayed long working hours coupled with lack of sleep. Although she hated bearing unpleasant news Fiona knew it would be wrong to keep this under wraps. 'Our dear friend Markham has been at it again. Take a look at this.'

James reached for the tabloid she was holding in her outstretched hand, his keen eye immediately focusing on the front page story.

Clueless Forensics, the headline blurted out in large bold print and underneath:

It comes as no surprise that the murder of Muriel Jennings remains unsolved. The process of Forensic Science is a slow and tortuous one. We need to ask ourselves how accurate and ultimately beneficial it all really is. Somewhere out there is a cold blooded murderer secretly laughing at the so far ineffectual efforts of the scientists and police, whom at the end of the day may get away completely scot free!

Perhaps we should enlist the aid of Inspector Gadget or better still The Infamous Pink Panther. Cartoon version of course!

James threw the newspaper across the room in disgust. 'The bloody nerve of that goon,' he seethed, 'what right does Tom Markham have to write such unadulterated crap. He can get stuffed for all I care.'

'No right at all,' Fiona chimed in, just as annoyed as her brother. 'Just because he inherited the rag he thinks he can print whatever he likes. Reason he does it is to flog papers and service his well-known addiction to the ponies.'

'That's as maybe, but I could quite happily throttle the little spiv,' James shot back with venom.

'Try not to let him get to you,' Katie wisely interjected, overhearing the proceedings from the back room kitchenette. 'Once this case is put to bed that smug grin will be wiped off his pock marked face.'

'Let's hope so,' James replied, still simmering as he made his way to the espresso machine. Up most of the night analysing fresh evidence had proved a dead-end. Lack of sleep and frustration strongly tempted him to add a dash of whisky to his large mug of cappuccino. Deciding against an Irish coffee he headed straight out to the lab to try and switch his mind from the article back to DNA replication.

Annoyingly his thoughts soon drifted back to Markham and the story. Although written with vicious intent he couldn't help thinking Markham had a point. It *was* taking rather a long time to come up with any hard evidence that might stick. That alone frustrated James who usually prided himself on fast results. The longer the case went unsolved the public had more reason to be concerned; always a drain on the morale for a team of forensic investigators.

***

Liz Palmer was denied sleep. She kept tossing and turning, frustration building by the minute. Insomnia had never been a problem in the past yet lately she'd been plagued by the damn thing. As a nurse, she was reluctant to take relaxants knowing the threat of addiction always lurked in the background. Maybe a warm glass of milk would do the trick.

Careful not to wake her husband, Liz slowly rolled over and slipped out of bed. She donned dressing gown and slippers which were close at hand and crept to the half open bedroom door. The old floor boards creaked and groaned as she padded along the landing making her way down stairs.

Fumbling in the dark she located the light switch situated just inside the kitchen door way. Instant light flooded the room. She stood still for a few moments whilst her eyes grew accustomed to the bright light.

Opening a nearby cupboard, she grabbed her favourite mug placing it on the kitchen table before moving across the room to grab the milk from the fridge. Only metres from the fridge she froze in her tracks, sheer terror on her face as she read the painted words on the fridge door: *Poor Muriel. Just think; You could be next.*

Instinct told her to run back upstairs to Simon but her feet remained firmly glued to the spot. Finally, she forced one foot in front of the other and raced back to the bedroom. She shook Simon from a fitful slumber and within moments they were both in the kitchen staring at the threatening words.

***

Katie heavy with sleep turned over onto her left side hoping to manoeuvre into a more comfortable position. The persistent ringing in her ears was driving her crazy. When it didn't stop, she began to wake recognising the quirky ring tone of her mobile phone.

She groped around on the bedside drawers, at the same time glancing at her electronic clock radio. It was 3:20am. This had better be good or heads would roll.

'Yes,' she snapped irritably.

'Katie, it's Elizabeth Palmer one of the book club members. I'm really sorry for contacting you in the middle of the night but we've had a break in.'

'Have you been in contact with the police?'

'Yes. They only left about an hour ago. I'm so sorry to ring you but I think the person who broke in is linked to the murder of Muriel Jennings.'

This was a huge assumption but one which couldn't be disregarded. 'Okay,' she managed, still sounding very lethargic, 'I'll head straight over. I'd appreciate a strong coffee when I arrive if you wouldn't mind.'

With James and Fiona away at a conference in Cardiff Katie reluctantly knew she would have to handle this on her own.

Within the hour, Katie was sitting opposite Liz and Simon making notes on her mobile phone voice recorder, interspersed with sips of industrial strength Colombian.

'You're sure you locked every door and window?' Katie asked.

'Quite sure,' Simon replied. 'Although the latch on the patio window wouldn't take much to prize open. It's been faulty for weeks, we keep meaning to get it fixed.'

'There's your answer,' Katie whistled softly. 'Easy access for a break and enter.'

'Yes, it's seems the most plausible way they gained entrance but what on earth for? We had no connections to Muriel Jennings other than my wife's association with her at the Bovey book club. She never socialised with her outside of those meetings.'

'It could be pranksters,' Katie suggested. 'Kids having a laugh at your expense. It doesn't take much for people to dabble in a bit of investigating and discover a few connections.'

'Let's hope your theory is correct,' Simon concluded not sounding too convinced. 'I take it you'll take prints of the kitchen?'

'Not me personally, but I'll send someone over first thing in the morning,' Katie advised. 'Try not to worry too much. I'm sure there's no connection at all with the murder of Mrs. Jennings. Like I said it's more likely to be kids messing about.'

Katie sounded confident as she spoke these words. However, later driving home, a permanent frown deepened on her forehead. Not for one moment did she think it was kids playing a sick joke. There was no doubt in her mind whoever wrote those words in red paint was directly linked to the death of Muriel Jennings.

***

With Fiona and James back from Wales Katie brought them up to speed on the incident involving Liz and Simon Palmer.

'It appears that a few of the book club members have been targets of either property damage or threats,' Katie informed them as they worked well into the evening going over the Jennings case.

Katie went through the events one by one, occasionally referring to the notes in front of her so she could relay all the facts.

'Firstly, Jane Anderson had her car vandalised. Someone maliciously smashed both mirrors and took a key or similar metallic object scraping it the entire length of the car. Shortly after Jane's incident, Liz Palmer discovered an intruder had been in her house leaving a threatening message on the fridge.

The third person to be affected was Ruby Smith, who contacted me just over an hour ago. She found a picture of Muriel Jennings pinned to the front fence and lying on the ground nearby was an old torch resembling the murder weapon.

Finally, to date we have a report just in that Cathy Munroe received an anonymous phone call from someone claiming to know Muriel's killer.'

'I just don't get it,' Fiona remarked. 'Why target members of the book club. It doesn't make sense.'

'Not much of this investigation makes any damn sense if you ask me,' James muttered.

Katie tried to bring calm to their growing frustrations. 'I have taken time to study the photos I found in the attic of Muriel's house,' she told her siblings. 'If you take the photo of the three children you can interpret it many ways;

the child with their face blanked out could just hate having their photo taken, on the other hand someone could be wanting to ensure their identity remains a mystery. If the latter is the case, then the mystery child could shed light on Muriel's past. There's also the possibility the third adult in the photograph with Mark and Stella is the child with the blanked out face.'

'In which case,' Fiona interrupted. 'Mark and Stella probably know who she is.'

Katie looked at her sister triumphantly, 'So all we need to do is take the photo and show it to Mark and Stella.'

'Not so fast,' James broke in. 'I think we should play this one close to our chests. At least until we've had time to unravel a few other clues. At this stage, it's hard to tell who's friend or foe.'

Katie lent back in her seat looking at the ceiling, 'Yes, you're right.'

'I still feel the book, 'The Sinner's Daughter', has major significance in this matter but for the life of me don't know why,' Fiona piped up. 'It wouldn't be a bad idea for one of us to meet with the author and see if *she* can shed any light on things,' making this statement Fiona was staring straight at her sister who let out a laugh.

'I get it,' Katie smiled, 'by someone you mean me?'

'You *are* the forensic psychologist,' Fiona reminded her, 'no one else would even get close to reading the mind of Lillian Webster.'

'What makes you think I'll have any luck?' Katie replied, pulling an abstract face. 'However, I'm happy to give it a go if you feel it would help? Another thing I want to do is get to visit the Jennings family Doctor; David Ashcroft. I'm almost certain he may have some inside information on Muriel's medical history, whether he will divulge or not is the problem. He's been away for the past few weeks but I plan to drop by after work on Monday and try to pry something out of him.'

With a semblance of new direction, the forensic team called it a night. All they needed was one lucky break or that piece of undeniable forensic evidence to provide clues to unravel the mystery. It was not uncommon for things to move swiftly along once that happened. They parted company all wishing for the same thing.

It was strange how the rain echoed through the damp basement. At first the drops were relatively quiet but becoming louder as day turned to night. There were parts of the stone wall that were soggy to touch as the moisture seeped through. Large puddles of water gathered on the floor creating small wading areas. Staring at the dank walls didn't seem a strange thing for her, it was almost comforting but within a split second that all changed. Figures appeared on one wall like a hologram with bright colours mixed with shades of grey, no longer a tranquil sight. She closed her eyes tight then opened them. A ghostly feeling swept over her. Casting her eyes once more around the basement she noticed the walls no longer looked damp, this time there were no puddles on the floor and all forms of life had disappeared.

CHAPTER ELEVEN

Stella opened the door clad in a pair of black corduroy trousers and a baggy yellow t-shirt. She wore a vacant expression and didn't seem at all pleased to see Katie and James standing on her front doorstep.

'We were hoping to ask you a few more questions about your mother if you can spare the time,' Katie muttered, wondering if they'd called at a bad time, noting the unwelcome expression on Stella's face.

'Of course, come on in,' Stella remarked, forcing a smile which didn't quite reach her eyes. She stepped swiftly aside to allow them access.

On entering the living room, they encountered Jane Anderson lounging on the settee reading a magazine. She looked up and smiled. 'Ms. Sinclair, how nice to see you again.'

Katie quickly introduced James trying to hide her surprise at seeing Jane.

'Jane looks after the marketing of our china clay exports,' Stella explained, waving for the guests to take a seat in the vacant arm chairs. 'When Mum was alive, Jane would drop by twice a month to go through marketing strategies and then stay for a light supper. I've now carried on the tradition.'

'Although it's probably about time I was heading off,' Jane announced, taking a quick glance at her mobile phone and easing herself up off the settee. 'I'll see myself out Stella.'

Then she turned to Katie. 'Goodnight Ms Sinclair. Nice seeing you again.'

'Likewise,' Katie mumbled. 'Good night Ms Anderson.'

Stella moved a pile of papers off the chaise lounge and sat down. Katie couldn't help but notice how frail she looked. 'How are you coping?' She asked with genuine concern.

'I have my moments,' Stella replied staring down at her hands to avoid eye contact. 'Dr. Ashcroft has prescribed a mild sedative to help me relax. To be honest when I'm alone I find things hard to deal with. I manage better when I'm around people. Less time to think I guess.'

She reached into her handbag retrieving a small glass bottle. With a swift shaky movement, she unscrewed the lid and threw a pill into her mouth, washing it down with a gulp from a glass of water. 'That's better,' she smiled. 'Now what can I do for you both? Do you have any new leads on Mum's murder?'

Katie shook her head. 'Not exactly, we wanted to ask a few questions in relation to the Bovey book club. We need to know if there is any member you have concerns about? Did your mother ever mention a particular member who disliked her in anyway?'

'No, she seemed to get on with everyone. Look Ms Sinclair I don't mean to be rude but I really do feel you're clutching at straws by asking these sorts of questions. I would have told you if I had reservations about any of the club members. After all, I want this matter cleared up as much as you do, perhaps even more so.'

Katie blew out her cheeks. 'Yes of course. I'm sorry,' then deliberately changed the subject. 'I must say the house looks spotless. I can tell you've done a bit of spring cleaning since we last called in.'

Stella managed a watery smile. 'Not me personally. I'm fortunate to have a great cleaning lady who comes in twice a week. I gave her some time off after mum died as I wasn't up to idle chit chat but now I'm back on track I felt the place needed a bit of sprucing up. God knows it needed it after the break in.'

Katie could have kicked herself. She was putting her foot in everywhere.

A few moments of awkward silence passed before James broke in with his own line of questioning. 'Stella, was your mother one for reminiscing about her youth, in particular her teenage years?'

Stella rolled her eyes. It was hard to decipher if this was because she hated these types of questions or merely found the subject of her mother's childhood boring.

James waited patiently for an answer.

'I don't recall mum ever talking much about her youth. I know she spent several months in Wales when she left school; that's where she met my father. Apart from a few stories relating to my grandmother she never really spoke about her childhood or teenage years.'

'What about *your* ex-husband, did he have a good rapport with your mother?' James asked.

'My mother and Patrick didn't really get along but if you're trying to insinuate he had anything to do with mum's murder forget it,' Stella replied with a sharp edge. 'Patrick lives in America with his new wife and hasn't set foot in England for over seven months.'

'I was fascinated to learn he's a well-respected analytical chemist,' James continued. 'I imagine he would have spoken a lot about his profession in the years you were married.'

Stella's brown eyes suddenly bored into James' blue ones. 'So now you think I killed my mother because I know how to cover up evidence,' she barked. 'Now I've heard it all. I think it best if you both leave.'

Katie reached out to touch Stella gently on the arm but she instantly drew back. 'We're not suggesting that,' Katie said softly. 'Murder investigations involve many angles of questioning.'

Stella's features softened slightly. 'Yes I'm sorry. I realise you're only doing your job.'

'One last question and we'll be off,' James announced. 'We discovered a photograph up in the attic of yourself, Mark and someone with their face blanked out. Would you happen to know who the mystery woman might be?'

Stella gave a small laugh. 'The lady in the photograph happens to be Jane Anderson, hardly a mystery. As I mentioned Jane does all our marketing for the china clay. Mum took that photo for the company newsletter. Not long afterwards Mark and Jane had a big disagreement and Mark decided to blank out Jane's face so the photo couldn't be used on the front cover. Just Mark being childish.'

'What about another photograph we found with two young children and an older child standing with a young woman. Can I presume the young woman is your mother and two of the children would be yourself and Mark?'

Stella nodded. 'Yes I think I recall that snap and before you're wondering the older child happens to be our cousin Janette. So no mystery with that one either I'm afraid. Just boring family and business photos.'

With that little puzzle cleared up James and Katie bid Stella goodnight heading back to their car.

'Well we can rule out the photographs as being leading evidence,' Katie grimaced 'At least that's one mystery solved.'

***

With the luxury of a two-day break and free of work commitments, Katie opted to ride over to Princetown, one of her favourite villages straddling the top of the moor. Katie rarely got to spend time on horseback so seized any opportunity to clamber into the saddle. Within ten minutes of leaving Bovey Tracey she entered the confines of Dartmoor; her grey Connemara a little restless, prancing around as the dust stirred up in the breeze. Even a plastic bag whipping past on the dirt track saw him side stepping in disgust.

Although a very experienced rider, Katie was forced to hold Polo Mint on a tight rein, soon growing tired of the pony's antics. What was meant to be a relaxing day was proving anything but. Reluctantly after a short period of time she dismounted, flipping the reins over the pony's head to lead him across the open moorland. At length on approach to Princetown Katie remounted to get a good view of Dartmoor Prison looming in the distance. It stood out grey and stark set against the back drop of the heathery moor. Katie shuddered at the thought of Ted Cartwright inside for the brutal murder of five women. There was nothing appealing in the prison architecture but then why should there be? It wasn't meant to be attractive. Dartmoor Prison was hardly listed as one of Britain's top ten holiday destinations; not one of its occupants had chosen to be there.

Mesmerised by the stone building in the distance Katie didn't see the deep blue sports car until it was almost too late. It careered around the corner on the wrong side of the road forcing her to canter on to the grass verge. Polo Mint snorted in disgust then as if to show who was boss decided to rear almost throwing Katie from the saddle. The driver of the flashy car jammed on the brakes screeching to a halt about 20 metres ahead. Seething inwardly Katie watched him exit the vehicle and begin strolling towards her, a grim determination on his strong features. He was tall, with a mass of silver flecked hair defining a man in his late sixties, early seventies.

When he was only a few metres away Katie could hear him muttering obscenities which she chose to ignore.

'Get your bloody horse off the goddamn road,' he bellowed. 'You'd be better suited to a bicycle,' adding as an afterthought, 'that's assuming you can even ride one.'

'I'm not entirely sure our close encounter was actually my fault,' retaliation, the forefront of Katie's wrath. 'You were driving way too fast over the open moors. Dartmoor is a national park where ponies and cattle roam freely. It's not a race track.'

'For your information madam, I have lived in this part of the country a lot longer than you have,' he snarled before marching back to his car, executing a wild U-turn and heading back at a rate of knots towards her.

'Bastard,' Katie yelled, as he screamed past in a cloud of dust without a backward glance, not that he would have heard, but it gave her some slight satisfaction. Her heart racing, she felt decidedly hot under the collar; only thing for it, a flat out gallop across the moors. Loosening Polo's reins Katie urged him forward with a moderate squeeze until he gathered speed. A gentle cooling sea breeze was blowing in from the coast and wisped across her fair complexion. She revelled in the sound of Polo's hooves as they occasionally pounded the soft ground. Travelling at such a speed she only caught fleeting glimpses of the straw-like heather which dotted the landscape. Feeling totally free she galloped on losing all track of time. It was almost five o'clock when Katie once more found herself on the edge of Princetown. Ominous grey clouds were now accelerating across the sky driven relentlessly by a chill northerly from a deepening storm in the Atlantic. Tired and lusting for a drink Katie was disappointed to discover all the shops in

the main street closed. The whole town appeared deserted save for a middle aged woman standing out on the pavement shaking a large tablecloth.

'It's turned into a cold day,' the woman chortled as Katie and Polo Mint walked past the Jubilee Memorial. 'Why don't ye come inside my warm kitchen me lover and I'll fix us up a nice cuppa. There's a small garden out yonder where you can tether your pony.'

Katie didn't need much persuasion. Her hands were numbed and her face was tinged purple from the cold. With Polo secured to a fence post in the pocket size back garden Katie followed the woman into a small white washed cottage. Instant warmth from a small wood burning stove surged through Katie's tired body as she stepped over the threshold into a quaint, rustic kitchen. It was a typical country workman's abode circa early 19th century with low wooden beams and local slate floors. The woman introduced herself as Mavis Partridge owner of one of the local gift shops.

'Let me get you a nice cuppa,' she volunteered. 'Milk and sugar?'

'Just a dash of milk, thank you,' Katie replied, fervently rubbing her hands together to restore circulation.

With the tea brewing on the old fashioned hob they sat at the kitchen table striking up conversation. Mavis was born and bred on Dartmoor and had owned her little shop for over thirty years. She claimed to know everyone in the town and nearly all of their business.

'I'd forgotten how close the prison is to the town,' Katie remarked, eager to bring the prison to the forefront. 'If those walls could talk I'm sure we'd all be amazed.'

Mavis laughed. 'Tis not for the faint hearted living around these parts that's for sure. Dartmoor Prison's seen some of the country's most notorious criminals you'll ever get to meet.'

'Or hopefully won't meet,' Katie jibed.

Mavis smiled. 'Yes indeed. My brother can tell 'ee stories dark and gloomy about the Prison. He works in the Prison museum located in the old dairy building. Some right rogues been inside them four walls that's for sure.' Mavis appeared eager to show off her local knowledge.

'Do you know much about Ted Cartwright?' Katie asked, enjoying her cup of tea as it slightly scolded the back of her throat. 'I believe he's an inmate at the prison.'

'Who doesn't know Ted,' Mavis replied, looking wistful. 'It's been many years since he committed those terrible crimes but to some folks it seems like only yesterday.'

'I understand the Cartwright family used to live on the edge of town, quite wealthy from all accounts,' Katie probed.

'You should go have a talk with Dexter Sims.' Mavis suggested. 'He was Cartwright's defence lawyer. If you continue along the main street for a few hundred yards, you'll find his house "Castaway" just before the bridge. Dexter can tell 'ee stories 'bout old Ted.'

Within the hour Katie excused herself, desperate to grab an opportunity to talk with Sims.

Katie found Dexter Sims polishing his sports car on the brick driveway. She stopped dead in her tracks on realizing it was same vehicle which had almost run her off the road earlier that afternoon. Dexter looked up and scowled, spotting Katie walking up the driveway, now leading a very docile Polo Mint exhausted from his long gallop across the moors.

'We meet again, how nice.' There was no disguising the sarcasm in this voice.

'I was wondering if I could have a word with you Mr. Sims?' Katie asked, tethering Polo to a nearby tree half expecting a vindictive tirade in reply.

'What topic would you like to discuss, the weather?' Dexter jibed. 'Or perhaps more fitting would be horse safety on the open moors.'

Katie curbed her tongue. 'How about the topic of Ted Cartwright. I believe you acted as his defence lawyer many years ago.'

'I can assure you I have nothing to say on the subject of Ted Cartwright and who the bloody hell are you anyway?' He snapped throwing his wet chamois leather into a nearby bucket before ascending a flight of steps up to the front door of his house.

Hot on his heels Katie followed suit. Squeezing inside Dexter attempted to slam the door in her face.

Katie quickly thrust a foot in the door preventing it from being closed any further.

'*You* may not have anything to say Mr. Sims but I can assure you *I* do,' Katie informed him, firmly trying desperately to keep her temper in check.

'I am not about to breach professionalism and talk to some low life journalist,' he snapped, 'so I'd move your foot if I were you unless you want to lose a few toes.'

'Sorry, no can do,' Katie said stubbornly. 'And just for the record I am not a journalist but a forensic psychologist. I would like some answers and I don't intend to leave until I get them.'

'You're wasting your time miss, you really are,' Dexter replied, a touch of softness creeping into his tone. 'What Ted did is best forgotten.'

'What if I was to tell you a recent murder investigation could have some bearings on Ted's killing spree.'

Dexter's face turned ashen and simultaneously he moved his frame out of the doorway allowing Katie instant access.

'You'd better come in,' he mumbled, beckoning with his hands. 'You can leave the mule tied to that tree. I'll see he gets some water before you head home. Poor beggar looks worn out. Lovely Connemara if I'm not mistaken. Fine Irish horse.'

Katie smiled inwardly. Dexter obviously cared a lot more about animals than people.

'Know much about horses?' she asked with interest.

'A fair bit. Been riding since I was a nipper but gave it up when I broke my leg in a fall about three years ago. Sorry, you'll have to excuse the mess,' Dexter remarked, showing her into an unkempt study. 'My housekeeper is away for a few days and I'm afraid cleaning is not my forte.'

Katie managed a grin. 'No need to apologize. I'm not one for housework either.'

Dexter moved to a small shelf retrieving a large bottle of whisky, then proceeded to pour himself a moderate amount. 'To steady my nerves,' he grinned sheepishly. 'Want one?'

Katie shook her head, warming a little to this eccentric old man. He reminded Katie of her late grandfather; a very hard exterior with a soft interior.

The arrival of a boisterous red setter had Katie feeling on edge. He bounded about barking madly almost knocking into the furniture. Katie was used to dogs but found the retriever a bit too skittish.

'Rally is an old softy, aren't you mate?' Dexter reassured Katie, as he fondled the dog's long silky ears. 'I've had him since he was a playful puppy. Old Rally wouldn't hurt a fly. So tell me missy. What makes you think I can help you with your murder enquiry? Ted Cartwright can't be your man. He's been behind bars for quite a while now. He's not likely to harm anyone else in a hurry.'

169

'We're just following a few leads and one of them is linked to the book which tells the full story of Cartwright's killing spree. Before I go into too much detail can I clarify that you did defend Ted Cartwright? You were his defence lawyer?'

Dexter let out an involuntary sigh, rubbing his left eye.

'Yes I did defend Ted Cartwright,' his tone was barely more than a whisper.

He saw Katie's questioning look and went on to explain himself.

'Well someone had to Miss. There was no other fool who was going to do it. Besides, Ted and I went to school together. I felt compelled to help the poor sod.'

This seemed a reasonable explanation but Katie wanted to know more.

'Knowing he had murdered five women couldn't have given you much cause to like him,' she postulated.

'My role as a defence lawyer doesn't allow me to like or dislike people Ms err...'

'Sinclair, Katie Sinclair. And, oh sorry I should explain I'm working with the Crown on a recent local homicide.'

Katie placed her card on the coffee table. Dexter leant forward to read the small print. 'Moorland Forensic Consultants, eh. Well, Ms Sinclair, you should know I was not allowed to form opinions. Besides a good defence lawyer must always believe his client to be innocent until proven guilty.'

'Yes, but you and I both know that's a myth,' Katie challenged. 'You must have known Ted was guilty by all the evidence provided, yet you still chose to defend him.'

'To this day young lady, I have my own beliefs,' Dexter answered softly, looking directly into her pale eyes. 'One of them being: Ted was wrongly accused of murders he didn't commit. The Ted I went to school with was a kind fellow. Not the person he allegedly turned out to be.'

'But people change over time,' Katie gently argued. 'Some adopt new traits and personalities that see them become a whole new individual.'

'Not Ted, he could never change. Certainly not into the monster people made him out to be.'

'Did his daughter Abby believe him to be innocent?' Katie probed.

'That I can't tell you,' Dexter replied. 'Abby didn't disclose her inner thoughts to me. I think deep down she will always have a great love for her father.'

'Do you still keep in contact with Abby Mr. Sims? After all I imagine you gave her a lot of support throughout the trial, becoming someone she felt she could always turn to.'

'I've not seen or heard from Abby for over ten years,' Dexter replied, finishing his drink and promptly pouring another. 'Each year on her birthday Abby receives a tidy sum of one million pounds. It is my job to see it goes into her bank account, nothing more, nothing less.'

Katie gave a gasp of amazement. This was the first she'd heard of any inheritance. She guessed the family was wealthy but not to that extent.

Dexter gave a hearty laugh. 'We're certainly not talking about an ordinary family here Miss Sinclair. You could actually write a lot of interesting stories on Ted Cartwright and his family.'

'So you have absolutely no idea where Abby could be?' Katie confirmed. 'Would the bank be able to shed any light on her whereabouts?'

'I can't for one moment fathom why you would be interested in trying to locate Abigail Cartwright,' Dexter mused.

'I believe Abby may have information vital to our current investigation,' Katie replied truthfully.

'An investigation you have not yet told me much about,' Dexter reminded her. 'What recent murder could possibly be linked to the Cartwright's?'

'The homicide of Muriel Jennings,' Katie dutifully told. 'Muriel was an aging woman murdered in her Ashburton home a few weeks ago. At the time of her murder she was reading "The Sinner's Daughter" by Lillian Webster. The book based on the Cartwright murders which…'

'Yes, I remember the reports on TV about Muriel's death. Pure coincidence I'd say, Dexter interrupted, turning to gaze out of the window at the Dartmoor landscape. 'Just because this lady was reading a book about Ted Cartwright just before she died doesn't mean there has to be a connection.'

'There's a possibility,' Katie said obstinately.

For a few moments, Dexter's mind seemed focused elsewhere as if he'd forgotten Katie was in the room. It was an eerie feeling. Then quite suddenly he appeared to return to the present continuing their conversation.

'Life is full of possibilities Ms Sinclair, but you need to know that Ted didn't need to murder any of those women,' Dexter's voice was barely a whisper.

'Then why did he?' Katie wondered out loud. Nothing was making much sense. She was determined to glean as much as possible from Dexter, especially Ted's mental state when he allegedly went on his killing spree.

Dexter sighed. 'Like I said, I still don't believe Ted murdered those women but if he did the only conclusion I have is Ted felt betrayed when his wife left him and wanted to make a final statement.'

'Some statement,' Katie mumbled, patiently waiting for Dexter to continue his explanation, which he did after a few silent minutes.

'When Jessica left Heather Lea, Ted lost his upstanding in the community. He was no longer the big shot he had once been so he turned to drink which eventually spiralled out of control. You see his pride was shattered.'

'How did the locals react when *you* took on the role of Ted's defence lawyer?' Katie enquired. 'I can't imagine life was made easy for you.'

Dexter pulled a face. 'I certainly had my fair share of hate mail. Windows were smashed, my car spray painted, I even received a few death threats.'

'Didn't any of this bother you?'

'To a point, but I'm a tough old bugger. Nothing was going to change so I tried to deal with things the best I could.'

'Tell me about the trial,' Katie pressed. 'I remember reading snippets in the local papers but I don't recall seeing or hearing anything about Abby at the time. Why was that? After all she was Ted's daughter.'

'Abby was protected by the government. It would have been damaging if she was brought into the limelight,' Dexter explained. 'Besides Abby didn't murder those women. She was an innocent young girl caught up in a living hell.'

'I see.' It was Katie's turn to momentarily pause the conversation. When she did speak again she wondered if her next statement would shock Dexter in any way. 'I met with Jessica Cartwright recently. She gave me some useful information but didn't disclose much about Abby.'

Dexter didn't look at all surprised when Katie disclosed meeting Jessica. His attitude was quite laid back as if Jessica was insignificant.

'Ah Jessica, she reminds me so much of a chameleon,' he grinned. 'I always found her so changeable.'

'Interesting choice of words Mr. Sims.'

He refrained from commenting, allowing a deathly hush to descend upon them. Finally, Katie broke the silence when it appeared he had nothing more to say.

'What else can you tell me about Abby?'

A small twinkle shone in his eyes. 'Ah yes, The Sinner's Daughter. There's so much I can tell you about Abby. I remember her being a gentle soul who always showed great compassion.'

Dexter shifted in his seat whilst toying with his whisky glass before changing the subject slightly. 'Tell me Ms Sinclair have you been inside the prison where Ted resides?'

'No I've only ridden past.'

'It's worth a visit,' Dexter informed her, draining the remnants in his glass and pouring another. 'Most of the inmates are non-violent offenders in line with the prison being a category C prison. Ted is a bit of an exception.'

'Have you ever visited Ted in prison?' Katie enquired.

'On one or two occasions, mostly during the trial but I've not had cause to drop by of late. By all accounts Ted is not a well man. I doubt he would even recognize me now. Some say it's early onset of Alzheimer's, other believe he's just quietly going insane. Whatever the case he will never be a free man.'

'I believe the one person who managed to escape Cartwright's clutches is buried not far from here. Is that true?' Katie asked, referring to information detailed by Fiona after her visit to Barney Rubble.

Dexter nodded. 'Her name was Sasha. She was the only woman who managed to escape from the house. The story goes she was assisted by Abby. The sad thing is she committed suicide several years later. Sasha's family believes she never got over being tortured by Ted and hence the reason for eventually taking her own life. Every day there are fresh flowers placed on her grave and no one knows who puts them there.'

'Hasn't anybody thought to hang around and see? I would have thought someone would be curious to know.'

'Apparently not,' Dexter replied. 'It is similar to the story of Kitty Jay. Kitty was a workhouse girl who lived in the Manaton area. She became pregnant and hung herself. You will usually see a bunch of fresh flowers on Kitty's grave. Legend has it not a day goes by when flowers haven't appeared there, even in winter.'

'Yes, I've heard the story, known to most as Jay's grave. My brother and I have walked from North Bovey through Easdon Down to the grave. Quite a climb in parts I recall.'

'You need to be fit to do that walk,' Dexter laughed. 'In my youth, I could practically jog that route now I'd be lucky to make it to first base.' Dexter rubbed the stubble on his chin a troubled expression creeping across his façade. 'Look miss, there is something I feel you really ought to know. It is bound to surface sooner or later if you conduct a thorough investigation and I'm not one to hold back on information that could be critical.'

He took another sip of whisky before taking a deep breath. 'Ted Cartwright had an affair with Muriel Jennings the woman who was murdered.'

Katie opened and closed her mouth like a goldfish. This news was totally unexpected but it shed depth of light in connection to Muriel and possibly the Cartwright murders.

'Well, perhaps affair isn't quite the right word,' Dexter continued sheepishly. 'Muriel was only a teenager at the time, Ted about twenty-four. Muriel ended up falling pregnant which was hushed up as much as possible. Muriel was sent away to Wales by her parents to avoid scandal. She returned to Devon several years later after marrying Bill Jennings.'

'Did she go through with the pregnancy?' Katie asked, unsure of exactly what questions needed answering. She was struggling to keep up with the information being provided. The news Ted and Muriel had been romantically linked came as a massive shock her hands were visibly shaking.

'One can only assume so,' Dexter replied. 'Rumour has it she gave birth to a daughter, I only learnt all of this when Ted was sentenced. It was sort of a confessional I guess. A lawyer is almost as good as a priest.'

Dexter let out a shallow laugh before adding, 'I tell you; the things one learns from criminals is mind boggling.'

Katie's own mind started to go into overdrive. The news provided by Dexter clearly linked in with the pathology results stating Muriel had another child. Some of the puzzle pieces were now starting to fit together. It now appeared that this child may also have been at the crime scene as the government path lab tests revealed a drop of blood from one of Muriel's offspring.

'Supposing she did go through with the pregnancy what do you think would have happened to the child?' Katie fired at Dexter watching him down another shot.

'I wouldn't have a clue,' Dexter solemnly replied, looking into an empty glass and debating if another was in order. The answer was obvious as he reached once more for the scotch bottle. 'Doctor Ashcroft Senior would be able to tell you more, though how his memory functions nowadays is anyone's guess. He's been the Jennings family Doctor since Muriel was a youngster. He'd be the one to interrogate.'

'Where will I find Doctor Ashcroft?' Katie asked, with some urgency.

'I believe he's now residing in a nursing home but I'm not sure which one. You could try talking to his son David who now runs the family medical practice in Chudleigh.'

'Thank you. One last question; In relation to the Cartwright family home, does anyone live there?'

'Not as far as I know. No local is game to set foot in a place where five women were brutally murdered. It's been on the market for years and the asking price well above the market. I think the realtor who's handling the sale is Trefor Jones, lovely Welsh fella who's not quite so familiar with all the history that lends itself with this particular property.'

Dexter stopped to come up for air before adding another sentence. 'I do hear rumours some folk claim to see lights flickering at Heather Lea on dark winter nights.'

The meeting with Dexter Sims came to an abrupt end as Polo decided to break free from the old oak tree and meander into the rose garden. Dexter wasn't too fussed but Katie took it as a cue to head home.

***

The following day, after briefing her siblings on the meeting with Dexter Sims Katie headed off on the chance of a meeting with Doctor David Ashcroft at his surgery situated in the small hamlet of Chudleigh, a picturesque village not far from the A38. The Chudleigh practice was a busy enterprise built over the years by Doctor Ashcroft senior and now run by David, his son. David, a good looking man in his late forties was well liked in the community, a trustworthy individual who took the trouble to get to know his patients. He was interested in their personal lives not merely treating their medical conditions.

Katie planned to drop in after surgery hours in the hope Ashcroft would have time to spare in answering a few questions. It was a long shot if he would allow her any time at all but worth a try.

Pushing open the surgery door she casually walked into a tidy little waiting room completely void of patients. So far so good she thought fronting up to the reception desk occupied by a disinterested young woman filing her nails.

Probably not the sort of filing the Doctor had requested, Katie observed as she tried to attract the receptionist's attention.

'Excuse me,' Katie began. 'I was wondering if Doctor Ashcroft was free?'

'Do you have an appointment?'

'Err no I don't.'

'I'll see what I can do,' the receptionist replied curtly, pressing a green button on the desk phone. 'Doctor, I have a lady in reception who would like to see you. Name of...'

'Katie Sinclair,' Katie obliged.

'No she doesn't have an appointment. That's fine I'll let her know,' she then turned to Katie. 'Please take a seat. Doc won't be long.'

Katie nodded but opted to stand and cast an eye over various medical certificates and diplomas spread around the walls.

After a few moments, the door to an adjoining room opened and a distinguished man in a white coat stood framed in the door way. He looked across at Katie, who confidently stuck out a hand and smiled.

'I don't recall having seen you before Ms. Sinclair, but my receptionist Amelia will take down some personal information and then I'll get you to come in to my rooms.'

'Actually, I'm not here as a patient,' Katie interrupted him. 'I'm a forensic psychologist with Moorland Forensics.'

'I see, in that case you'd better come through into my office. I can spare you about ten minutes.'

'I'm looking for information regarding Muriel Jennings whom I believe was a patient of yours,' began Katie, now comfortably ensconced in a black leather designer chair opposite Ashcroft's desk. 'I understand you've been the Jennings family G.P. now for some years?'

'That's correct although my father Doctor Ashcroft senior has been acquainted with the family a lot longer than I have. I'm not sure I'll be able to give you what you're looking for Ms. Sinclair. On graduating as a Doctor, you take the Hippocratic Oath, as you well know. Providing answers to your queries could jeopardize my career which frankly is something I'm not prepared to do.'

'In that case, would it be possible for me to take a look at her file notes? Then I won't need to ask any questions,' Katie produced her best disarming smile knowing she was unashamedly pushing the boundaries already surmising what his reply would be.

She predicted correctly; David Ashcroft shook his head a single curl of brown hair falling across his forehead. He managed a crooked grin. 'Nice try but that is definitely out of the question I'm afraid.'

'Could you turn a blind eye for once?' Katie persisted, laying on the charm again.

'I understand you are investigating Muriel's death, but at the same time I need to protect patient confidentiality.' David continued firmly. 'I could lose my registration if I were to disclose highly sensitive information.'

'What if I were to seek a court injunction?' Katie shot back at him, her niceness rapidly disappearing.

'That would be an entirely different matter,' he replied equally curt. 'However, until you have that piece of paper giving you the authority to have access to a patient's file I will not be producing any documentation.'

Katie was deflated, wishing for once she would come across someone willing to bend the rules. She hated red tape and bureaucracy in general.

As if reading her mind David Ashcroft quickly scribbled an address down on a piece of paper and placed it in her right hand. 'Try my old man,' he suggested. 'You'll find him ruling the roost at The Manors nursing home. He's not so fussed about protocols now he's retired and he may just give you the information you are after.'

Katie gave him a grateful smile, 'Thank you.'

'You're welcome, but if anyone asks; we never had this conversation.'

Katie held tight to the piece of paper as she hurried to her car. As soon as possible she would be calling on Ashcroft Snr.

***

Deep in thought James was heading back late to Bovey navigating his Land Rover through the dark back country Devon lanes, the radio tuned to the BBC, his mind faraway drinking in the final majestic chords of 'The Sinfonia Antartica' on Radio 3. He wasn't expecting his mobile phone ring tone to shatter the serenity. He pressed the hands free button cursing who could be calling him at this ungodly hour.

'I understand you are investigating the death of Muriel Jennings?'

James didn't recognize the male voice on the other end of the phone. At a rough guess, he'd pick the caller to be in their sixties or seventies. No spring chicken.

'Who is this?' he demanded, tightening his grip on the steering wheel and willing the 4wd through a particularly nasty bend.

The caller chose to ignore the question James fired at him, instead offering a statement. 'I know very little about Muriel's death but am convinced someone had her book marked. Who killed Muriel, not I, not I said the fly? Who shall I tell, why thee will I tell, as I sit alone in my tiny padded cell.'

Before he could comment the party hung up. James found a sudden tightness welling in his chest and pulled off to the side of the road, thoughts rushing through his head. Was the caller Ted Cartwright? The age and gender certainly matched. He attempted to trace the number but to no avail.

James continued to ponder over the conversation as he drove into North Bovey. Perhaps it was a prank caller, someone who knew James had been assigned to the Jennings case. It wouldn't be difficult to discover who was heading up the forensic investigations into Muriel's death. His name was mentioned in several newspaper articles and at recent press conferences. His mobile number was also easily accessible through directory assistance.

Pulling into the driveway of his duplex at the bottom of Indio Road, he grabbed the small note book and pen always kept in the glove box and quickly scribbled down a few details. The information the caller gave could have value further down the track. As with all investigations nothing could be discounted.

A short while later, James sat relaxing with a hot chocolate in his lounge room reflecting on the call. *I am convinced someone had her booked marked.*

What exactly did that mean? Either it was someone taking the piss or it was someone who knew quite a lot about the death of Muriel Jennings. If James had been wrong with his assumption the other party had been Ted Cartwright, could it have actually been Muriel's killer? He shivered at the thought. One thing was certain: Ted Cartwright couldn't commit a murder from the confines of Dartmoor Prison. That was one name that could be struck off the list of suspects.

James recalled classic text book cases which gave evidence showing it was not uncommon for killers to make themselves known to police and investigators. They often enjoyed playing cat and mouse pushing boundaries until they were caught, sometimes visiting and revisiting the crime scene. The current problem Moorlands Forensics faced was the killer hadn't been apprehended, they were still at large with every possibility they would strike again at any moment. A doubling of their efforts on the case was urgently required.

**

'Who is it,' cried Katie as a ring of the front door bell interrupted her bedtime routine.

'It's Matt. Hurry up and open the blasted door it's freezing out here.'

Katie grabbed a robe, donned slippers and shuffled down the stairs. 'What on earth are you doing coming round this time of night?' she demanded, opening the door. 'I get very little kip time as it is without a midnight invasion.'

Matt grinned, stepping over the threshold and producing a bottle of red wine from behind his back. 'I brought us a little nightcap.'

'Fine, but you're not staying long,' Katie replied firmly, reluctantly ushering him into the living room still warmed by the faint glow from the wood burning stove. She produced a couple of long stemmed wine glasses from the kitchen and watched half asleep while Matt opened and dispensed the wine with practised aplomb. He passed Katie a glass as she sat down on the sofa, her feet curled up beneath her bottom.

'I believe a member of this book club you've been investigating is harbouring a secret, a very big secret,' Matt began, sampling the red's bouquet and looking her straight in the eye. 'Want to hear more?'

'Go on,' Katie turned to face him, her interest rising.

'I'm fairly sure one of them happens to be Abby Cartwright – Ted Cartwright's daughter.'

The revelation shook Katie from her drowsiness. 'Abby, a book club member, no way,' Katie blurted, now fully awake and desperate for details. 'How the hell do you know that?'

'Ah no,' Matt squirmed. 'I'm not about to reveal my source. Besides at this stage I'm only about 80% sure.'

'Surely you can give me a bit more information?' Katie pleaded, pointing her glass in mock anger at Matt, spilling half the contents on her robe in the process.

'Unfortunately, I can't. The person who provided me with this knowledge swore me to secrecy. I don't want to end up breaking the law. Not even for you sweetheart.'

'I'd come and visit you in prison,' Katie teased. 'Just a few crumbs? Any idea which member of the book club it might be?'

'Sorry, no can do,' he reiterated, leaning forward to plant a soft kiss on Katie's sultry lips. 'That's a down payment for the news I've divulged tonight,' he informed her once their lips parted. 'I'll collect the balance later if I can come up with the goods.'

Long after Matt had gone Katie mulled over their conversation. It seemed unreal Ted Cartwright's daughter could be a member of the Bovey Book Club, someone she'd already met. The past week had been filled with revelations. First Dexter Sims breaking the news Ted Cartwright and Muriel Jennings were lovers, now this intriguing titbit from Matt. Katie digested it all, now realising the next step was to unravel the identity of the book club member. No easy feat. The best way to garner that would be by the process of elimination. There were only about four women who would fit the criteria by definition of age. Abby had to be in her twenties so that narrowed things down a bit. On the other hand, how ethical was it for Katie to try and unearth Cartwright's daughter? Perhaps it was not a wise move to delve that deep into the past. Unravelling the truth could prove fatal for Abigail Cartwright, who obviously wanted her secret kept that way. Katie only slumbered that night. Her mind buzzed with activity. There were white roses, pretty women, men in blue sports cars and dark damp cellars all floating around on the ceiling.

The flowers were placed on the table next to a Tiffany Vase. How lovely they would look when the girls came to dinner. They would all be given a white rose. Realising there were ten roses in total she grabbed a pair of scissors to behead the unwanted roses. There that was better. She didn't need all those white roses, that would be silly.

CHAPTER TWELVE

Moor View, an independent co-ed school set within 64 acres of land lay just on the outskirts of Newton Abbot. The uninterrupted view from the grand manor house taking in a large chunk of the Dartmoor escarpment; a vista to surely seduce any prospective parent contemplating sending their child to Moor View. Not only a day school; it also offered term and weekly boarding.

James and Fiona drove in through the grounds parking Fiona's red TVR directly outside the main office. The Registrar, a Mrs. Butler, had agreed to see them on short notice, James being keen to find out exactly why Muriel had agreed to pay school fees for someone else's child. Initial gut feeling told him blackmail was involved.

'Do come in,' Mrs. Butler greeted them warmly. She was a sprightly woman deemed to be in her early seventies with no immediate plans for retirement. Her hair was neatly tied up in a bun with not a sign of a grey hair. Regular trips to the hair salon helped retain some of her youth.

They followed the Registrar up two narrow flights of stairs to a compact but inviting office with a small window overlooking a deserted, high walled courtyard.

'Great advantage point for monitoring any unruly students.' Sandra Butler smiled, motioning her visitors to two small country chairs. 'Now I understand you'd like to talk to me about the account of one of our students. Of course, I'm more than happy to answer any of your questions, but I doubt I'll be much help.'

'What exactly can you tell me about the fees being paid by JC Holdings?' James asked, retrieving notebook and pen. 'I assume the girl in question is somehow related to the company's late director Mrs Muriel Jennings?'

'The girl in question is Rebecca Marsh, a student in year ten,' Mrs Butler informed them. 'Beckie has been here since kindergarten and a full-time boarder residing in Manor House. Like all the other students she goes home at the end of each term. Her adoptive parents currently reside in France. Her biological parents we know nothing about.'

'What sort of adolescent is Rebecca?' Fiona asked with interest. She knew the school fees were in the top bracket so most people would be hoping for a good return from their investment.

'Quite a remarkable one,' Mrs Butler answered. 'Beckie is an attractive young woman who's always near the top in her subjects. She's very athletic with a bubbly personality. You couldn't wish for a better student.'

'Do you know much about her adoptive parents?' Fiona ventured.

'Not a lot. They own a champagne vineyard in the Bordeaux region of Southern France. Quite wealthy by all accounts.'

'So doesn't it strike you as odd that someone else pays Rebecca's school fees?' James quizzed, now dismissing his theory of blackmail. With parents that wealthy there would be no need to extort money from someone else.

Mrs Butler looked flustered, colour flooding her pale cheeks. 'It is not my job to question why someone pays another child's school fees Mr. Sinclair. Rebecca is not a charity child if that's what you're implying.'

'The thought never crossed my mind,' James replied truthfully.

'Can you recall any changes in Rebecca over the past few weeks, anything unusual?' Fiona interjected quickly, taking a softer approach. She knew at times that people often took James' direct manner the wrong way and didn't want to get Mrs Butler off side.

Sandra Butler paused to think for a few moments before answering. 'I can't say I noticed any changes in our Beckie. However, a little over three weeks ago, we did receive a handwritten note to advise her school fees would no longer be paid by JC Holdings. If I remember correctly it was not long after Muriel Jennings died.'

This was news to James who sat bolt upright. 'Does this mean Rebecca will be leaving Moor View?' he enquired.

Mrs. Butler leaned closer to James as if afraid someone would overhear their conversation. 'Thankfully no, I have it on good authority her parents in France will continue paying for her education. Although there is one other thing you should probably know about.'

'Yes,' James pressed, his own voice barely more than a whisper.

'Muriel Jennings was a frequent visitor to the school. Every Friday afternoon at around four o'clock she would collect Rebecca and take her for afternoon tea in Bovey. This was all approved by Rebecca's parents who welcomed this outing for their daughter.'

'Would we be able to meet with Rebecca?' James asked. 'Just to establish a better feeling on her rapport with Muriel Jennings?'

Mrs Butler shook her head. 'I'm afraid Moor View has strict confidentiality policies. If you want to seek further clarification I suggest you speak with the management at JC Holdings, they are the only ones who can authorise a meeting.'

Fiona let out an involuntary sigh. Once more they had hit a brick wall. Whether Mark Jennings knew about Beckie, or not, it was certain he would not permit Moorland Forensics to conduct a meeting with her.

'There is one person who may be able to shed some light on your questions,' Mrs Butler said, seeing Fiona's despondent look. 'I can't promise anything but our bookkeeper Gladys Banks may know more in relation to Beckie's school fees. After all she's the one who handles all the cheques. I'll see if she's in her office and enquire if she knows anything.'

A few minutes later Mrs. Butler returned with a rather timid looking Gladys.

Gladys mumbled a brief hello before stuttering through her next sentence. 'I really shouldn't, I mean I could get into a lot of trouble, but you see…'

'It's okay,' James reassured her. 'We just want to see if we can help Beckie.'

'Yes of course. Well, I… err… well… I… err… stumbled on the information accidentally. Not that I was prying mind you.'

James felt his patience waning as he tried to keep his temper in check. He just wanted the woman to spit it out.

Gladys looked as if she was about to pass out but stoically continued. 'I understand you want to know more about those mystery school fees being paid for Rebecca Marsh. It's no mystery really: Beckie is the granddaughter of the late Muriel Jennings. You know, I saw this on one of the cheques when I went to cash it. Normally the payments were through a direct transaction into our account but on a couple of occasions cheques were sent instead.'

James eased himself up out of his chair. 'Thank you, Gladys. You've given us something really valuable to proceed with. We appreciate your time.'

'So what do you make of that?' Fiona enquired of James, as they returned to the car. 'We didn't for one moment connect Rebecca as Muriel's granddaughter. Also quite clearly; we were wrong in assuming Rebecca's school fees were being coughed up as a form of blackmail. I feel a bit bloody stupid in hindsight.'

James turned to face his sister. 'Possibly, but I don't think we were entirely wrong,' he replied, 'we're just not quite on the right track.'

'That sounds like a riddle,' Fiona said, an edge of frustration in her voice, 'do enlighten us!'

'Well let's stop and think about this,' James said, leaning against the hardtop of the TVR. 'If Rebecca Marsh is Muriel's granddaughter, this would surely mean Rebecca's biological mother is the child Muriel Jennings had with Ted Cartwright, assuming Dexter Sims was correct with his assumption Muriel gave birth to a daughter following her affair with Ted. If we're on the right track, then blackmail or at least some type of extortion could well have been taking place; that blackmail being carried out by Muriel's illegitimate daughter.

***

Lillian Webster's home, "The Hawthorns", stood sentinel on the main by-road approach into Chudleigh, a massive old rambling residence now succumbing to the ravages of time and neglect. Katie warily pushed open the rustic, creaking wooden front gate which suffered the ignobility of rudely parting from its hinges when she tried to close it.

Although Lillian Webster hadn't replied to Katie's numerous emails proposing they meet Katie decided to strike without announcement as time was now of the essence. Eerily, as if Lillian had been expecting her, the front door opened before Katie even reached the bottom step. A bubbly matronly figure in her mid-fifties greeted Katie with gusts of enthusiasm. Her rotund countenance either by chance or design matched her outfit; a pair of black cotton trousers with a baggy t-shirt.

'Entrez-vous,' she gushed cheekily, 'no need for introductions. I can spot a psychologist a mile away.'

Katie wasn't sure if this was a compliment or not so refrained from saying anything.

Lillian led her through a dark, narrow hallway into a modestly furnished, spacious study, reeking with the smell of stale tobacco smoke and dominated by one wall completely filled with books and various publications. Opposite, a large pair of French doors lay flung open revealing a dazzling vista of meadows and woodlands rolling down to the sprawl of Exeter just visible in the hazy distance.

'Not all mine,' Lillian smiled, indicating towards the books, 'although, in total, I'd say I have over one hundred that were scripted by me.'

'Well, that's about one hundred more than I've ever written.' Katie laughed, trying to make herself feel at ease. 'I never excelled at composition writing, always struggling with university essays.'

'I find that hard to believe Ms. Sinclair,' Lillian gushed. 'Writing comes from the heart my dear girl. Some form of writing lies within us all. It just takes a little determination and a lot of patience. You may think it's a bridge too far but I'm always saying if you set your mind to it you would pen something others want to read.'

'Perhaps,' Katie, not quite so convinced, watched transfixed as Lillian pulled a cigarette from out of her desk, pushed it into an absurdly long gold cigarette holder, and lit up blowing the smoke nonchalantly in Katie's direction.

'Self-doubt is your problem,' Lillian informed her. 'Unusual for a psychologist. Now, a drink?'

Katie accepted this offer waiting patiently while Lillian busied herself in the kitchen. This was the perfect opportunity to nosey around seeking snippets of information on Lillian's lifestyle. Porcelain cat ornaments were strategically placed around the room. All photos on display were also of felines; obviously Lillian Webster was a great cat lover.

'I appreciate you taking the time to see me today,' Katie began when Lillian returned. She took a seat in one of two leather arm chairs accepting the fine china tea cup passed to her, not at all surprised to see dainty Siamese cats painted on the sides. 'I'm not sure if you are fully aware of the reason I am here to see you?'

'From the way your emails were worded, I have a vague idea but perhaps you had better fill me in with more detail so I can try and be of some assistance.' Lillian instructed her.

Katie started to explain how the forensic team believed there may be a connection between the death of Muriel Jennings and the book Lillian had penned "The Sinner's Daughter". She deliberately kept a lid on her recent discovery that Muriel Jennings had been romantically linked to Ted Cartwright. She wanted to see if Lillian volunteered that information. There was every chance she didn't even know about the relationship.

'I'm certainly happy to answer all your questions,' Lillian said briskly, 'but whether I can be any real help remains to be seen.'

Katie retrieved note book and pen from her bag flipping to a blank page.

'I guess my first question is an obvious one but I need clarification. You did write the book about the Cartwright murders, didn't you?'

'Yes I did.' Lillian drank noisily from her cup not seeming to care much for etiquette.

'And have you written previous books based on real events?'

Lillian shook her head giving a hollow laugh and waving her cigarette aimlessly around in the air. 'Good god no, this was my first. It's also likely to be my last from all the unwelcome publicity it attracted. Most of my books are romance novels set around the Greek islands. I don't normally do non-fiction but this one tugged at my heart strings. I also happen to know Professor Neil Bradbury who ran the psychiatric institute where Ted Cartwright's daughter Abigail got admitted. It was Neil's suggestion I put pen to paper.'

'What sort of unwelcome publicity are we talking about?' Katie enquired, whilst jotting down notes.

'When you write about real life tragedies you inevitably stir up a sea of mixed emotions,' Lillian replied, stubbing the remains of her cigarette on the desk. 'There were some people who clearly felt the book should never have been published and the evidence to back this up was through all the hate mail I received. However, we journalistic types are pretty thick skinned. Water off a duck's back as far as I'm concerned.'

There was no denying Lillian Webster was a tough individual who didn't let much get the better of her.

'How long did the book take to write?'

'All up about fifteen months. It wasn't easy rounding up the pertinent material. Some of the victim's families were reluctant to talk. Then I came across others with such hatred for Ted Cartwright it became difficult to determine fact from fiction. Plenty of people were willing to rant about Ted being the personification of evil itself but didn't have much to back up their stories. Of course you can't put that sort of unreliable stuff in print.'

'What facts *did* you base the book on?'

'I spent an eternity wading through the trial transcripts tapes, mostly the submissions from the defence lawyers and prosecution. I also interviewed the victim's families.'

'What about information relating to Abby. How did you come by that?'

'From Abby, of course.'

Katie couldn't hide her look of surprise. 'You met with Abby?'

'Yes. We met on several occasions. In total, I'd say at least ten times. You look surprised Ms Sinclair, why is that?'

Katie blushed, uncomfortably discovering Lillian's eyes boring into hers.

She stammered her answer, 'I just didn't realise you were given the opportunity to get so close to Ted Cartwright's daughter. I didn't even entertain the possibility.'

Katie pulling herself together continued questioning. 'So Abby actually consented to providing all the material you needed to write the book?'

Lillian gave a hearty laugh. 'Let's just say I didn't need to sit down and draw logic on this one. At the time of writing the book Abby was a young teen. She was also in a mental institution. Her mind was detached from reality so she never even knew what day of the week it was when I rocked up to see her. Before the book was published her lawyer spoke to her about the pending publication; she didn't seem to mind. I can assure you everything was legal and above board.'

Lillian had managed to indirectly answer the question, a cunning trick of a good journalist.

'How often did you meet with Abby?' Katie asked.

'Generally, once a week for about an hour, there were always two hefty security guards present. We never met alone. This ruling was set in place by Abby's legal team and I had to comply with these stringent conditions. Not that it bothered me mind you.'

'Do you know what happened to Abby? Where she could be now?'

'All I know is she was discharged from the psychiatric hospital but where she went I wouldn't have a clue. Some believe she fled the country, others say she went insane. What you can be sure of though is that her identity would have changed. Probably her appearance as well.'

'At the end of the book you refer to *the one who got away*. Can you elaborate a bit more on that?'

'If you've read the book Ms Sinclair and I'm sure you have, you'll know Ted Cartwright murdered five women in total but persecuted six. One had a lucky escape. Hence *The one who got away*.'

'I see. Do you know much about her, the one who got away?'

'I've never met her if that's what you mean.'

'So you never had a chance to get her version of events?'

Lillian looked annoyed as if this in itself plagued her. 'I did my best to get as much information for the book but sometimes you come up against brick walls.'

'How well would you say you got to know Abby whilst writing it?'

'Well enough to know she wasn't off her trolley.'

'What about her father?'

'That's a different story. When I asked him why he murdered those poor women he looked directly at me and said, "If you're that fuckin' clever figure it out".'

Katie waited for Lillian to drain the dregs from her cup before continuing. 'Now that's a sure sign of one messed up individual don't you think?'

Or someone who could be entirely innocent, Katie thought but refrained from commenting. His utterance could be interpreted the way Lillian had interpreted it. Perhaps Ted was being a smart arse and asking her to step inside his head. However, through her years working as an experienced psychologist it could also be Ted's way of saying he didn't actually kill those women.

The interview came to an abrupt termination when one of Lillian's cats slinked in and unceremoniously plonked itself on a pile of papers which Katie assumed were latest novel drafts in progress. It was clearly apparent that although Lillian adored her cats disturbing the paperwork was out of bounds. All of a sudden Katie ceased to exist as Lillian, her demeanour changing became engrossed in picking up papers and pedantically shuffling them back in some kind of meaningful order. Lillian didn't even acknowledge Katie's presence. She scolded the cat, sat down at her old electric typewriter and began to type, muttering softly.

Katie realised no more was to be gained from the visit today. Lillian Webster was a little eccentric but had certainly thrown new light on the Cartwright's. She quietly exited the house, wondering what really went on in the bizarre mind of an individual such as Lillian Webster.

The bottle of pills sat on the cold stone floor. There were one hundred and five little white tablets at last count. She didn't rely on them, even though people thought she did. It could be days, weeks even before she felt the urge to pop one of those tiny pills, always taken with a cold glass of water. Besides why take them when she liked hearing the voices that crept into her head? After all they kept her company especially at night time. As soon as she popped a little white pill the voices vanished and she was left all alone; all alone in the cold basement staring into emptiness.

CHAPTER THIRTEEN

The sanatorium lay half buried amongst mature elm trees on the outskirts of Totnes. An unattractive, three storey building of dark red brick construction it was partly obscured by large unruly overgrowths of ivy which covered the walls creating an unsettling feeling of neglect.

Katie knew it was a gamble arriving unheralded and negative thoughts mingled with doubt filled her sub conscience as she swung her car into a vacant spot opposite the main entrance. Nevertheless, the tactic had worked often in the past and in some respects, it was the best approach with certain types, to catch them with their guard down. Countless attempts to arrange an appointment to meet with Professor Bradbury had been fruitless. The lady claiming to be his secretary insisted a very full schedule with no available time in the near future.

To one side of the imposing gothic style main door dangled a long rope pull conjuring visions from a 60's Hammer Film Dracula movie. Katie tugged tentatively on the device resulting in a loud clanging on the other side. 'What in hell's name was that!' a dumb founded Katie gasped, almost falling off the steps.

Before she could regain her composure, the door swung open, a stern faced, middle aged woman filling the doorway. 'Can I help you?'

A wave of uneasiness swept over Katie. She sensed being under surveillance from unseen CCTV the moment she drove in, a feeling compounded by the speed with which the doorbell was answered. She tried to exude an air of confident professionalism. 'I was hoping to see Professor Bradbury for a few minutes.'

'Your name?' the woman barked, in a voice almost robotic in nature, devoid of obvious life or emotion.

'Katie Sinclair.'

'Regarding?'

'I'm sorry but I do not wish to divulge that information,' Katie replied, quickly realizing she was fighting a losing battle and her request to see Professor Bradbury would almost certainly be declined.

'I take it you don't have an appointment?' the third degree causing Katie to bite her lip and mentally refrain from lashing out.

Katie shook her head predicting almost word for word the woman's next sentence.

'I'm sorry Ms. Sinclair but the Professor doesn't see anyone without an appointment.'

'I understand that may be your policy but perhaps you could just notify the Professor of my presence,' adding as an afterthought, 'if you wouldn't mind.'

Katie stood her ground, folding her arms defiantly projecting a look that indicated she'd remain there all day if necessary.

'Very well, wait here,' the woman advised abruptly, closing the door in her face.

Katie waited for what seemed an eternity. The wind was picking up and a sudden chill swirled around the nape of her neck. Resigned to the fact that she had been rudely dismissed Katie turned and started to descend the steps when without warning the door opened again, this time by the Professor himself. Katie instantly recognized him from the photographs which had accompanied articles and papers he'd written over the years; now in his early seventies sporting shoulder length silver hair with wide rimmed tortoise shell glasses perched on the tip of an elongated beak-like nose. Unflattering features notwithstanding, Bradbury enjoyed a ranking among the top echelon of UK psychiatrists being held in high regard by his peers in the medical academia; rumour had it he would soon be invited to the Palace.

'I believe you have requested to see me?' Bradbury smiled warmly, as he offered his hand, which Katie instantly accepted. A dramatically contrasting reception to the one handed out by the Dragon Lady.

'That's right,' Katie replied deftly producing a business card.

The professor held it close to his eyes studying her name and title carefully.

'You'd better come in Ms Sinclair,' he instructed. 'I'm afraid I can only grant a brief hearing. I'm chairing a conference workshop session in Ivybridge at two.'

Katie grateful for the unexpected windfall of a few minutes dutifully followed him through a long, poorly illuminated corridor flanked by plain white doors leading off on both sides. Opening the first one on the right he motioned her into a small treatment room which doubled as a make-shift office.

Professor Bradbury eased himself onto the edge of a large oak desk, his long legs swinging like a pendulum.

'Now how can I help you Ms Sinclair? We've not had the pleasure of meeting before but I've heard of your forensic work. From all accounts your little team have put in quite a sterling effort on some of the more challenging criminal cases in the last few years.'

Katie blushed slightly at the compliment. 'I'd like to ask you a few questions in relation to Abigail Cartwright,' Katie began, sounding a little nervous. 'I'm well aware you may not wish to speak with me as I am not an advocate for your client. Also the information I do obtain is not guaranteed to be kept confidential.'

'What exactly would you like to know?' Professor Bradbury asked, sounding rather bemused as he made direct eye contact momentarily forcing Katie to look away.

'I understand you treated Abby here at the hospital for a number of years? Exactly how long was Abby a patient of yours?'

'Abby is still a patient of mine Ms Sinclair,' Bradbury said quietly. 'She comes to see me once a week for a two-hour session.'

'In that case, can you advise of her current mental state? I need to know if Abby is capable of murder.'

He gave a shallow laugh. 'I'm sorry Ms. Sinclair, I am unable to divulge confidential patient information. Although, really I suppose I do admire your tenacity.'

'You're unable or unwilling to provide me with that information?' Katie fired back at him, her frustration bubbling to the surface.

Bradbury stood up and made his way to the door. Katie realising this was probably her cue to leave, followed close behind.

'Look Professor, any information you can provide me with is crucial to our investigation.'

'Yes, I'm sure it is Ms Sinclair, but I don't really appreciate your prying into my professional affairs.'

Katie, annoyed he was being so resistive, felt compelled to tackle him one more time.

'Even if people's lives are in jeopardy?' she blurted out, following him to the front door.

He swung around so their faces were only inches apart. She could smell pipe tobacco on his breath. 'I'm afraid so,' he replied, his countenance showing no emotion. 'Now if you'll please excuse me I did mention I have a meeting to attend.' He dismissed her with a salutary wave of his hand before turning and striding off down another bleak corridor.

Katie found herself once more with a closed door in her face. A disappointing encounter undoubtedly, although one valuable fact had surfaced: Abby was still a patient at the Institute.

Katie hurried down the drive way. Just before reaching the car something made her glance instinctively back towards the building where she caught a fleeting glimpse of a face at a second storey window. A face she thought she recognised.

***

"The Manors" was a purpose built, dual level nursing home, boasting three wings offering a variety of accommodation. Situated in a small hamlet on the edge of the Dartmoor escarpment it commanded sweeping panoramas across the moor and surrounding countryside. To the casual observer, it resembled a luxury country resort hotel surrounded by extravagantly landscaped gardens and sweeping lawns.

Katie, following the signposts up the long meandering driveway to the visitor's car park, was mindful to keep to the ten mile an hour speed limit, coming to a halt in the first available parking spot only a short walk from the main entrance. Retrieving her handbag from the rear seat she made her way the short distance along the gravel path to the front entrance.

A blast of cold air greeted her as she strolled into a large reception room occupied by several cane arm chairs spread evenly along the back walls. A heady cocktail of disinfectant, furniture polish, and freshly cut flowers filled the space, which was dominated by a large vase of gladioli set imposingly on a marble plinth in the centre of the room.

The duty nurse seated behind the reception desk looked up and smiled as Katie approached. She had dark brown bobbed hair already showing speckles of silver grey. Her pale blue uniform was immaculate; a nurse's badge shinning next to a silver fob watch. Whilst signing the visitors book Nurse O'Mara, with obviously nothing much else to do was only too happy to engage in conversation with Katie, providing interesting and colourful anecdotes on some of the residents, or 'inmates', as she affectionately referred to them. Maintaining an air of professionalism, she openly chatted about Doctor Ashcroft Senior whom she claimed to be a particular favourite. After a good ten minutes, she pointed Katie in the direction of Doctor Ashcroft's room and then immediately returned to the filing she had been in the middle of processing when Katie made her entrance.

Katie walked slowly along the newly carpeted, main corridor glancing into rooms which had their doors open. They were all tastefully decorated in an individual style to suit the occupants. A lot of time and money had obviously gone into creating a cosy environment and Katie well imagined the hefty sums being forked out by family members to support their loved ones at The Manors.

Doctor Ashcroft's room was in the left wing, commanding views as far as Salcombe and the Channel. Katie spotted Ashcroft sitting by a large bay window a pair of binoculars glued to his eyes. He sensed someone entering the room and spoke to Katie as she stepped over the threshold.

'I'm always impressed with the landscape, especially at this time of year. Do come in Missy. Is it too early to offer you a sherry?'

'A tad,' Katie replied, moving across to the window and looking out at a view dominated in the distance by the familiar granite outcrop of Haytor. 'I'd say you have one of the best views in the house Doctor Ashcroft. Quite breathtaking.'

'Please, I prefer Colin instead of this Doctor business,' he told her in a marked tone. 'I've not practised as a GP for many years. I now leave all that to my son David.'

'He's a credit to you Colin,' Katie gushed. 'I had the pleasure of meeting him the other day. In fact, that's the reason why I'm here today.'

'Yes, he phoned me last night and mentioned you were coming to see me. He also filled me in on the reason for your visit. Now don't just stand there like a bitter lemon. Have a seat and let me see if I can possibly help you with your investigations. I know you wouldn't have got much from David and quite rightly so. As a practising GP, he needs to maintain confidentiality at all times. Me, however, that's a different matter altogether. No one's going to bother two hoots about a senile old goat prattling on about the past. Although not everyone's completely gaga in here you know.'

'The thought never crossed my mind,' Katie reassured him.

Colin gave a mischievous grin before adding. 'Old Bert in room fourteen can be a bit forgetful at times. I once saw him try to eat a boiled egg with a knife and fork. In his prime he was quite a clever business man. Owned "Pixies Sweet Shop" in the centre of Newton Abbott and can still quote the price of a bag of sherbet pips.'

Katie smiled and sat down in anticipation on the bed opposite Colin keen to hear his stories especially new details he might offer up on the Jennings family. According to David Ashcroft, his father had looked after the Jennings family ever since Muriel was about twelve years old. She saw in his eyes a kind considerate man who would have taken his role as a family GP very seriously.

Ashcroft Senior cast a quick look towards the door to ensure the coast was clear then with a spring to his step moved to a small cupboard where he proceeded to remove a small crystal glass and a bottle of dry sherry. He deftly poured himself a double nip returning to his seat and taking a hefty sip.

'That's better,' he grinned sheepishly. 'Now let's see if anything I have in my memory banks is of any use to you.'

He proceeded to launch into a methodical background history on the Jennings family. Although handicapped by a partial deafness he still possessed all his faculties and knew how to spin a good yarn. He related how Muriel's father Victor had laboured in the stone quarries on the moor dying fairly young, early forties, from silicosis. Her mother Cecily had worked part-time in a corner grocery store, the rest of the time spent at home raising her six children, only one who was still alive, Muriel's sister Connie who lived in Truro. Back then Muriel had been known as Muriel Townsend.

Katie listened to Colin's story enthralled by the history lesson. He only stopped to throw down more sherry and then continued, 'That was of course until she married Bill Jennings in the sixties I believe. His family weren't short of a quid as they owned a few farms and the old woollen mill in Bovey which is where they started a textile business. It was several years later when they had dosh behind 'em that Bill bought into the clay industry. He never looked back as far as business goes. However, I've jumped ahead of myself as the interesting facts lie before she met Bill. That's what you'll be interested in.'

Katie watched Colin down another mouthful. He seemed to be quite a natural story teller and obviously enjoyed having company. Doubtless he led a lonely existence in the nursing home compared to his life before as a busy G.P.

The next bit of news came as no real surprise to Katie as Dexter Sims had already informed her of Muriel's ties to Ted Cartwright. However, she still managed to look amazed at what she was hearing. Colin was watching her face and took some delight from her reaction as his story unfolded.

'Oh yes,' he laughed. 'It was a shock to a number of us in the know. A teenage pregnancy back then was certainly not the norm, the stuff of movies really. The immediate Townsend family were of course insistent it remain a secret.'

'How did the family take the news Muriel was pregnant?' Katie asked, her eyes keenly fixed on Colin.

'The news hit them like a ton of bricks. The Cartwrights and the Townsends never saw eye to eye. They fought over Bovey land for many a year. The pregnancy news drew even more of a wedge between the families. Muriel was sent away to keep out of harm's way. She eventually returned to Devon after she'd married northerner Bill Jennings. By then her parents had died and past conflicts were somehow forgotten.'

'What happened to the child Muriel had? I'm assuming she did have the child?'

'Oh yes, she had the child, a little girl by all accounts. I seem to recall that the word around was she was adopted by a mining family in South Wales.'

'Are Muriel's other children aware of their half-sister?'

'I very much doubt it. Although, we are a relatively small community, some secrets can be kept if you try hard enough. The Jennings family being respected pillars of the community around these parts it's not the sort of publicity they'd be craving. Something like that coming out after so many years could do a lot of damage; a revelation they would want kept under wraps especially after Ted's murder conviction.'

'How old would you say Muriel's daughter would be now?'

'A rough estimate, I'd say forty-seven.'

'One final question: who actually knew about the pregnancy?'

Colin scratched his head and rolled his eyes.

'There was myself of course, I actually confirmed the pregnancy. Victor and Cecily Townsend, the local rector of the parish, who at the time was the Reverend Corbett Trigg, and Joan and Stan Cartwright. There was no need to tell anyone else.'

'And you're completely confident the people you just named are the only ones who were privy to the pregnancy?'

'One hundred percent, no doubt about it.'

Katie stayed talking to Colin Ashcroft for a further half an hour before retracing her tracks to the office. If no one knew about the pregnancy Katie calculated, then it could have little or no relevance to Muriel's death. It was just coincidental that she had found out about Muriel's shady past.

***

James and Katie lounged at their desks staring at a whiteboard covered by their summaries of all the pertinent facts gleaned over the last two weeks of investigations. They were trying to piece things together to see if they were any nearer to finding Muriel's killer.

'This is what I think,' James spoke at last, dropping his glasses and rubbing his eyes slowly. 'Someone discovered Muriel's secret past and started blackmailing her for money, large sums of money. Christ knows there's no way Muriel would want anyone discovering she bore a child to Ted Cartwright. Think what damage you could potentially inflict on Jennings Clay; Muriel bearing a child fathered by a serial killer! The mind boggles. The media would be rabid. I'm damned but that's all I can come up with.'

'Yes, but old Doc Ashcroft is adamant no one else knew about the pregnancy,' Katie replied firmly. 'He came across most convincingly that not one of the people who had knowledge of the pregnancy would ever disclose that information. You can't be right in your assumption on this one James.'

'What if someone found out from another source?' James pressed, determined not to give up that easily.

Katie looked keenly at her brother wondering what he was alluding to. As far as she was concerned Muriel's secret had remained just that; a secret. She didn't for one moment believe the secret was breached. She waited for James to deliver his reasoning.

'Medical records would seem the obvious way to gain access to Muriel's shady past,' James said smoothly. 'It would be relatively easy for someone to sift through Muriel's files. Any one of the Ashcrofts' receptionists would have access to confidential information.'

Katie gave a low whistle. 'That's definitely a possibility. Why didn't I think of that?'

'Not clever enough maybe,' James replied smugly. 'It takes brains to work that one out.'

Katie grabbed a ruler from her desk and flicked it at her brother, striking him in the middle of his forehead.

'Bugger, that hurt,' he grimaced, rubbing his head vigorously.

'It was meant to,' Katie grinned sheepishly. 'That's what you get when you try to take the piss.'

'Okay we'll call it quits,' James said, rising to his feet 'I'm off to have a bite to eat with Nick. A ploughman's at the pub in Widecombe, so that's where I'll be if you need me.'

Alone in the office, Katie pondered over the possibility someone *had* got hold of Muriel's medical records. If this was the case the finger would definitely point at current or previous reception staff working for Ashcroft Senior and Ashcroft Junior. With this information at hand there was no telling what someone might do for money. They may start with blackmail but eventually resort to murder.

The footsteps echoed across the cold, grey flagstones. Up and down, up and down in the silent dead of night. She lay in her bed listening to the relentless patter. Not for a single second did they cease. Up and down on the basement floor all night long. In despair, she covered her ears to block out the sound.

CHAPTER FOURTEEN

Katie cursed the onset of the flu which inevitably inflicted her whole body. Unable to lift her pounding head off the pillow a visit to Doctor David would have to wait.

It was Sunday anyway so what did it matter if she spent the whole day in bed? There was nowhere special she had to be. With her bedside clock showing a quarter to nine she rolled over onto her right side and drifted back into merciful slumber, only to be rudely woken some forty minutes later by the shrill ringing of the phone. Reaching out to pick up the receiver she managed a very weak hello, followed by a sneeze.

'Katie it's Matt. Are you doing anything today or can I pop over? I've got some very interesting information that I'd prefer to give you in person.'

'Sure, come on over but don't blame me if you catch my bug,' she replied, before sneezing again.

Matt laughed, 'I'll see you around three.'

Katie dropped the phone on the floor, reset the alarm for eleven, climbed back under the covers and was asleep instantly.

After devouring a croissant and two paracetamol washed down with the requisite double espresso, Katie spent the rest of the morning lazing in a garden hammock flicking through gossip magazines. With the sun directly beating down on her face she dozed off, eventually woken by the sound of a car door closing. As she shielded her eyes from the bright sunlight she saw Matt smiling down at her. 'Hello sleepyhead. I thought you might like some good news: I've discovered Professor Bradbury is away overnight at a conference. This will give you the perfect opportunity to snoop around the psychiatric hospital and see what else you can find on Abigail Cartwright. And, get this, I've also been able to establish it was initially a Doctor Allan Rogers who treated Abby and he's still in residence at the institute. You may find he's more willing to cough up some pertinent facts, word is; he's a bit more laid back than Bradbury.'

Katie sat up in the hammock careful not to move too suddenly for fear of landing in a heap on the grass. It took a few moments for her brain to process what Matt was saying. She'd completely forgotten they'd discussed her visit to the psychiatric hospital over the phone the other night, now it all came flooding back.

'What makes you think Rogers will talk to *me*?' Katie asked, curiosity mixed with a small dose of scepticism. In her experience, all psychiatrists were joined at the hip, never willing to breach patient confidentiality.

'Apparently, the Prof and Rogers don't always see eye to eye,' Matt explained, 'therefore if Doc Rogers knows Bradbury won't talk to you about Abigail then maybe *he* will.'

***

Doctor Allan Rogers M.D. himself opened the door when Katie arrived at the psychiatric hospital the following morning. There was no sign of the Dragon Lady who'd most likely accompanied the Professor to his conference to ward off any unwanted individuals who encroached too much on the Professor's personal space. After a brief introduction and explanation for her visit Katie was ushered into a small office with the door quietly closed behind them.

'Please sit down Ms. Sinclair.' He pointed to a well-worn black leather club chair that creaked slightly as Katie sat down. 'Can I get you something to drink, tea or coffee?'

Katie shook her head. 'No thank you. I know I'm not meant to be here and wouldn't want to compromise your position by attracting too much attention. I'd be happy to settle for a glass of water.'

'I appreciate your consideration.' Rogers smiled warmly, fetching them both a glass of water from the nearby water cooler. He then sat down in a chair opposite Katie. 'Now how exactly can I help you today? I am guessing you would like to ask me a few detailed questions about Abigail Cartwright. I was brought up to speed by Professor Bradbury after you visited last week. I'm also aware he was very reluctant to answer any of your questions.'

'Why was that exactly?' Katie fired straight from the hip. She was eager to find out if Professor Bradbury had anything to hide. On the contrary, the reply from his colleague was quite straight forward with no ulterior motive for Bradbury not divulging information requested, other than moral reasons.

'Our Professor does everything by the book. He has very high professional standards and believes strongly in his code of ethics,' Rogers explained. 'To compromise patient confidentiality would go against his principles.'

'I see. How about *you,* Doctor Rogers? Are you under the same ethical code of conduct as the Professor?'

Doctor Rogers gave a hearty laugh. 'Let's just say I bend a few rules from time to time if I feel the circumstances warrant it,' his face broke into a broad grin.

'Now shall we press on in case I change my mind and suddenly acquire a conscience.'

Katie warmed to his relaxed demeanour. Time to strike while the iron was hot before he did develop a conscience.

'Do you remember what medications you prescribed Ms. Cartwright?'

'I remember exactly,' Doctor Rogers said, looking at Katie's keen face.

'Are you able to share that information with me?' she blushed a little when she realised he was studying her closely.

'I mostly treated Abby for depression and anxiety. The drug prescribed was Fluoxetine. Not uncommon as you know, half the country's on it.'

'Was she compliant with taking Prozac?' Katie asked, using the brand name she was used to.

Doctor Rogers nodded. 'Always. Abby understood how much this medication would help her.'

'So it was a successful medication for her to be on?' Katie continued, taking a sip of water.

'On the whole yes, but we eventually introduced Olanzapine which seemed to produce a much better effect.'

'Tell me Dr. Rogers; when Abby was in your care did she ever discuss the murders with you?'

'The topic never came up and I was instructed by my superiors not to raise the subject under any circumstances.'

'Why was that?'

'Two reasons really. One was because the case had not yet gone to trial when Abby initially became my patient and secondly because Abby was very fragile. Saying the wrong thing could have tipped her over the edge.'

'Would Professor Bradbury have asked Abby about the murders?'

'Probably, my job was to treat Abby's condition but Bradbury's role was to gather as much detail as possible in order to submit evidence at the court hearing. From what I learnt Abby provided very little that was of use. You need to remember Ms. Sinclair, the house where the homicides took place is quite extensive. It's highly probable Ted Cartwright committed the murders without Abby having any idea what was going on.'

'I'm not quite sure I follow. Are you trying to say there's a chance Abby knew nothing of the murders even though she lived in the same house as her father?'

'It's a strong theory. When Jessica moved out along with the servants Ted and Abby would have been totally lost rattling around in that old place.'

Katie still looked perplexed.

Rogers continued, 'We're talking about a very large residence here Ms. Sinclair. It would be easy to wonder around and not see another person for days, weeks even. Ted lured his victims into the house and locked them up in the basement. After keeping them imprisoned for several months he finally took to torturing and murdering each and every one of those wretched women.'

Katie shuddered at the morbid picture conjured up in her mind, glad Ted Cartwright was now safely behind bars and his vicious killing spree had ceased.

'I understand that when Ted lured the last woman into the house Abby managed to help her escape. Can you give me any more details on what actually happened?'

'From all accounts, Abby stumbled on the young woman as she went in search of a skipping rope she'd misplaced. She wandered down to the basement, found the woman bound and gagged, then led her safely to freedom. One can only imagine what that poor child saw in the basement. When first admitted here Abby didn't speak for months. It was gentle coaxing from a team of experts before she uttered her first coherent sentences. Even then she never really spoke about what happened.'

'She must have spotted the five other women strangled and murdered in the basement?' Katie spoke her thoughts out loud.

'One can only assume so,' Allan Rogers replied, letting out a hefty sigh. 'Not something anyone should witness, even less so a child.'

'I'd be surprised if she was ever able to go on and lead any sort of a normal life after being subjected to that,' Katie said. 'Those images would stick in your mind for ever.'

'Not necessarily,' Doctor Rogers replied. 'As a practising psychologist, you would know how powerful an instrument the mind can be Ms Sinclair. It's my belief Abby subjectively erased a lot of the memories from her subconscious. Similar to the way Midazolam works on the brain.'

'So it could be possible for her to be living a fairly normal life retrospectively?' Katie said thoughtfully.

'Absolutely, after her release from here she would have continued to receive a lot of support and counselling. She still sees Professor Bradbury on a regular basis but due to our rather restrained professional relationship he never divulges exactly what they discuss in his therapy sessions. What you need to understand is this; Abby was very much a victim in all of this. The support she received was amazing. Everything was done to help her get over the traumas she experienced.'

'Is there anything else you remember about Abby?'

The psychiatrist stroked his chin and turned his gaze slowly to the window. 'You know, she always had sad eyes. I remember those big brown eyes that seemed to bore straight through you.'

Katie refrained from comment.

214

'Abby also had nightmares,' Doctor Rogers advised. 'When she was an inmate here she would often lie awake at night fixedly staring at the ceiling for long periods. Then all of a sudden, she would let out a piercing scream. Staff would come rushing in only to find Abby sound asleep. On questioning her the next morning she had no recollection of these nightmares.'

Katie then took the plunge. 'Do you think Abby is capable of murder Doctor Rogers?'

Doctor Rogers didn't seem at all surprised by Katie's blunt question. When he didn't answer, Katie fired another question at him. 'Could she have been the one to murder those women and not her father? After all, the transcripts from the trial kept stating Cartwright was adamant he hadn't killed those women. Perhaps he was shielding his daughter? Maybe Abby's story of looking for a skipping rope was invented. Reality could be she got bored of murdering and decided to let the last one go.'

Rogers forcefully shook his head. 'No I really can't accept for the life of me Abby is capable of murder, especially at such a tender age. Abby is no more a murderer than you or I Ms Sinclair.'

'I just don't get it,' Katie said, sounding frustrated. 'Usually people have some motive for killing even if it's hard core anger. I've gone over and over all my notes on Ted Cartwright, yet he doesn't fit the profile of a serial killer.'

'Then perhaps possibly, maybe he *was* convicted of a crime he didn't commit.' Rogers spoke softly. 'It wouldn't be the first time a person has been wrongly sent down for a felony not of their doing. Half of the inmates on death row in America are probably innocent. Justice is blind they say Ms Sinclair and I'm sure it won't be the last.'

'One last question; are you aware of any medical conditions Abby has?'

'I do know she's a diabetic but can't recall if she was having insulin injections or if her diabetes was controlled by diet. Of course, all the medical information we have on file is only up until she turned about fifteen so things may be different now.'

Katie looked up at the wall clock and decided she had probably got just about everything she could from Rogers. 'Thank you for seeing me today,' she held out her hand. 'I really appreciate your time and the information provided has been extremely helpful.'

'Glad I could have been of some assistance. I'll show you out.'

Doctor Rogers led Katie to the front door and escorted her outside into the grounds. Katie glanced back at the old building and grimaced. From the outside, it looked shabby and badly in need of urgent refurbishment. As if reading her thoughts Doctor Rogers gave a brief explanation seeming a need to justify his place of work.

'The hospital exterior certainly appears a trifle run down but I can assure you the individual rooms inside are in much better condition. The care our patients receive here is next to none. One last thought before you go Ms Sinclair; it takes lots of practice to put yourself into the mind of a serial killer but it can be done.'

***

Katie was only half listening to her brother as he provided an update on Muriel's case. She kept remembering the last statement Doctor Rogers had made. What exactly did he mean, *'It takes lots of practice to put yourself into the mind of a serial killer but it can be done'*? It all seemed a bit cryptic.

'You haven't listened to a word I've said, have you?' James enquired of Katie, as she sat playing with some papers on her desk.

'Huh what, sorry.'

James tried again. 'The gov'ner of the prison intercepted this letter which was addressed to Ted Cartwright. It appears to be from Cartwright's daughter, Abigail.'

James passed the folded piece of paper to Katie who unfolded it and read with interest.

'You're not my father. You're nothing but a murderer.'

Although the words were typed in large print they didn't cover much of the white paper.

'That's odd,' Katie said reading over the words until they became a mass of jumbled letters. 'It doesn't make sense. When I was chatting with Ted Cartwright's lawyer Dexter Sims, he made it perfectly clear Abby still acknowledged Ted as her father and conveyed she would always love him despite the things he'd done. If this is the case, why would she write something like this?'

'Perhaps she suddenly realized what a monster her father really is and love swiftly turned to hate,' James said candidly, 'that's not uncommon.'

'Sorry but I don't buy it,' Katie continued, 'a leopard doesn't change its spots, not that easily anyway.'

'Perhaps she was never a leopard in the first place,' James laughed, watching his sister as she raised her eyebrows questioningly. 'What if all along she was a tiger and you only thought she was a leopard?'

'Don't try and get technical with me James my boy,' Katie smiled affectionately.

'I'll try not to,' he grinned. 'By the way did you manage to contact the prison to find out if Ted has access to a telephone?'

Katie gave a brief nod. 'Yes, I did. Once a week he's allowed to make a ten-minute phone call.'

'Any particular day or time and are the calls monitored?'

'No set day or time but the calls are monitored. However, when I tried to talk to one of the prison guards about this monitoring system he shrugged his shoulders, more or less implying no one was going to bother listening in on an old man's conversation.'

'Oh great, so in other words they prefer to sit with their feet up watching television than do the job we pay them for,' James seethed.

'Yep, that sums it up, what did you expect?' Katie replied. 'There is no way of clarifying the recent call you received came from Ted Cartwright but we can't rule it out either.'

As James headed out to the lab Katie turned her attention to researching local real estate agents on the internet to find out who was handling the Cartwright family home, Heather Lea. She'd already been advised the estate agent was a Trefor Jones, but needed details on the realtor he worked for. Reading through several articles she learned the house had been on the market for a very long time, which was hardly surprising. No one was likely to request a second viewing if they knew its history.

Jones & Clifford estate agent was handling the sale. Their Devon branch was located in the main high street of Newton Abbot. J & C Property Analysts, as they liked to be known, were an elite organization with established branches in nine other counties. They dealt mainly with high end million pound properties, not your average run of the mill, three-bedroom stuff.

Deciding to pay Jones & Clifford a visit on the spur of the moment, Katie grabbed her handbag and car keys before quietly heading out the back door. It didn't take long to reach their two storey office, even managing to snare a parking spot right outside the front door.

Trefor Jones had just returned from an open house when Katie strolled in hoping to catch a few minutes of his time. She was in luck; he wasn't due out to his next appointment for at least three hours. Seizing the opportunity to find out more about Heather Lea, Katie decided it was easier not to admit any involvement in an investigation but instead to punt the story she was in the market for a residence in the area. She relayed this message to the young girl on reception who then went in search of Jones.

Trefor Jones was a young man in his late twenties who seemed eager to please as he came bustling up to Katie dressed in an immaculate dark grey business suit and bright blue tie. His sandy coloured hair was parted neatly to the left.

'How can I help you?' Trefor began, thrusting out his hand. 'My receptionist informed me you are looking for a character property on the moors.'

'Yes, that's right. You see I'm an author and I'd like something with charm and character,' Katie lied convincingly. She wasn't really sure how credible she would come across pretending to be a millionaire but she'd give it a go.

'An author how wonderful,' Trefor seemed suitably impressed so far. 'Do you have a budget in mind?'

Christ that dreaded money question had cropped up so soon!

'Not really,' Katie tried to sound confident, even matter of fact. 'I like large houses so let's not bother with anything less than nine hundred thousand. Manor houses and executive estates are my definite preference.'

Trefor was a little overwhelmed with Katie's confident, laid back demeanour. Not his usual client type. Turning to his laptop he flicked through some pages on the firm website before enquiring, 'How many people are going to be residing in this house?'

'Oh just me,' Katie replied casually, wondering if she really could convince this shrewd estate agent she had loads of dosh and enjoyed living alone in oversized properties. As he passed across some leaflets portraying properties he thought she might be interested in Katie's confidence soared even higher. Must be doing a decent job convincing him she was a genuine house hunter. The front seemed to be working. Barging in and demanding access to a listing as part of a forensic murder investigation would probably cause Trefor to clam up and put him offside.

As Katie flicked through the coloured brochures the fifth one came up trumps. '*Heather Lea*' she read '*A home boasting character and charm, set on eleven acres of rugged moorland*'. It was listed at a little over two million with twelve good sized bedrooms.

'This one catches my eye,' Katie remarked, as she held up the glossy brochure to show Trefor. 'Has it been on the market for long?'

Trefor seemed taken aback as she continued to wave the brochure under his nose.

'It's been listed for a couple of years,' he replied softly 'there's not really been much interest with this particular property. It's rather big and requires considerable repair work. I'm not convinced it's what you're really looking for.'

Katie kept a straight face at his comment in relation to the property being on the market for a couple of years. More like ten she thought to herself but for Trefor to admit that would certainly decrease his chances of making a sale. She also loved his comment about what he thought would suit her. A typical sales man convinced he knew best for his customer. Yet really, he knew nothing about her; nothing at all!

'What can you tell me about this one?' she pressed. 'I do like the look of it. Definitely a writer's dream, located on all that moorland.'

He hesitated for a few moments as if choosing his next words carefully. 'The previous owners moved away suddenly. It has lain empty for quite some time, sadly falling into a sorry state. I am convinced if someone took the trouble of doing it up and restoring the place to its former glory it would be magnificent.'

No mention of murders here Katie smiled to herself. As for the owners moving away suddenly he'd got that one right. With Ted Cartwright whisked away to Dartmoor Prison, he could hardly have delayed such a move!

'When would I be able to view the property?' Katie asked at last, holding onto the brochure with a firm grip.

'I could arrange for early next week if this suits?' Trefor informed her, grabbing a black leather diary lying within easy reach.

'Perfect.'

***

Katie waited patiently for Trefor Jones to finish his telephone conversation. A viewing had been arranged for Heather Lea, where Ted Cartwright had lived for approximately six years before the grisly discovery of bodies in the basement.

At last Trefor put down the receiver and turned to Katie with a broad smile. 'Ready to go?'

'Absolutely.'

They took Trefor's car as he was familiar with the location of the house. It was off the beaten track and the estate was given a thorough workout as it bumped along the dirt road leading up to the property. Katie was vaguely familiar with this part of the moor but would most probably have got lost had she attempted to find the place by herself.

First appearance held her captivated by its serrated beauty. Its sheer size and location alone were impressive. It was a magnificent structure, obviously designed by a prominent architect in the gothic revival style, around 1860 Katie guessed, situated miles from any other inhabitants with the village of Widecombe just visible in a distant vale.

Before going inside Trefor showed Katie the outside of the house and the vast estate lands attached to it. At the back of the property stood an overgrown apple orchard and located not far from the established trees, half buried in the long grass, lay an old wooden cider press.

'You know it's rather odd,' Trefor informed Katie as they walked back around to the front of the house, 'Not long after I met you last week I had another lady interested in this property. You know how it goes; no interest for ages then a rush of enquiries all at once. I didn't have time to bring her up here so she came to look at it by herself. I've not had any feedback so I assume it's not the place for her.'

'How interesting,' the news was a surprise to Katie. 'Do you know if she happened to be a local woman or perhaps here on holiday?'

'I'm not entirely sure as one of my colleagues handled her enquiry. Now, as we stroll around the house you will need to mind your footing,' he instructed, 'there are parts of the house deemed unsafe. I am aware of the major hazard areas which we won't go near but that's not to say we mustn't tread carefully at all times.'

Trefor produced a large metal key from his pocket leading the way up the crumbling front steps to a covered in porch. Katie was pleased she had dressed sensibly in jeans, t-shirt and walking boots.

Trefor had a few problems trying to turn the key in the lock. 'It appears someone's tampered with the lock in an attempt to break in,' he remarked impatiently. 'I'll have to file a report and get someone out to fix it. Probably kids looking for a lark.'

Katie was not quite so convinced.

They began their tour of the property on the ground floor in what had once been the main reception room. A strong musty smell hung in the air a result of the house being closed up for long extended periods. A thick coating of dust was prominent on the windowsills and skirting boards. A few pieces of furniture lay idly in one corner draped in sheets but apart from an authentic, highly decorative fire place and original Aesthetic Period features the room was empty. For some reason the door to the old scullery kitchen was jammed. No amount of pressure would force the lock.

Fifty-five minutes later they negotiated a large wooden staircase to view the first floor rooms. The master bedroom was spectacular dominated by three large, arched windows facing south across the moors. All twelve bedrooms were massive in size, some with elaborate ensuites. *Obviously, the country retreat of a Victorian industrialist,* surmised Katie now understanding what Doctor Rogers meant when he said two people could easily live in the house and go weeks without seeing each other. The thought of that gave her goose bumps.

'I take it you're not interested in seeing the basement?' Trefor mumbled, as they made their way back down to the ground level.

'On the contrary I'm particularly interested to see the basement,' Katie replied with gusto. 'It will be fascinating to gain insight into how much space is under a house of this magnitude.'

Trefor appeared startled by Katie's keenness to view the underground levels. Finding laughter welling up inside she had to forcefully turn away to disguise her amused look. Trefor clearly hadn't bargained on having to show anyone the depths of Heather Lea – the basement where Cartwright had slain his victims.

The basement ran the entire length and width of the property. Shining Trefor's torch in front so she could see where she was going Katie stepped from the final stone step onto the damp concrete floor. A nervous glance around indicated the place had become home to a large family of spiders. Closing her eyes tight she tried to picture what the place would have seemed like to the poor frightened women who'd been forced to live here for several months before their final demise. She shuddered before opening her eyes and ascending the stairs to where Trefor was patiently waiting for her, having only braved a few steps.

'I think I've seen enough,' she instructed, swept by a wave of nausea, desperately in need of fresh air.

'Are there any other properties you'd like to view?' Trefor asked anxiously, as they made their way outside. He was regaining some of his colour after turning a pale shade of green when Katie had insisted he show her the basement.

Katie shook her head. 'Not at this stage,' she replied truthfully. 'This place has given me quite a bit to mull over.'

***

Katie and Matt finished a home cooked meal and were enjoying one another's company reminiscing about cases they'd worked on over the years. They'd shared a bottle of red and were now comfortably seated on the lounge in Katie's small terrace house. A warm evening lingered after a balmy day and the door to the patio was slightly ajar allowing a cool breeze to drift in.

Both were a little tipsy from the wine and as they sat in cosy silence Matt's arm came up around Katie's shoulder. At first she let it rest there enjoying the serene environment.

But after a few moments she felt the need to brush his advances aside. 'Matt I can't. It's too soon and I'm really not ready.'

The frustration on his face was turning to annoyance as she fumbled to quickly fasten the buttons on her blouse which he'd leisurely undone. Katie felt annoyed with herself more than with him. She thought she'd be over it by now but clearly, she wasn't. Maybe it was something she'd never get over. Her psychiatrist had warned of relapses and as a psychologist herself she knew she had a long way to go before she felt truly comfortable in a sexual relationship.

'For god sake Katie,' Matt blurted out, clearly irritated by the rejection, 'you don't have to remain a nun for the rest of your life.'

Before she could take control of the situation Katie found her hand moving upward striking Matt across the side of the face; a hard slap that resounded throughout the entire room.

'Don't you dare; you have no fucking idea what I've been through!' she screamed. 'Why can't you at least try to understand?'

'That's what I do all the time Katie,' he fought back, 'but after a while I get bored of finding how sensitive you've become.'

Katie felt the tears welling up in her eyes, her hands were clenched together as anger kept close to the surface. 'Get out before I throw you out,' she urged.

Matt sighed heavily, got up slowly and grabbed his jacket from the back of the chair. 'It's always about you, isn't it?' he shouted, shaking his head in disbelief. 'Always the victim Katie. You know for once I'd have thought you could put the bloody past behind you and move on. Hell knows, you need to at least try.'

Stunned to silence Katie watched him head out the door with not even a look of remorse.

Katie's mind flashed back to her honours year at London University. She began to tremble as vivid memories came flooding back, causing a cold sweat to break out. She was angry she hadn't quite learnt to put things into the dark recess of her mind.

It happened just before her twenty first birthday; a time when she should have been celebrating. Had she been naïve or unlucky?

Glancing out the window towards a blackening sky her thoughts returned to the dank corridor on the third floor where she'd been ambling back to her room after spending an hour in the common room with friends. She held an old coffee mug in one hand and a folded newspaper in the other.

'Hello Katherine, not planning on spending the night studying, are you?'

Katie tossed back her golden curls giving an infectious laugh. 'No not tonight, I plan to make a coffee and do a little reading,' she indicated mug and newspaper.

'I'll escort you to your room if you like.'

As they arrived outside room thirteen, her digs for the past six months, Katie took out her key fumbling an attempt to unlock the door. Her hands full made the task rather difficult.

'Here let me help you,' Frank offered, taking the cup from her hand. Grateful for assistance Katie finally unlocked the door. 'Coffee?' she offered.

'Yeah, why not.'

Once inside the room it happened so quickly. He'd forced her onto the bed, removing her lace panties with dominance. She tried to scream but her head was thrown in such a way she could hardly breathe. Within a matter of seconds, he was inside her. That innocence she was saving for someone special whisked away instantly. After he'd gone all she could do was cry. Icy tears full of hate and remorse. To this day, she could still taste the abundance of salt as the tears trickled into her mouth. What happened that evening left scars for life.

Never for one moment did she ever think she could trust a man again.

Of all the nights for her car to break down it had to be tonight. Why did it happen when she had to go somewhere in a hurry? She sank down by the river toying with the damp grass. The night was deathly cold with bright stars twinkling alongside the silvery moon. She suddenly sprang to her feet and jumped into the cold water. Her feet were bare so the chill grabbed her unexpectedly. For about ten minutes she danced about, her white dress an apparition of a female ghost. She sang in a high pitched voice no longer afraid of what might happen. She wanted it all to end. It had been a tortuous ride and now she wanted the road she travelled to stop suddenly.

CHAPTER FIFTEEN

Matt stood outside his old farm house cursing softly as he waited impatiently for the taxi. After several harassing phone calls from Katie they'd finally come to a truce on their recent feud. As the way of a peace offering he'd also begrudgingly agreed to try and obtain the much needed information they required on which member of the book club happened to be Abigail Cartwright. Accordingly, he needed to travel to New Scotland Yard and attempt a covert break into their data base.

The taxi ride took about twenty minutes. On arrival at Newton Abbot Station he paid the cabbie and hurried to the small lobby where he glanced at the overhead screen confirming the next train for Paddington was departing from platform two at seven fifty-four. The indicator showed it running to schedule. Perfect. Any delays would not put him in the best mood for the day's tasks ahead.

Checking the pre booked ticket in his hand confirmed a seat reserved in Coach C. As the train rumbled into the station he climbed aboard locating his spot by the window and throwing his laptop and small bag on the adjacent seat. He would move his belongings if anyone came to sit down otherwise they would stay there for the duration of the journey.

As predicted the express city service pulled out of the station right on time, always a good sign.

With levels of hunger rising, and craving an overdue breakfast, he made his way to the buffet car situated in coach E at the rear. As the train gathered speed he clung to the side of passing seats to steady his footing against the lurching carriages. Being one of the first to reach the travelling diner he was served immediately, thankfully avoiding the long, snaking queues which often formed on UK rail journeys. He ordered a double hot chocolate, a chicken salad sandwich, and a packet of plain crisps; as an afterthought adding a muesli bar to the list as a hedge against ebbing sugar levels.

It was an uneventful trip up to London passing silently and swiftly through the bucolic countryside, making only two stops, one at Exeter St David's, the other at Reading on the outskirts of London.

As the train drew slowly into Paddington Station a little before eleven Matt gathered up his laptop, bag, phone, and jacket and disembarked joining the usual hive of London activity. Single minded travellers, baggage in hand hurried to catch the Heathrow Express, others mostly sightseers and tourists headed for the underground West End services. Matt, blending seamlessly into the throng, immediately made his way to the tube to alight the Jubilee line to St James' Park. This was by far the nearest and quickest station to access New Scotland Yard. The journey was relatively short and Matt soon found himself heading towards his old stamping ground; the large grey, unremarkable, modernist glass slabs which housed The New Scotland Yard on Broadway in the Borough of Westminster. A warm drizzle drifted aimlessly in the air as he hurried along, the clouds hovering low, enhancing the sense of claustrophobia which Matt had come to hate about London.

Outside the entrance, he fished out the old ID badge from the inside of his jacket pocket reverently hoping Tel Halligan was still one of the main security guards on duty. Tel would allow him access without the third degree. Upon entering the building Matt was delighted to spot Tel seated behind the front desk and breathed a sigh of relief. So far so good, luck was on his side.

'Well if it ain't me mate Matty,' Tel greeted him warmly, as Matt strolled up to the front desk. 'I've not seen you in a long while. What you been up to man?'

'This and that,' Matt tried to sound as casual as possible, but inside his nerves was shot to pieces. Damn Katie Sinclair. If he was nabbed falsely obtaining inside information from the Yard he would face a lot of probing questions and possible hefty charges, not even counting the severe embarrassment.

Before Tel could enquire Matt's intentions his portable communication device started ringing demanding his full attention. He pressed the button hidden below the desk which released the door allowing Matt instant access, waving him through as he took the call.

Fortune favours the brave.

Matt made his way along the wide, sparsely decorated corridors to the elevators housed at each end and pressed the 'up' button. He only had to wait a few minutes before the lift arrived to take him up to the third floor where he had once shared an office with a couple of other officers along with his old boss Barbara Hill.

He encountered Barbara on exiting the lift, almost knocking each other over as she hurried past engrossed in reading a file.

'Hello there Matthew,' she smiled with genuine affection recognizing Matt. 'I've not seen you in a long time.'

Matt gave a boyish grin. He liked Barbara who was always upbeat. She'd been an excellent boss and mentor, although jokingly known as 'M' around the building. Despite enjoying his current role in IT he missed the comradeship that had gone with his job at Scotland Yard.

During the four years he'd been seconded to The Yard, he'd made some invaluable friends, Barbara being one of them.

'I guess it has been a while,' he replied, planting a kiss on the side of her cheek. 'I see you've changed the purple hair to pink, looks great.'

'Something different.' Barbara laughed, giving a little twirl. 'Are you here for a special assignment? Lex must have forgotten to tell me about it. I swear his memory gets worse by the day. You can use my office if you like as I have to go out for a couple of hours. I'm desperately in need of lunch and want to sample this new little Bistro on Victoria Street.'

Matt smiled inwardly. Barbara had always been fond of food, although it didn't show. She had a trim little figure and was in fine shape for a woman edging towards sixty.

Matt was pleased Barbara was working on assumption in relation to his visit so he didn't need to directly lie a reason for his unexpected presence. He watched her slender figure disappear along the corridor before turning towards her office which lay almost directly opposite the lifts. Just outside the office stood a vending machine offering an array of hot beverages; overcome by sudden thirst Matt dropped some coins in the slot and retrieved a frothy cappuccino. Coffee was never that great when you had to drink out of a cardboard cup but it would have to suffice. Besides he didn't want to venture to the staff canteen and run the risk of being caught by overzealous security staff or bailed up by an old acquaintance.

Balancing the coffee in one hand and belongings in the other he carefully managed to open the office door by flicking down the door handle and pushing it open with his foot. Once inside he closed the door and placed drink and case on Barbara's desk, which as usual was clean and tidy with not a scrap of paper or stray pen in sight. Matt constantly marvelled at how Barbara could be so efficient in her work yet never appear to be heavily involved in any real projects. He guessed that as usual all her active files were neatly stowed away in one of the two large cabinets lining the opposite wall.

Matt switched on Barbara's computer then lent across to draw the Venetian blinds shielding the windows from the corridor. Drawing attention to himself and having to survive interrogation was the last thing he needed. Not only that, he needed 100% focus. Shadows moving along the hallways would cause distraction.

Sitting himself at the desk Matt cursed heavily under his breath as he frantically tried to recall passwords and codes. He could hear his heart pounding away in his chest and sense small droplets of sweat forming on his forehead while his fingers systematically worked the keyboard. 'Still haven't fixed the bloody a/c' he mumbled to no one.

For the first half hour, he didn't come across anything remotely interesting. Matt knew that Babs bizarrely used access codes and passwords associated with James Bond movies. Becoming increasingly confident as the minutes ticked away he broke into more complex files and brought up the folder that gave him in-depth information on the Cartwright murders. It was code named 'White Rose' and after what seemed like an eternity he finally recovered the 2001 data base he was looking for using the access code "SMERSH", very predictable. Matt knew exactly what he was searching for but it would still eat up precious minutes trawling through the documents to retrieve the vital data. Staring at the screen the name suddenly shot out at him like a thunderbolt, *Abigail Miranda Cartwright.* Bingo. He'd struck gold. Time didn't allow analysis of all the details now. Instinctively he immediately saved the text to his USB. Then clicking print, for hard copy insurance, he heard the printer warming up on the table next to him and waited, tapping his fingers expectantly for the five page document to be spat out. Retrieving it he swiftly checked again that the information on the pages was correct before placing them into his case. Thanks to Babs, a job well done, but now he had to get out of here without being caught.

Matt kept his head bent and made directly for the fire stairs opting to avoid the crowded lunchtime lifts in the hope he wouldn't bump into anyone else he knew. Security cameras lined each corridor which he deliberately tried to avoid.

He'd almost made it to the ground floor exit when he heard someone call out his name. 'Matthew Tyler! What a nice surprise. What brings you back to The Yard?'

Matt swung around to see Lex De Cruz, one of the head honchos, standing only metres away. Lex had been Commander of the technical division Matt worked for.

'I came to see Barbara,' he lied, before quickly changing the subject. 'You're looking well Lex. I heard you had a triple bypass at the start of the year. By the looks of things, it all went well?'

Lex nodded. 'Yep, everything appears to be back in working order. Fine set of medical staff at Charing Cross Hospital. Don't care what people say about the NHS, they did a great job fixing my plumbing.'

'Good to hear, well I must scamper, I've got a train to catch.' Matt replied, gently patting Lex on the back, leaving him with a quizzical expression as he made good his escape.

It was only when he stepped outside, refreshed by a now constant rain that Matt finally felt he could allow his breathing to slow down to a more acceptable rate. He didn't plan to do any more data break-ins anytime soon so Katie Sinclair could think twice before asking.

The way his own heart had fluttered over the past few hours nearly saw *him* become a bypass candidate. He would be pleased to get back to Devon to continue with his relatively normal life. He was passed living off adrenaline.

Liz Palmer hurried through the hospital corridors, well aware she was running late for the start of her afternoon shift. The migraine she'd been plagued with over the past few days just wouldn't go away. She'd taken as many pain killers as she dared.

'Are you feeling okay?'

Liz jumped at the unexpected question by Anne Johnston one of her nursing colleagues. In her own little world, she hadn't noticed Anne standing by the entrance to the ward.

'Just a bit off colour that's all,' Liz replied, accompanying Anne to the nurses' station. 'I've been covering a lot of nights lately. It seems to take me weeks to get back into a normal sleep pattern, especially the older I get. You know what it's like.'

'You don't look at all well, Liz,' Anne continued, sounding genuinely concerned. 'Why don't you let one of the duty Doctors take a look at you. We can always try and cover your shift if you need to go home?'

'Don't fuss Anne, I'm fine, really I am,' Liz scolded. 'Why don't you make us both a strong coffee, that should do the trick.'

At first Anne looked reluctant to do as she was told and kept trying to persuade Liz to get one of the Doctors to examine her. Liz stood her ground steadfastly refusing. Conceding defeat Anne headed towards the ward kitchen returning some ten minutes later with two steaming hot coffees and a plate of biscuits.

Liz was already seated behind the nurses' desk looking through the patient admission list. 'I've a feeling we're in for a fairly busy evening,' she remarked, helping herself to a biscuit and accepting the drink Anne was holding out. 'I see Mr. Witherspoon has joined us again. How that man

234

keeps going is beyond me. I'd have thought his emphysema would have finally got the better of him.'

'We're too damn good at our job,' Anne laughed. 'All this modern medicine is certainly keeping people alive much longer.'

Liz found her vision blurring but still tried to focus on the duty list written on the white board.

Her head felt like it was about to lift off. She had no idea what was happening but inside knew these aliments couldn't be normal. She'd been feeling like this for days now and the symptoms were only getting worse.

How she managed to get through the shift was a mystery. She literally crawled into bed that night feeling like she was on a merry-go-round. With a pounding head, eyes barely focusing and continual nausea she feared not even waking in the morning. What was it Deirdre once said "Death beckons to us all eventually".

***

When Katie arrived at David Ashcroft's surgery just before 6pm she noticed a low light burning in one of the front rooms. All the doors were locked but she needed to talk to Doctor Ashcroft as a matter of urgency. She suspected he was inside finishing up before heading home. Katie produced a piece of paper out of her coat pocket, which had his on-call number scribbled in red ink. Carefully reaching into her bag she retrieved her mobile and dialled the number.

It took several moments before he answered but she instantly recognized Ashcroft's voice on the other end of the line. Katie swiftly explained her whereabouts and the reason for the visit, then waited patiently for him to unlock the front door.

'Ms Sinclair how lovely to see you again, do come in.' He sounded genuinely pleased to see her as they both stepped inside out of the crisp evening air. 'I must say I'm surprised to see you here at this time of night.'

'I took a gamble you'd still be here,' Katie confessed. 'I have a few additional questions I'd like to ask and wanted to wait until you were on your own. I don't think you'll mind assisting me with this one as its nothing too confidential.'

'I see. By the way did you manage to pay my father a visit?'

'Yes I did. He's an amazing man. Lots of anecdotes to tell.'

David grinned sheepishly. 'He's a fine man and in his prime, was an excellent Doctor. If I can manage to be half as good as him, I'll be happy.'

They were soon ensconced in David's office. A seductive calmness pervaded the surgery now it was devoid of patients.

'I wanted to ask you about the reception staff you've hired over the years,' Katie began. 'I'm just following some new leads in relation to Muriel's murder and this information would greatly assist me.'

'Well I can't say there have been that many,' David replied, scratching his head and leaning back in his chair. 'Brenda Mills was employed for over thirty years by my father and then when Colin retired she worked for me. When Brenda retired, my daughter Gemma helped out for a few years and recently Amy Forrester, who has been with me for almost four years. You met Amy when you called in the other week. We also have a part-time receptionist to relieve Amy on her days off; Maggie's her name, she's a distant cousin of mine. That's about it.'

'Do you ever get in casual staff?' Katie asked.

'No, never, that's too costly and they wouldn't have any knowledge in relation to our patients or where to locate files. It's not a job you can teach someone in five minutes.'

Katie was surprised at how few receptionists the practice had employed over the years.

'Can I ask how much these receptionists would be paid per annum?'

'Colin and I have always believed in paying well,' David grinned. 'Amy's remuneration is about forty thousand pounds a year which I concede is well above industry. Mind you she does a great job and often stays back to finish things off even after closing hours.'

Katie sat up with interest. 'Would she ever be here alone after everyone else has gone home?'

David looked surprised at this question. 'Occasionally. If you're implying Amy is taking drugs I can assure you she isn't. Firstly, all medications are safely locked away. I am the only one who has a key. Second, she has no clear signs or symptoms to indicate she's abusing narcotics or psychotropics.'

'I'm not thinking or suggesting anything of the sort,' Katie replied truthfully. What she was really trying to find out was whether Amy had access to patient medical records and that answer was clearly a 'yes'. It would be easy for Amy to go through file notes when she was by herself in the surgery; easy for her to access knowledge on a patient's medical history, general condition, and any treatments they were receiving.

On reflection, Katie was thankful she still went to visit Dr. Walker in Exeter when requiring occasional medical attention. It was certainly worth driving the extra miles for peace of mind. His surgery installed high-tech security cameras so no one could get into patient notes after hours without others knowing about it. At first when Doctor Walker informed her of the proposed new scheme she'd scoffed at the idea, now she was beginning to realize the benefits.

'Would you mind if I took a quick look at Amy's personal file?' Katie asked. 'I'm keen to do a background on her. I need to explore all avenues with our murder investigation. We just can't leave anything to chance.'

'Be my guest,' Doctor Ashcroft replied, handing over a slim folder he retrieved from the top drawer of his desk. 'I can't help thinking you're wasting your time Katie but you're welcome to peruse it.'

Katie flipped through the first few pages where there was an address and details of Amy's next of kin. She quickly copied the information into her pocket notebook then thanked Doctor Ashcroft for his time. As she strolled outside into the still night her mind started working in overdrive thinking about how easy Amy Forrester could obtain detailed confidential information on Muriel Jennings. Could she be the person they were looking for in this murder investigation? Anything was possible.

Her mind raced ahead in leaps and bounds until she wondered if her head would actually explode. She was annoyed no one had ever taken her seriously and thought it was about time she taught them all a lesson. It was him she hated the most. He had said it would be alright but it wasn't. She banged her fist against the wall until her knuckles bled. If there was pain she didn't feel it.

CHAPTER SIXTEEN

Jane Anderson jogged at an uncompromising pace, determined to burn as many calories as possible. Her white t-shirt clung to her slim figure, the perspiration increasing with every stride. Jogging for Jane was a great way to release built-up frustration or anger. Today she felt she could run to Land's End and back the hate burned so intensely. As she headed further across the moor the black mood she'd woken up with slowly started to subside. The entire day had been a living hell with Mark Jennings at the centre of it all. His verbal stream of abuse had begun the moment she'd set foot in the office at a quarter to eight. He was an arrogant bastard as far as she was concerned. Someone who deserved to have bad things happen to him. With these thoughts foremost in her mind, she stumbled across the house quite unexpectedly. Rounding a bend and heading back towards Widecombe the edifice loomed in the distance looking neglected amongst the backdrop of ancient oak trees. Jane's knowledge of Heather Lea was sparse. She'd only read snippets of information in local publications. Heather Lea – the house where Ted Cartwright had murdered five innocent women.

Curiosity swaying her decision Jane stopped jogging to carefully walk across the springy heather until her feet led her up the crumbling steps to the front door.

Naturally she assumed the door would be locked so it came as a shock when she turned the handle and the door opened with ease. Stepping over the threshold an instant calm swept over her. There was a soothing ambiance she hadn't expected.

The house itself didn't really intrigue; she was more interested in the panoramic view to be gained from the second level. As she carefully made her way up the curving staircase she jumped when the floor boards creaked unmercifully. A shiver tingled down her back turning around to look behind, believing she was being followed. Then she took control of her senses, if someone was stalking her she would hear their tread on the stairs. Entering the master bedroom, it didn't disappoint, the view from the dormer window across the open moor was amazing. Dartmoor stretched to the far horizon, breath-taking in its rugged beauty.

As if being transported to another dimension the view soon became forgotten as Jane closed her eyes to visualize what death would be like, what death had been like for those innocent women who'd spent their last remaining days in the cold dark basement? Normally afraid of being in unfamiliar surroundings the house suddenly became a familiar place. It was as if she and the house were one, a place she knew so well. Jane no longer wanted that beautiful view. Her focus was to see the basement. Down the stairs she trod with single purpose in mind, down into the bowels of the house where the bodies had lain – five pretty maids all in a row.

***

The day of the Bovey Tracey Annual Fete dawned bright and clear. Scattered, fluffy off white clouds scudded across an opaque sky but no rain was predicted; the North West wind would most likely propel them out to sea. As early as six o'clock event staff started arriving; a large canvas marquee was erected in the centre of the field to serve refreshments, wooden tables lined the edges of the field where stall holders would exhibit and hawk their produce or wares; and rides were erected for those seeking excitement. The fete was an important cash generator for local businesses and attracted punters from all over the county.

Cathy Munroe, the principal fete organiser, paced up and down parallel to the field gate consulting a map and directing people with much waving of arms to their designated areas. A permanent frown developing on her forehead as she bustled about.

The Sinclairs, volunteering to give pony rides, were reversing two horseboxes into their allocated spot. They were happy to have a day away from their busy schedules, glad to temporarily put the world of forensics aside. They had jointly decided that Polo and Briar were not suitable mounts for trots around the field so as back up they'd borrowed two docile ponies from the family stables; Bilbo & Baggins.

'As usual, a huge event,' James remarked leading Bilbo down the ramp of the horsebox onto the lush green grass. 'Cathy Munroe must have the patience of a saint to organize something of this calibre.'

Fiona nodded, casting her eyes around the two-acre field wondering how long it took to pull something like this together.

Katie was soon well into her element handing out leaflets on The Dartmoor Pony Society. She spent a lot of her spare time campaigning and volunteering in support of the Pure Bred Dartmoor Ponies. It angered her to think that over the years the breed had nearly been wiped out, basically through carelessness and greed.

By ten o'clock the fair was well underway with a substantial crowd of purveyors and sightseers already intermingling. A multitude of fun events and games were on offer including James's favourite, bale tossing. A bent nosed woman dressed in gypsy clothes and overlarge ear rings called out to passers-by, ''Ave your fortune told by Madam Zola, only ten quid. Come along girlie, let me know if that fella's the one for you.'

Katie stood and watched with amusement as a young couple decided their fate rested on the reading from the elderly woman. After a bit of half-hearted haggling they reluctantly handed over ten pounds which was pocketed immediately, then followed her into the small tent.

'Perhaps it's something you'd be interested in Miss Sinclair?'

Katie swung round to discover Tom Markham standing only inches away, grinning like a Cheshire Cat. Having been so engrossed in proceedings Katie hadn't noticed his approach. She deliberately turned away, not at all interested in his repartee. Seemingly unperturbed by the rebuff Tom continued to mouth off. 'Maybe the old bag can look into her crystal ball and tell you who murdered Muriel Jennings,' he gave a shallow laugh. 'She's more likely to get it right too.'

'Get lost,' Katie muttered under her breath. She was not in the mood for his ridicule. 'Why don't you have *your* fortune told Markham? You might learn what a dickhead you are.'

With that cutting riposte Katie stormed off, heading straight for the refreshment tent desperately in need of a large glass of wine.

'Nothing like a cool cider to quench your thirst on a day like this,' James smiled, as he joined Katie lounging on the makeshift bar. 'I always knew my talents as a forensic expert would lead me to better things one day.'

Katie smiled, glad of the company. 'I just bumped into Tom Markham, how I detest that little weasel.'

'Don't let him get under your skin,' James advised. 'As long as we're involved in our line of work we'll always come across his type.'

'Yes, I know. I just find him worse than most journalists I've encountered over the years,' Katie said with venom.

James, glancing around the tent, was pleasantly surprised to sight Stephen Tilly, an old friend from University propping up the other side of the bar. He looked relaxed as he stood with his arms draped around an attractive member of the opposite sex. James walked up to him clapping him firmly on the back. 'Stephen Tilly me old mate.' The two men shook hands and then exchanged a brief mate's embrace, 'You're the last person I expected to bump into.'

'We've just bought a house in Bovey Tracey,' Stephen explained. 'You'll be seeing a lot more of me in the future. I'll be coming to you for expert forensic advice.'

'Very glad to hear it,' James smiled. He looked at Steve's companion quizzically. The last time he'd seen Steve was a little over six months ago and he'd been with a leggy redhead called Alison.

'This is my wife Rachel,' Stephen informed James, edging Rachel forward.

'Nice to meet you,' James remarked, endeavouring to hide his shock. 'When did all this happen? I had you down as a confirmed bachelor.'

'A little over two months ago,' Stephen replied, turning slightly red. 'We got married in Rachel's home town of Dublin. It was pretty well a rushed affair as Stephen junior is on the way.'

'Congratulations, a marriage and a baby all in the same year. That's amazing. Are you also a scientist Rachel?'

Rachel shook her head laughing. 'Nothing that exotic I'm afraid. I own a small florist shop in Totnes a few yards from the Eastgate Arch, The Lilly Pad.'

She handed James a business card which he dutifully accepted and popped into the back pocket of his jeans.

'Are you still working at Exeter Uni?' James enquired of Stephen, waving to a barmaid for more drinks.

'Yep, I'm now head lecturer in the science department. I even have my own office and secretary.'

'Good for you,' James remarked sounding genuinely pleased for his friend. Katie came to join the small group and soon the two women started up their own animated conversation whilst the guys talked about old times and the latest scientific literature. Finally, after about an hour James and Katie returned to find Fiona leaning against one of the horse trailers.

'About time,' Fiona scolded as she saw them approach. 'Now you're here you can help get the horses back into the lose box so they can be ferried home. Alfie's just arrived to collect them.'

'Yeah sorry we took so long,' James apologised sheepishly, winking at the stable hand as if to say *women.* 'We bumped into Steve Tilly and his new bride.'

Fiona raised her eyebrows. 'Steve Tilly got married. Wow I never thought that day would come.'

Once the horses were safely on their way back to Dartmoor the group were free to scout around the fete. They wandered over to the makeshift bandstand and stood listening to a local band *Doctor Who and The Cider Men* who were surprisingly good for a bunch of school kids. Fiona remembered seeing them at a pub in Crediton once. Tapping along in time to the music James couldn't help but notice a low slung, Italian red super car making its way across the field to where the classic car show was in progress. He gave a low whistle. 'What a machine. That little baby must be worth at least 100 grand. How on earth can that young female behind the wheel afford such a gem?'

'That's Amy Forrester,' Katie enlightened him. 'Amy's the receptionist in Dave Ashcroft's surgery.'

'Hells' bells, am I missing something. Receptionists must be paid more than I thought to be able to prance around in a brand new Alfa Romeo,' James replied dazed. 'I'm definitely in the wrong business.'

'Doctor Ashcroft informed me she's on an annual cop of forty thousand pounds which is certainly not enough to buy that automobile,' Katie replied with assuredness, pleased to be able to shed light on the matter.

'Probably family money,' Fiona suggested. 'Or maybe she's got a rich boyfriend. She's very attractive. I doubt she'd ever be short of male admirers.'

Katie lowered her voice a notch. 'I have my suspicions Amy Forrester could be linked in with the suspected blackmailing of Muriel Jennings. I have a few leads I need to follow up on but she's certainly someone to look more closely at.'

'Had you not thought to share this information with us before?' James remarked, sounding put out. 'We don't keep secrets when we're investigating a murder.'

Katie picked up the undertones in his voice so tried to smooth things over. She casually informed him she *was* intending to share this bit of news but wanted to investigate a few things first. Besides it was more a hunch that anything.

James appearing satisfied with this hasty explanation led his sisters away from the band to take a closer look at the car.

Exiting easily from behind the wheel Amy sidled up to James. 'Amelia Forrester,' she held out her hand. 'My friends call me Amy.'

'James Sinclair. My sisters and I were just admiring your car. I've read up on the latest Alfa but never seen one in the flesh. The closest I get to such a beauty is by flicking through pages of a classic car magazine.'

'Yes it really is a delight,' Amy replied proudly, 'an absolute dream to drive, attracts a lot of attention.'

'Must have cost a tidy packet?' James remarked, now genuinely confused how any one especially a GP's receptionist could shell out for the latest high end offerings in Italian exotica.

Amy gave a cheeky grin. 'It's not stolen in case you were wondering. Bought it straight off the stand at the Frankfurt Motor Show.'

James put up his hands in mock horror. 'The thought never crossed my mind,' he replied honestly.

'However, to curb your curiosity I do happen to have very wealthy parents who are happy to throw money at me all the time. This little rocket was a present for my birthday which happened to be last week. It even came wrapped with a large gold bow across the bonnet. I'll take you for a drive if you like?'

James was tempted momentarily but shook his head. 'Maybe another time. Happy birthday for last week.'

'Let me know if you ever want that drive,' Amy laughed as she headed across the field towards the marquee, leaving James still engrossed in the car's sensual lines.

'I think she fancies you,' Fiona laughed, giving James a gentle shove. 'Maybe even marriage material.'

James shot his sister a cynical look. He hated the thought of settling down. His biggest fear was being stuck in a loveless marriage with no means of escape. He particularly relished the excitement of seducing married women, meeting at a secret rendezvous to give the relationship an extra buzz. When he got bored with one woman he could move on to the next.

'Amelia Forrester is the type of woman who would fancy any bloke,' James grinned. 'Just look at the way she's draping herself all over Mark Jennings.'

Fiona watched as Amy planted a passionate kiss onto Mark's lips not seeming to care in the slightest who witnessed this show of affection. In response Mark placed his arms around her waist pulling her in tight to whisper in her ear. Amy seemed to find what he'd said extremely funny and started giggling. They were acting like two love struck teenagers.

'At least knowing Amelia has well to do parents solves the query on where she got the money from,' James said to his siblings. 'Although her lack of class is apparent if she's carrying on with Mark Jennings.'

Fiona was about to turn away when she spotted Deirdre Mulligan bowling along near to where Mark and Amy were still locked in a firm embrace. Deirdre clearly preoccupied and unsighted almost collided with the couple.

'I'm sorry,' she muttered. Then a surprising thing happened; instead of moving away from the twosome she remained riveted to the spot: her eyes became two wide saucers before she turned a deathly white, as if she'd witnessed a ghostly apparition.

Fiona, fearful Deirdre was about to collapse onto the ground, raced across the grass taking a firm grip of her arm. 'Are you alright?' she enquired, as Deirdre started to sway.

'Yep, all good,' Deirdre muttered, sounding a little dazed. She allowed Fiona to lead her away from the crowds showing her to a disused wooden box which would double as a seat.

'I thought I saw someone I recognized but must have been mistaken,' Deirdre explained, colour slowly seeping back into her cheeks. 'I also missed breakfast so I reckon my blood sugars are a bit low.'

Katie joining Fiona had also witnessed Deirdre's reaction on seeing Amy Forrester and puzzled over the meaning. She tried to come up with a plausible answer but eventually speculated it was probably a case of mistaken identity.

After ensuring Deirdre was OK the Sinclairs agreed to call it a day as the sun sank inexorably lower in the sky. Heading towards the exit they encountered Matt Tyler clearly enjoying the company of an attractive blonde wearing a skirt so short it resembled nothing more than an oversized floral handkerchief tied around her slim waist. Matt had one arm firmly around her shoulder leading her towards the marquee stopping every few seconds to plant a kiss on her lips.

Katie stopped dead in her tracks. She hadn't expected to encounter Matt, especially in the arms of another woman. She felt a sudden tightness welling up inside, quickly reaching into her bag for the asthma inhaler she always carried. She'd not had an attack for a while but felt one coming on as she watched Matt canoodling with this tart. Taking three quick puffs Katie then threw the inhaler back into her bag.

Unable to pretend she didn't care, Katie fled towards the car park fighting back an upsurge of tears. It was vital to get home before she crumpled in a heap. She could try and explain the sudden disappearance to her siblings tomorrow, although it would be quite obvious why she'd left in such a hurry.

Anxiety building, she threw the little Punto erratically out the main entrance narrowly missing a combine harvester and knocking over a stack of straw bales only momentarily slowing her speed, before sending a group of Morris dancers scattering in all directions.

Needing desperately to calm down and ward off a major asthma attack, Katie eased her foot off the accelerator, gradually bringing the car under control. She started to work on thought processes flashing in her head.

What did she care if Matt had found himself a girlfriend? She and Matt weren't exactly dating, they were just good friends. Not one of them had ever spoken of uniting their passion. Perhaps it was Katie's interpretation that they both secretly desired the same thing but Matt didn't seem to share the same understanding.

Back in the sanctuary of her own home Katie walked over to the fridge, peering inside. Locating a bottle of sparkling shiraz, she knew was in the back compartment, she angrily popped the cork, filled a flute and rabidly consumed two glasses in quick succession. Striding out into the garden she plonked down in an old cane chair and stared, transfixed at the greenhouse.

Jolted annoyingly from the trance by the prompt tune from her mobile she noted five missed calls and three new messages. She was in no mood to converse with anyone. The callers could wait.

It now became apparent Matt was only interested in sex and when Katie had declined his advances he now turned to the first floozy he could get his paws on.

The last drop drained from the bottle, Katie picked up the flute and hurled it forcefully at the side of the garage. The satisfying report of shattering glass echoed loudly in the still evening. Staggering slowly to an upright position she headed back inside. Tightly gripping the hand rail as a wave of nausea swept over her she climbed the stairs to her bedroom. Flopping onto the bed fully clothed she slipped into unconsciousness within a matter of seconds.

The next morning Katie had difficulty dragging her unyielding body out of bed. She was tempted to phone in sick before realising she'd made an appointment with an

249

associate professor at one in Crediton; pretending to be sick was not an option.

Walking into the office Fiona greeted Katie with a questioning look. 'Boy, do you look rough.'

'Don't start, I'm not in the mood.' Katie snapped, heading into the kitchenette to concoct a strong espresso, adding the requisite two heaped teaspoons of sugar. If this didn't bring her back to life nothing would.

Fiona knew better than to quiz her sister when in 'one of her moods', rightly guessing it was man trouble, probably associated with Matt and knew better than to ask questions. In time, Katie would divulge snippets of information but not now. Fiona returned to the demanding task of verifying the mass spectrum of a synthetic opiate pretending Katie didn't exist, the best option under the circumstance.

For the entire morning, Katie immersed herself in a large pile of paper work. Eventually unable to concentrate as the headache grew she pulled open her top drawer retrieved a bottle of aspirin and rapidly swallowed three large white tablets with a full glass of water. She threw up three times in the space of a couple of hours, wondering how she could have been so stupid to consume a bottle of bubbly on an empty stomach. It reminded her of university days which were long gone. Back then she was young and foolish, last night it was just plain foolishness.

Katie mercifully managed to keep the one o'clock meeting brief. Unable to indulge much in conversation she nodded in all the right places before returning to the office. The sun had already disappeared behind enveloping grey cumulus clouds and the air had cooled noticeably. After an hour staring into space Katie switched off her computer to wander up town in search of something for dinner.

She was surprised to discover the small supermarket practically deserted, normally at this time of day it was a hive of activity. Waiting in line at the checkout Katie glanced towards the shop window spotting Amy Forrester standing on the pavement talking on her mobile and struggling with a large bunch of flowers. 'Good afternoon,' she smiled warmly as Katie approached with shopping bags in tow. 'Picking up something last minute for dinner?'

Katie nodded. 'Yes, my cupboards were looking very sparse. Those flowers are beautiful, I love freesias.'

Amy laughed. 'Yes, they're for my sister Cher. She has always loved flowers. Sorry to rush but I didn't realize it was so late. Cher is expecting me.'

Katie watched Amy walk away, annoyed to discover a tinge of jealously sweeping over her. Amy Forrester seemed to have the perfect life: a steady job, stunning looks and endless money to boot. What more could a girl ask for? Katie then forcefully dismissed these crazy thoughts. Her own life was one others would envy so she couldn't complain.

Katie so deep in thought didn't notice Liz Palmer approaching until she spoke. 'Ms Sinclair, can I have a word with you?'

Katie turned quickly, almost overbalancing with the weight of her shopping. Although not keen to strike up conversation Katie forced her best smile. 'Why of course, what's up?'

Liz looked over her shoulder. 'Could we go somewhere private? I don't want our conversation overheard.'

'We can head back to my office,' Katie suggested. 'It's only a five-minute walk down the road.'

Liz was relieved, pleased to be given an opportunity to talk.

Katie showed Liz into the front office, motioning towards a seat.

'I wanted to let you know that several book club members have recently received white roses,' Liz began, still lowering her voice afraid of being overhead.

'Roses,' Katie looked puzzled.

'Yes, white roses. Just like the cover of Lillian Webster's book, although I have no idea what it all means.'

'Any note with the roses?' Katie asked, absorbing this new revelation.

Liz produced a small piece of torn paper, handing it over with a shaky hand. Katie read the note which simply said, 'For the dearly departed.'

'When did *you* receive *your* rose?' Katie asked, a sickening feeling creeping into the pit of her stomach. The person sending these roses must be seriously twisted.

'Early this morning,' Liz replied, almost on the brink of tears. 'I got in my car to go to work and found this note tucked under one of the windscreen wipers alongside the rose.'

'Who else has received a rose?' Katie enquired.

'Four of us in total; Jane Anderson, Deirdre Mulligan, Cathy Munroe and of course me.'

'I'd like to keep this note if you don't mind?' Katie informed her. 'I will need to chat with my colleagues but please don't mention the roses to anyone else.'

After Liz left Katie called the team together for an urgent meeting.

'What I don't understand is how someone found out the history behind the white rose,' Fiona remarked. 'This information was kept from the general public and certainly wasn't mentioned in the book. Admittedly the front dust jacket depicts a white rose but nowhere on the actual pages does it mention about a rose being found on each victim.'

'If that's the case we can be certain we are looking at someone who had inside information into the Cartwright murders,' James speculated.

'Well, surely no professional would stoop so low.' Fiona remarked.

'I was thinking of someone actually linked to those murders,' James replied softly. 'The more we learn about Ted Cartwright the less I'm inclined to think of him as a murderer. Perhaps all along he was convicted of crimes he didn't commit and the real killer is still out there.'

***

Katie sat propped up in bed unable to come to grips with the program on the Discovery Channel. Her hangover now finally subsided, anger took its place. It had been a trying day, she was irritable and tired. The only way to work the wrath out of her system was to go and confront Matt about his bit on the side.

Not bothering to dress Katie climbed out of bed, wrapped her dressing gown around her and drove onto Dartmoor heading for Matt's humble abode.

He opened the door without smiling. 'Here to give me a lecture?'

'You don't seem to care about anyone except yourself,' Katie fired back at him, 'to you the whole world is one merry-go-round and you think you can trample on people and treat them like shit.'

'You're being melodramatic, lighten up a bit,' Matt retorted.

'How do you propose I do that?' Katie asked, with a dose of irony in her voice. She stood shivering on the doorstep.

'Well if you weren't afraid to lose your knickers once in a while perhaps you'd start to be a bit more fun,' Matt jibed, taking hold of her wrist and twisting it in a firm grip. She let out a painful cry. Silence reigned for a few moments before Matt spoke again.

'Wow, you really are bitter and vengeful aren't you Katie. You don't realise I carried out some dangerous and very borderline stuff for you over the past week. If I'd have been caught borrowing from Scotland Yard's data base it might have been the end of my career. What did I get out of all this? Nothing.'

'Oh, how clumsy of me,' Katie said, in barely a whisper. 'I naturally assumed you did those things to help me. When all you really did it for was an attempted fuck.'

'Don't be ridiculous,' Matt's face was bright crimson; his anger shooting to the surface.

'Me, ridiculous, I'm not the one being ridiculous,' Katie fought back. 'I'm merely spitting out the truth. When you didn't get what you wanted, you ended up screwing a twenty-year-old bimbo. Good, was she?'

Matt hit his fist hard against the panel of the door. 'Yeah, she was good. Damn good,' he replied through clenched teeth.

Katie turned away fighting back tears. She ran the short distance to her car staggering into the driver's seat. This was wrong, all wrong and she only had herself to blame.

There was nothing left in the basement. It had all been cleared away. Now who would want all that old rubbish? She sat on the cold damp floor wondering if the past would only be a distant memory. It wasn't a bad place quite cosy really, definitely specious. Should she attempt to put a bit of sparkle into the joint? It was something she could think about. No rush to make alterations. She wasn't planning on going anywhere else. No, she was here to stay.

CHAPTER SEVENTEEN

'Where were you yesterday afternoon?' James asked Katie as he put the finishing touches to a lab report. 'I wanted your opinion on a new amphetamine designer drug.'

'I was pottering around on the Heath in an attempt to de-stress,' Katie replied.

'Find anything of interest?'

Katie held up an earth encrusted object.

James reached for the artefact before brushing away some dirt and placing it under a magnifying light. 'Not bad. You've done alright this time.'

'What's your opinion?' Katie asked.

'It looks like the brass hilt of a sword; probably Royalist. The Historical Society would love this for next month's Battle of Bovey Heath Exhibition.'

'No way,' Katie jibed. 'This is going into my collection.'

***

Mark Jennings stared at the office clock; it was two minutes off midnight. Gathering up his mobile and car keys he eased himself up from his desk. It was much later than he thought. Almost robotically he flicked on the security alarm, turned out the lights, then made a quick dash through the front door locking it before the alarm could be activated.

Outside, a chilled air greeted him. Above a few stars sat motionless in a dusky sky accompanied by a waxing crescent moon which cast an almost supernatural light on proceedings.

Placing the keys in the ignition of his BMW he was surprised when the engine refused to fire. He cursed under his breath. The car had been a new purchase only four months prior so there was no excuse for an electrical hitch. After another three attempts, it finally burst into life, settling into a gentle purr. A relieved Mark engaged drive, planted his right foot and exited out through the security gates heading towards Exeter. He tuned in the radio on the centre touch screen console with a verbal command and wound down the driver's window for some fresh air. At the bottom of Holden Hill, he eased his foot onto the brakes but with no response, his heart rate skyrocketing. He tried again to gently apply pressure and the foot pedal went straight to the floor. Almost instantly the black coupe spun out of control skidding in a broadside off the road and landing in a shallow ditch head first. On impact the front airbags exploded but a millisecond too late to prevent Mark's head smashing sickeningly against the windscreen. Black out was instantaneous.

***

The sun was already rising when James made the call to Fiona shortly before seven. Although it was Sunday he knew she'd be up pottering around, preparing breakfast. Fiona was never one to lie in, even on a day off.

'You'll want to hear this. I've just received a call from a sergeant at Exeter Hospital,' he informed his sister. 'Mark

Jennings has been admitted to the emergency department following a car crash. His vehicle ran off the road exiting Holden Hill. The report is a cut to the head and moderate concussion but otherwise they say he's reasonably OK.'

'Why are we being told about this?' Fiona replied, flipping a couple of bacon rashers in the pan, listening to the sizzling sound and enjoying the aroma emanating the room. 'I would have thought this information should be relayed to his next of kin.'

'Stella has also contacted me,' James explained. 'She was very concerned. Her theory is someone tried to kill him. We're waiting on examination by a local mechanic but even at this early stage it would appear someone tampered with the brakes on the Beemer, there was no fluid in the hydraulics.'

'Any traces of alcohol in his blood stream?' Fiona pressed, sounding rather sceptical. 'Mark does have a tendency to drink. Perhaps he wants us to think someone else was at fault to avoid any charges.'

'On this occasion the breathalyser showed no evidence of Mark having touched a drop of alcohol, surprising as it sounds,' James enlightened his sister.

'Wow.' Fiona felt the wind taken from her. She really had expected a reading off the scale.

'They did do a preliminary check for other substances in a blood sample,' James continued, 'but they're waiting on a full lab toxicology screen tomorrow.'

'Drugs,' Fiona said, sounding triumphant. 'There you go. He was taking illegal drugs, which in my opinion are not much different to alcohol consumption.'

'Perhaps,' James said, not sounding convinced. 'Mark is adamant he has never exposed his body to drugs and I have a strong tendency to believe him. If Mark is telling the truth, there is the possibility someone *was* trying to finish the old boy off.'

'Still only an assumption,' Fiona chided, dishing up her bacon. 'The blood results will be ready soon enough James. I'd bet my life on it Mark Jennings is working on a cover up, besides who would want to kill him?'

'Any number of people,' James replied earnestly. 'I think we need to speed up the Jennings case Fi. If we don't, we may find ourselves with a lot more dead bodies.'

***

The driveway stretched for almost a mile before coming to a halt outside the grand entrance of a classic Palladian style house built in the 1920's; a copy of a 17th century Italianate villa.

Noticing movement from an adjacent greenhouse Katie ventured across the manicured lawns locating an elderly gardener attending small seedlings. As she pushed through the glass doors heat engulfed her entire body, forming instant beads of perspiration on her pale complexion.

On hearing footsteps, the old man momentarily looked up before continuing to water the tiny saplings. 'Can I help you miss?'

'I hope so,' Katie volunteered. 'I'm looking for the occupants of the house. Would you happen to know where I might find them?'

'Ms Ilbert is currently in France,' he replied, with an air of caution etched to his croaky voice. 'I'm afraid she won't be back for several weeks. Is there anything I can help you with? Jim Pike's my name, I'm head gardener of this very fine piece of real estate.'

Putting down his watering can he offered a soiled hand for Katie to shake.

'Katie Sinclair,' she answered, managing a brisk handshake. 'I'm looking for Mr. and Mrs. Forrester. I was under the impression *they* owned the house?'

Jim shook his head. 'You've got that wrong Missy. Georgina Ilbert owns Valley View, has done for the past thirty years. Prior to that it was owned by Admiral Long.'

Katie once more studied the address on the crumpled piece of paper she was holding. Yes, this definitely matched the information Amy wrote on her application form when applying for a position with Doctor Ashcroft.

'Who did you say you wanted again?' Jim asked, attempting a sneak peek at the hand written note in Katie's right hand.

Katie repeated the names. 'Robert and Dana Forrester.'

Jim scratched his head. 'I have to admit those names do sound familiar. Let me go and speak with Mrs. Cox the housekeeper. She's bound to know of any Forresters. She's lived in these parts since she was a nipper and knows everyone who's local and most of them that ain't.'

Jim disappeared in the direction of the house returning several minutes later with a sprightly lady suffering from severe scoliosis. Despite this impairment, she sported a roly-poly figure and a merry smile to match.

'Jim tells me you're looking for the Forresters?' she cackled.

'Yes that's right. Would you happen to know where I might find them?'

'Bob Forrester died over two years ago,' Mrs. Cox informed her. 'Poor bugger had chronic emphysema. They say he smoked over forty cigarettes a day. As for his missus, she's around town somewhere. You'll catch her in the local boozer. Bit of a drinker is our Dana, has been for ages.'

Katie tried to make sense of what she was hearing. 'So they don't own Valley View?'

Mrs. Cox gave a hearty laugh. 'Good god no. What gave you that impression? They both worked here for a short time. Bob was hired as the odd job man and Dana was assistant cook. Funny you should think they owned the place though.' She gave another high pitched cackle.

Katie didn't want to elaborate on the confusion so just mumbled. 'My mistake. I must have misunderstood the information I was given. Where did you say I might locate Dana?'

'I'd try Drake's Folly,' Mrs Cox volunteered. 'If you continue along the A38, take the Dartington turn off, you'll see it nestled between trees on the left hand side of the road, about half mile along.'

Katie thanked them for the information before hopping in her car and driving the few miles in the direction indicated.

To a casual observer, the exterior façade of Drake's Folly public house was anything but welcoming. In parts, large fragments of paint and plaster had fallen off the walls, exposing the ancient brick work. Broken pieces of rustic outdoor furniture were strewn over the tiny lawn adding to its down at heels look. Inside was no better. Dimly lit, it smelt of stale booze and body odour, not the sort of place anyone would visit for a quiet relaxing drink. The juke box was belting out an old seventies song approaching pain threshold levels, drowning any attempts at conversation. Katie wondered why the place hadn't been bulldozed eons ago. She crossed the room trying not to breathe too frequently as she approached the barman who stood clearing glasses from a corner table.

'Excuse me,' she shouted over the top of the music. 'Could you tell me where I might find Dana Forrester?'

He pointed to a woman slouched at a nearby table, wine glass in one hand, cigarette in the other. Her tousled hair could have doubled for a bird's nest; it was obvious she'd not used a brush in years. Her clothes were no more than old tattered hand me downs far too big for her petite figure.

Katie thought there had to be some mistake. Surely this unkempt woman wasn't Amy's mother, a woman of great wealth and fortune?

Trying to mask the immediate shock Katie summoned up the courage to confront Dana, and walked up introducing herself as one of Amy's friends.

Dana seemed to accept the plausible story Katie provided. When she also realised Katie was a psychologist Dana turned the conversation into a counselling session.

'I was never always in this state,' she explained, making a conscious effort not to slur her words, without much success. 'I've been in and out of rehabilitation clinics more times than I care to remember. Don't do me much good though. Most quacks have all but given up on me now.'

'Drink can be an unforgiving demon,' Katie remarked, as she pulled a chair up to the table. She studied the woman's fine details, noticing how the ill effects of alcohol and smoking had played havoc with her complexion.

'Once upon a time Bob and I owned our own home,' she said sounding proud. 'We'd paid off the mortgage and were living the high life.'

'So what changed?' Katie asked, listening with interest as Dana's story unfolded.

Dana gave a small sniff. 'A few years ago, our youngest daughter committed suicide. That was the start of our demise,' Dana explained. 'Bob started to suffer from deep depression and I took refuge in the bottle. Our days were consumed betting on the dogs until eventually we had no money left. Our house was repossessed to pay debts, we hit rock bottom. At the time, it was our mechanism to numb the pain. Stuffed lungs got poor Bob in the end. The reality was he just ran out of puff, literally. As for me, see for yourself. I can't go more than a couple of hours without wanting a drink. Lord knows I've tried.'

'Losing a child is dreadful,' Katie remarked softly, feeling the pain of the other woman through the sorrow in her eyes. 'It must have been difficult for Amy losing her sister.'

'Amy was distraught. Wouldn't speak to a soul for a very long time,' Dana replied.

'Did she receive counselling?'

'Of a sort, but she tried to cope in her own way. The strange thing is; about a year ago, she suddenly seemed to accept what happened, becoming very resilient. She decided to finally make something of her life. Good kid my Amy, smart too, but you'd know that being her friend.'

Katie, lost for words, only managed a compliant nod. 'She seems to have done alright for herself. The car she currently drives is beautiful. Must have cost a tidy sum?'

Dana gave a hearty laugh. 'I understand she has a well-paid job. Like I said she's a good kid.'

It became apparent Amy had lied about the car being a birthday gift from her parents. This begged the question as to where exactly the cash had come from. Even on a good wage she wouldn't have been able to afford such extravagance.

'Was Amy anything like her sister in personality or looks?' Katie asked, watching Dana signal the barman for a double whisky.

'Oh yes, they shared similar features.'

Katie decided to call it a day. There didn't seem to be anymore to be gained from Dana who was now knocking back the hard liquor rapidly. Back on the A38 heading home her mind kept wrestling with the mystery of how Amy Forrester had found the money for her high end auto. She was now top of the list of suspects who could have been blackmailing Muriel Jennings.

It was late when she reached the prison. There it stood dark and dreary just as she always remembered. It had been over seven years since she'd seen Ted and even now she wasn't sure she could do this. What would they talk about after all this time? Would he even want to see her? Perhaps it was time she faced her demons and told him what had really happened. She then gave a shallow laugh; Ted already knew. How could he not know? Her laughter rang out through the misty rain settling on her flushed face.

CHAPTER EIGHTEEN

Not bothering to wash her hair, Katie tied it neatly in a tight ponytail and held it in place with her favourite antique, Japanese tortoise shell comb.

It was a glorious day, and a hike across the moors would be perfect to blow away the cobwebs.

Bluebell Woods lived up to its name. The spreading earthy floor was a swathe of rich lavender-blue flowers mimicking a large wool carpet. With the sun's rays reflecting off the ancient deciduous trees the entire copse bathed in luxuriant purple haze, the ambience forming a harmonious bond with Katie's inner being.

Katie remembered reading somewhere that the bluebell was a protected species under the Wildlife and Countryside act of 1981. She often squirreled away quirky bits of information in the back of her mind. You just never knew when it could prove useful, especially in her line of work.

Large honeybees were in abundance, humming away as they went from flower to flower looking for pollen. Holly was also in abundance, a dark emerald green without the bright red berries which would accompany the bush during colder months.

Exiting the woods near an old bridle path, Katie bent down to tie a loose shoelace and in the process placed her fingers into the water of a babbling steam. The icy sensation made her withdraw her hand quickly and shake it vigorously to restore warmth. How mad she was to imagine the water in early spring would be anything but freezing.

Idly meandering along, the distant sound of tractors intruded into her senses, competing against the dazzling early morning cacophony of birds and insects which buzzed all around. Unusual for this time of year there were only a few new born lambs frolicking in the fields. Ponies were more in abundance as they grazed the open moorland looking for rich heathery grass to munch on. Not many of the ponies were true Dartmoor ponies, most were mixture breeds.

Nevertheless, they made a timeless image in an immutable iron-age landscape. Rounding a corner near the walk car-park Katie happened upon Amy Forrester. She was taken by surprise. The moors covered a vast area, it was rare to bump into anyone you knew.

'Hello again,' Katie smiled. 'It's a lovely day to be out walking.'

'Yes,' Amy replied crisply, not looking too pleased to have encountered Katie.

'Another beautiful bunch of flowers I see,' Katie remarked, noting the bouquet Amy was carrying.

'Yes, symbolic white roses.'

Amy headed off along the bridle path as Katie turned back towards her car. As she hurried along an Arctic chill swept over her as Amy's words flooded back into her mind. What had she meant by 'symbolic white roses'. To Katie the thought of white roses brought with it the Cartwright murders. Could there be a connection to the Cartwright murders and Amy Forrester?

Over fish and chips back at the laboratory, James and Fiona listened as Katie relived her recent encounters with Dana and Amy Forrester.

'It's bloody clear to even blind Freddie Amy was lying in relation to how she obtained the money for that flashy lifestyle,' James said bluntly. 'Perhaps she was the one blackmailing Muriel Jennings. After all, Marshall Davidson was adamant he knew nothing of the reason why Muriel frequently removed large sums of money from the company back account. He was almost convinced someone held something pretty devastating over her.'

'Don't you reckon Amy could have despatched Muriel?' Fiona asked, in a voice sounding a little shaky. 'I also wonder what her remark meant about symbolic white roses. I find that particularly weird.'

'It's possible Amy killed Muriel,' James replied. 'However, right now we have nothing physical on the forensic side linking her to Muriel's murder.'

'Here's another thought,' Katie piped up, 'If Amy read Muriel's medical records she'd discover Muriel had an affair with Ted Cartwright. That's a perfect reason for threatening Muriel. There's no way Muriel would want any of that information out on the streets.'

'I think it's about time we alerted DCI Rose to bring Amy Forrester in for a few words,' James advised. 'I'll get on to it straight away.'

Beating the girls to the last piece of battered cod James picked up the lab phone and put a call through to Exeter Police Station.

***

It was cramped, hot and stuffy in the small interview room. Amy Forrester sat opposite James, who in turn sat next to a senior detective. A big burly police constable was standing near the door and next to Amy sat a small guy with Italian features; her lawyer. An interested spectator, Detective Mick Rose viewed proceedings via a two-way mirror.

266

'Commencement of interview 20:25 hours 25th May 2016,' the detective confirmed. 'Could you please state your full name.'

'Amelia Frances Forrester.'

'Are you aware that you are being questioned today in relation to the murder of Mrs. Muriel Jennings back in March 2016?'

'Yes.'

'Do you understand that anything you say may be held as evidence and used in a court of law?'

'Yes.'

'Can you confirm where you were between the hours of three and seven on the evening of the 4th March 2016?'

'I was having dinner at the Comfy Pew near the Cathedral in Exeter. It was a friend's birthday and a group of us had gone there to celebrate.'

The police officer looked at the lawyer, 'Can we confirm that?'

'Yes we can. All seven people attending the dinner party can confirm Amelia was there that night, arriving around 5pm.'

'See, I didn't kill Muriel Jennings,' Amy stuck out her lower lip in a pouting fashion. 'Although I'm not sorry she was murdered. Served the cow right, got exactly what she deserved.'

The solicitor shot her a firm stare, which quite plainly told his client to shut up.

'So if you didn't murder Muriel Jennings why did you blackmail her?' James was playing a wild card by asking this question. Reality being he had no idea if Amy was the one who'd blackmailed Muriel Jennings.

Amy's lawyer answered for her, 'My client is not guilty of murder so unless you have good reason to detain her on those charges I suggest you let her go. This is clearly a waste of time for all concerned.'

'I would like an answer to my question,' James shot back at him, 'a simple yes or no would suffice.'

Amy looked at James with loathing. 'I plead not guilty.' she said crisply. 'Now, as my lawyer has already instructed; I am to be released if I am not being charged with murder.'

Amy stood up to leave. The interview was terminated.

***

Options were now running out. Acting on a hunch and impulse and annoyed he hadn't been able to gain anything of value from Amy Forrester, James calculated it was worth the aggro of another confrontation with Mark Jennings and picked up his mobile. He located him at his small Teignmouth terrace house recovering from the recent car accident. Remarkably, Mark was far from rude when James turned up, even inviting him in for a light lunch. Slightly taken aback James accepted this friendly gesture as it was nearing lunchtime and he'd skipped breakfast.

'How's the bumps and bruises?' James enquired, taking a seat at the kitchen table laden with a variety of freshly made sandwiches.

'I'll survive,' Mark replied, offering a lopsided grin. 'Unfortunately, the car's not in such good shape, a write-off I believe.'

'We're waiting on lab reports for fingerprints and hopeful we may get lucky,' James advised. 'All we need is permission from you to cross match with your employee records? I understand all your employees undertake a formal screening prior to commencement of work with Jennings Clay which includes finger printing.'

Mark nodded, popping another sandwich into his mouth. James continued with his questioning.

'I am sorry to bring up your personal life again but I'm working on a bit of a hunch; can you clarify if you often buy expensive gifts for Amy Forrester? We originally thought Amy may have been blackmailing your mother, now we believe differently.'

Mark gave a shallow laugh. 'Yes, it's something I shouldn't really do but I never have been able to resist a pretty woman. I smother Amy with gifts and she gives me the sort of affair I'm looking for – no strings attached.'

'I know we've been over this before Mark, but can you think of anyone on the payroll who might want to wish you or your mother harm?'

Mark pondered the question for a few seconds before replying. 'I must admit; I don't have the closest rapport with Jane Anderson. She's very pushy. For some reason my mother insisted on keeping her on in the marketing role but god knows why. In my opinion she's useless, is shit with our major customers, and hasn't really increased sales figures in the past few years she's been assigned to the post.'

James sat up and took note as Mark continued. 'There's also an instance I was working back late one evening when I received an anonymous phone call from a female. I'd had a fair bit to drink but looking back on it now I wonder if the voice on the other end belonged to Jane. I vaguely recognised the voice but was too drunk to get instant recognition.'

'What exactly did she say?'

'Oh, I don't know, something about me thinking I'm smart, not giving a damn and the last bit was really puzzling now I come to think about it. She said something about *wanting what is rightfully hers*, whatever the hell that means.'

James listened with intent. That did seem a very odd thing to say; *wanting what is rightfully mine*. He stood up to leave thanking Mark for his time and promising to be in touch as soon as they had further developments.

***

Deirdre Mulligan caught her reflection in a passing shop window. Her natural rosy glow was tinged grey and her pale blue eyes resembled sunken pits.

Previously, she'd thought the cramping pains in her stomach were caused by a bout of salmonella poisoning from a take away kebab but now she believed differently. The effects of tainted food didn't last for weeks. A basic medical knowledge lent enough insight to surmise she was being slowly poisoned. The problem was she didn't quite know what to do about it; there were certain things that needed to be kept quiet. With these thoughts mulling in her head Deirdre didn't see Fiona Sinclair approaching.

'Hi Deirdre, here to pick up a few bargains in the Spring Sales?' Fiona said brightly. 'Elders has some brilliant fashions on the upper floor.'

Deirdre managed a brief nod, as Fiona hurried on her way with the minimum of banter.

After ten minutes' aimless window shopping Deirdre at last finally decided to drop unannounced into the Chudleigh surgery on the way home. Doctor Ashcroft would be able to diagnosis the crippling ailments without too much fuss.

How she drove to the medical centre Deirdre had no idea. It was all she could do to stagger up the three flights of steps and open the main door. Once inside the cool reception room objects started spinning. Deirdre instinctively knew at any moment she would pass out.

'Are you okay?' Doctor Ashcroft asked, reaching out a steadying arm. Deirdre losing control of her legs tumbled to the floor, slipping mercifully into unconsciousness, everything around turning black.

***

When Fiona returned to the office, a little after 10pm, James was still working in the lab. 'Are you still at it?' Fiona enquired, surveying James immersed in changing lamps on the AAS.

'Yep,' he replied, not bothering to look up. 'By the way, I've just received a call from Dave Ashcroft who's on his way over with some urgent blood and urine samples and swabs. He's had three patients call in to the surgery today, all with signs of poisoning. Not doing anything tonight are you as I could do with some help on this one?'

'Somehow, I get the feeling this is not the usual run of the mill GP stuff,' Fiona remarked casually. 'OK, I'll be only too happy to assist.'

'All three happen to be members of the Bovey Tracey Book Club,' James threw in unexpectedly.

Fiona nearly fell off the bench she was seated on. 'Go on.'

'Deirdre Mulligan, Liz Palmer and Jane Anderson have all reported suffering from intense cramps, sweats, headaches and vomiting. Tell me sis, if you were going to poison someone, what would be your preferred method?'

'Wow, that's a leading question,' Fiona replied, jumping off the bench to flop into a nearby chair. 'I'd need to think about that one.'

'I'd just like to know what *you* would do if you didn't want to get caught.'

271

'Most times people get caught, inevitably,' Fiona replied, earnestly, 'but if I wanted to make it quick and decisive I suppose I'd go with an obscure plant alkaloid; strychnine or brucine. Tropane alkaloids from the belladonna group perhaps or maybe something a bit more topical like ricin. They're generally extremely toxic in small amounts causing very agonising, rapid death.

On the other hand, you have the more insidious option, which is probably easier to get away with. A heavy metal like Arsenic, Lead, Antimony, Bismuth, Barium Cadmium, Mercury, the list goes on. Easy to get hold of as they are common in the environment, difficult to trace and diagnose – take your pick. I'd use Thallium just to be satanically different, an old rat poison favourite years ago.'

'How would you go about getting the poison into the body?'

'Easy. Most people drink coffee. I'd go with that technique, although there could be collateral damage. You do run the risk of knocking off more people than intended if you opt for this particular method.'

By the time David Ashcroft arrived at the Moorland office with patient samples in hand James had rounded up Nick and Katie who were anxious to be part of this new development. Ashcroft provided a brief account of his patients' symptoms while Fiona started on some routine preliminary toxicology tests.

'I've already ruled out food poisoning,' she began, 'and the symptoms don't look to me like alkaloid ingestion. I think we're dealing with heavy metals here something like the classic inheritance powder. I'll start by checking cells for Leukonychia before conducting some basic blood and urine tests. The urine samples were collected within the past 24 hours so we should be able to get an accurate gauge of any acute exposure.'

Fiona went straight into the classic Marsh Test developed by James Marsh in 1830 to determine the

272

presence of arsenic. A relatively simple test to perform and highly sensitive based on the production of arsenic hydride vapour, it still required high levels of concentration. James weighed in and set to work warming up the atomic absorption spectrophotometer and going in search of an arsenic hollow cathode lamp; he wanted undeniable spectrographic confirmation of any heavy metals.

After an hour of intense, meticulous work Fiona removed her gloves and mask. The others sat around in silence as she scribbled a few notes before checking the results.

'The tests are all positive,' Fiona informed her small audience. 'High levels of arsenic are present in all six samples and I purposely ran four separate heavy metal tests for confirmation.'

'Yep, no doubt,' chimed in her brother as he waved a print out of the AAS results for Arsenic above his head.

'This is amazing stuff,' Doctor Ashcroft said, wiping a creased brow. 'All three women were sent over to Torbay Hospital so I'll phone through authorising the administration of biomethylation to covert the arsenic to a less toxic form. We'll also treat them with dimercaptosuccinic acid to sequester the arsenic away from blood proteins. They'll also require supplemental potassium.'

Fiona sat down totally wrung-out. 'Well, it certainly appears members of the Bovey book club have been deliberately poisoned. It is highly probable Muriel Jennings was poisoned the same way.'

Right now, she hated them all. It was their fault this had happened. Perhaps it was even his fault. He knew, of course he knew. The only problem was he had paid the price. Did it matter? How could it matter? Nothing mattered anymore. Life started and life ended. Sometimes there was a middle, but always there was a beginning and an end.

CHAPTER NINETEEN

James went in search of Katie, eventually finding her out in the small courtyard reading a book. She looked up and smiled as her brother approached.

'Sis, after you'd met with Ted's barrister you mentioned something about Ted receiving letters in prison from Abigail?'

'Yes that's correct,' Katie replied, placing the book on the small wooden table next to the hammock.

'What if the letters weren't from Abby?' James said. 'Suppose they happened to be from Ted's other daughter, the one he fathered from his relationship with Muriel.'

Katie shielded her eyes from the sun, looking up in surprise at James. She hadn't thought of that possibility.

James went on with his hypothesis. 'You distinctly said Dexter Sims believes Abby would always have a great love for her father yet the letters Ted received in prison stated otherwise. It's a good indication the letters weren't written by Abby after all.'

'This certainly shows things from a different angle.' Katie admitted.

'The other point to make is these letters may contain finger prints which could help identify Ted and Muriel's daughter.'

Within an hour one of the letters Ted Cartwright received whilst in prison had been carefully placed into a clear plastic bag by a police forensic liaison officer and handed over to Fiona for analysis. There was a slim chance a test could be conducted to reveal finger prints.

Carefully holding the letter with tweezers and plastic gloves Fiona held up the letter and explained the test she was about to conduct and why.

'I know the chemical treatment of documents can be damaging and destroy crucial evidence but I don't feel we're left we any choice. I'd really like to examine the letter sent to Cartwright by running a ninhydrin test for proteins. I can't guarantee the test will work but if it does, the results should be impressively clear.'

Fiona mounted the letter in the fume cupboard and sprayed it gently with a fine mist of triketohydrindene hydrate solution commonly known as ninhydrin. She applied two more coats and waited patiently, alternatively passing the document over a steam source and heating with a hair dryer. Bingo! At last dark blue images materialised. She had achieved the result she wanted. Now it was up to Regional Police Forensic technicians to find out exactly whose prints were on the letter.

***

Katie sat chewing on the end of a pen. Something was niggling in the back of her mind but she couldn't put her finger on it. Getting up from her seat she began pacing the room until she almost felt the carpet wearing out underfoot. Stepping outside for some fresh air she grabbed her mobile bringing up the number for Dana Forrester.

'Dana its Katie Sinclair. Sorry to bother you but I have an important question I'd like to ask.'

'Katie how lovely to hear from you,' Dana sounded chirpy, genuinely pleased to hear from her. 'Your visit the other day made me take a good hard look at myself. I've not had a drink for three whole days. Too early for a major breakthrough but it's a start.'

Katie listened to a completely different sounding Dana on the phone. Her speech no longer slurred there was a pleasant lilt to her voice. 'That's wonderful news. I'm really pleased for you.'

Dana gave a small laugh. 'Now what question do you have for me?'

'I hope you don't mind me asking but I'm interested to know why your eldest daughter committed suicide. I imagine she suffered from some form of depression?'

For a few seconds a silence descended, Katie even wondered if Dana had hung up. Then she heard her shaky voice down the line, barely more than a whisper. 'I'm surprised Amy didn't tell you seeing you're such good friends. Ted Cartwright subjected my daughter to months of torture, holding her captive in his grimy basement. When Sasha finally escaped, we all thought it was over, that the past would eventually be forgotten. Five years later she took an overdose. She could not lead a normal life after what he did to her. Cartwright's an animal. That bastard can rot in hell for what he's done.'

After putting down the phone, Katie grabbed coat and bag fumbling for car keys; it was paramount she speak with Dana in person.

Katie reached Dana's small Paignton apartment in High Street half expecting to find her slumped in a chair cuddling up to an empty bottle of scotch. It was a pleasant surprise to find her stone cold sober making a small snack.

'I thought you'd show up,' Dana confessed. 'I know you'll want some questions answered.'

Katie sat down in one of two tatty armchairs balking at the smell of stale cigarettes and damp carpet. The small flat was dark and dingy with only a small window letting in a glimmer of light.

'I'm sorry to drag up the past and such painful memories,' Katie began apologetically. 'I had no idea your daughter was subjected to months of torture by Cartwright.'

Dana gave a wistful smile. 'It's not something I broadcast.'

'It can't have been easy for any of you.'

'No it wasn't. I think it hit Amy hardest of all. She closed up for several months, not even communicating with Bob and myself. She doted on her sister and found little purpose in life when Sasha died. She looked for answers Ms Sinclair but I don't really think she found any. What logic can there be behind such an atrocity?'

Katie fell silent for a few moments; no words felt appropriate after Dana's last statement.

'You moved from Princetown not long after Sasha's death, didn't you?' Katie surmised.

Dana sighed heavily, her hands visibly shaking at having to relive the horror of that particular time in her life. 'Yes, I couldn't bear to be so close to Sasha's grave. I felt as if I'd let my darling girl down, not being there to protect her from such a monstrosity. Amy stayed in the area and every day without fail she would take fresh flowers up to Sasha's grave. She would sit with her sister for hours on end to seek solace. I worried in winter when the snow was knee deep whether Amy could still make that pilgrimage. She told me that if ever a day came and she couldn't make it across the rugged moor she no longer wanted to live.'

Katie felt Dana's pain, the worry that at any time she could lose another daughter. No wonder she sought comfort in alcohol, there wasn't a great deal left to live for.

'She is okay, isn't she?' Dana asked softly. 'You will take care of Amy, won't you?'

Katie nodded. 'I will see she gets all the help she can to move on from the past.'

Dana gave a sigh of relief before taking a firm grip of Katie's hand. She then openly wept whilst Katie sat stroking her dark curls. There were no words to offer; Dana had suffered in silence for so long. It was too late for anyone to show real compassion.

Katie left the Paignton flat wondering what justice was really all about. Dana and her family had suffered in silence, in a world where no one really cared.

***

After three days' intense treatment in hospital Doctor Ashcroft discharged all three of his patients; Jane Anderson, Deirdre Mulligan and Liz Palmer.

To celebrate her road to recovery Deirdre planned to have dinner with some close friends around seven. The chirpy mood she'd woken with soon vanished when her car stubbornly refused to fire. Damn. What was wrong with the bloody thing? It was only serviced a week ago and the mechanic assured it was as good as new.

Cursing, she repeatedly tried the key in the ignition but knew it was no use, continuing in this vein would only flood the engine. There was no choice but to catch the bus. It was nearly seven now and she'd planned to catch up with Liz for a quick drink in the town before they went on to join the others for dinner.

The bus was on time but it still meant Deirdre was running late. Finally arriving at the Frog and Toad she rushed in panting her apologies, 'Car trouble, sorry I'm late.'

'I thought you'd just got that fixed?' Liz questioned, raising her eyebrows.

'Don't go there,' Deirdre replied, still sounding a little out of breath. 'Cost me a fortune too. I'll be having words with that so called 'mechanic' when I get the chance.'

The two women, happily chilling out over a glass of wine, spoke of their recent ordeal and who could have been responsible for such an act.

As they stood up to leave Deirdre noticed she'd forgotten her mobile. She felt lost without it. 'You go on to the restaurant,' she advised. 'I'll catch a cab home, find my lifeline and be back by the time you're all ready to order.'

'I'll text you what's on the menu,' Liz laughed. 'That way you can pre-order.'

Deirdre grabbed her coat and bag, quickly making for the exit. It was dark outside, the moon lost behind thick clouds. Heading for the taxi rank she fumbled in her jacket pocket for the small torch she always carried. No sooner had she seized the tiny object it inadvertently slipped from her hand onto the concrete pavement, Deirdre let out a sigh of frustration. Kneeling down to retrieve it she felt a forceful blow to the side of her head and a damp cloth being placed over her mouth and nose. She tried to struggle and call out but the street was deserted. Her cries were in vain. With her vision failing, Deirdre could only make out distant shapes, until suddenly she passed out as everything drifted into darkness.

***

Deirdre reached a shaky hand to her forehead just above the right eye. The throbbing was intensifying with each passing second. Her fingers connected with warm blood beginning to congeal. Exactly how long had she been unconscious? It could have been minutes, even hours.

Gradually focusing she found her in surroundings all too familiar as she made an attempt to crawl around the dimly lit room hoping to discover a door or other means of escape. She'd been here before but couldn't quite place it.

After several failed attempts to locate an exit she sank down onto the floor groaning from frustration and pain. In sheer desperation, she banged her fists hard against the icy walls crying out in anger; she was a prisoner with little chance of anyone hearing her cries for help.

***

James took the call as he was working in the lab. 'James it's Nick here. I've got the final results back from finger prints lifted off Mark Jennings car. They belong to Jane Anderson, no doubt about it. The technicians were able to get nearly 12 points of reference.'

James gave a low whistle. 'I half expected that.'

'Ah but there's more,' Nick continued. 'I'm coming right over. Please make sure the girls are around. I think we may have solved the Jennings case.'

It was a tantalising time waiting for Nick to arrive. Katie kept fidgeting like a small child.

Nick's news was certainly a quantum leap. He'd taken the results from Fiona's letter testing and they matched perfectly to the prints on Mark's car. It became apparent Jane Anderson was Muriel and Ted's illegitimate daughter.

'All roads lead to Jane as the murderer,' Nick concluded. 'She certainly had the motive. Mick Rose agrees.'

'Barney Rubble also mentioned blood found at the crime scene indicated different DNA to that of Mark and Stella,' Katie piped up. 'It would certainly appear Jane is the one we've been looking for.'

Within the hour police were alerted to arrest Jane on suspicion of murder. She was handcuffed and taken to Exeter Police station.

'Jane Anderson, you are under arrest for the murder of your mother Muriel Jennings. You do not have to say anything but what you do say, may be used as evidence in a court of law.'

Jane refused the offer of a lawyer as she sat on a hard wooden seat with a defiant look on her face, arms folded. The initial statement recorded by the police sergeant jarred in her consciousness as she listened to the accusation of murder.

'You're wrong,' she snapped, puffing on the cigarette she'd been allowed to have. 'I didn't kill Muriel Jennings.'

'Do you admit to the fact Muriel Jennings is your biological mother?' James asked, his eyes keenly locked on Jane's.

Jane smiled sardonically. 'Well worked out. I wondered how long it would take your forensic team to come to that conclusion. Mind you, it took long enough. I was right under your noses and you didn't spot that one, did you? Surely there must be some resemblance.'

James didn't reply. He was reluctant to point out that with so much cosmetic work Jane probably didn't have any family resemblance left. It was also probable she looked more like her father Ted Cartwright, whom James had never met.

'Let's start from the beginning,' DCI Rose interjected. 'Why did you hate your mother?'

'Easy, she prevented me from having part of what is rightfully mine; Jennings Clay. I even tried blackmailing the bitch but that didn't work. She gave me money, which at first I accepted but she wouldn't change the will to include me as a beneficiary to the business. I didn't want her small handouts; I wanted what is rightfully mine.'

'So that's why you killed her?'

'I didn't kill her. I admit to poisoning her but that didn't do much good. The old bat was as tough as nails.'

'Do you also admit to poisoning some of the book club members?'

'Yes, it was the easiest way to get to Muriel. She loved coffee.'

'What about the threats on the club members. Were you behind those?'

'Yep, that was me,' Jane replied triumphantly. 'I did it to create confusion and deflect the blame.'

'We discovered Muriel was paying for your daughter's school fees,' James broke in. 'Was that part of your blackmailing scheme?'

Jane laughed. 'Muriel doted on Beckie. She lavished her with expensive gifts, quite natural for a grandmother.'

James tried a new approach to his questioning. 'Your blood was found at the crime scene. How can you deny that?'

'I'm sure it was at the scene but I didn't kill my mother. I arrived at the house to try and do the bitch in but someone beat me to it. If I knew who that person was I'd give them a medal.'

'So how do you explain your blood in the house?' James continued, beginning to feel hot under the collar from Jane's casual responses.

'No problem in explaining that,' Jane smirked. 'I cut myself on that damn table in the hall housing the telephone. If your forensic people do further analysis, they'll discover the amount of blood they found is consistent with a small cut to the finger. Look, I've still got a slight abrasion; it was a fairly deep cut.' Jane held out her right hand and sure enough she appeared to be telling the truth. 'Now, if we're done here I'd like to go home. Sorry to have wasted your precious time but I am not my mother's killer, although God knows I wish I were.'

***

'So you honestly don't reckon Jane killed Muriel Jennings?' Katie quizzed, as her brother returned to the office, completely washed out.

'No I don't,' he sighed. 'It's all circumstantial. I think she might have eventually committed the crime given half a chance but someone beat her to it, now we need to find out who that person was.'

'Has she been charged with the poisonings and tampering with the brakes on Mark's car?'

'For the poisoning yes, however, Mark is not pressing charges, he wants as little publicity as possible on this one.'

A sharp knock at the emergency side exit door stopped their conversation in its tracks. It was getting late. Not expecting any visitors Katie cancelled the alarm and opened the door with caution.

'Ms Sinclair it's Liz Palmer. May I come in, it's urgent.

Katie stood back to allow Liz access.

'I'm worried about Deirdre,' she blurted out. 'She was meant to join a group of us for dinner tonight but didn't show up. She isn't answering her home or mobile numbers. That's not like Deirdre, it's totally out of character.'

The siblings detected real concern in Liz's tone. Liz caught hold of Katie's arm. 'I'm not sure if you're aware Ms. Sinclair but Deirdre is an insulin dependent diabetic. She requires insulin three to four times a day and without this she's in very serious trouble.'

Katie wanted to impress on Liz that she was a forensic psychologist not a detective, but decided against it. Liz was visibly distraught.

After sitting Liz down with a strong cup of tea and plenty of sugar James advised that unfortunately this wasn't really a situation where they could assist; Liz would need to report her concerns to the police. It was not a matter for Moorland Forensics.

After Liz had been ushered out the door Katie and James poured themselves a nightcap and were once more deep in conversation when the phone rang.

'This is turning into some evening,' Katie grumbled, picking up the receiver and barking a 'hello.'

'Ms Sinclair. It's Professor Bradbury,' an element of urgency in his voice, which Katie found quite disturbing. 'I really need to speak with you. Where can we meet?'

'I can come to your office if you like?' she suggested, looking up at the office railway clock showing a few minutes to witching hour.

'Are you able to get here within the hour?' he sounded quite breathless as if something was troubling him. 'I have something really important I need to relay to you and your brother.'

'Yes, we should be able to make it,' Katie replied, pulling a face wondering what the emergency was.

Within an hour, Katie and James had arrived at the psychiatric hospital. They found the main door unlocked assuming it had been left open for their benefit. Passing through a deserted reception area they headed straight for Bradbury's office. The door was slightly ajar, sending a narrow shaft of yellow light into the darkened corridor.

Katie went to speak as James pulled her back; Doctor Bradbury sat slumped in a chair one hand clenched tightly around the telephone hand piece.

James moved forward reaching out to feel for a pulse but quickly shook his head confirming what they already suspected. He was still warm to touch, his death only minutes before.

James reached for his mobile to make the necessary calls.

'I want this place searched thoroughly until we find exactly what we are looking for,' James instructed Nick and his team when they arrived some fifty minutes later clad in their forensic gear. 'It is highly improbable Professor Bradbury died of natural causes.'

The room had suddenly gone cold. Katie shivered as she took in the surreal environment. She was only speaking with the Professor a short while ago. It felt surreal that his life had ended so swiftly.

Nick briefed his team and ordered photos to be taken before beginning the search. It didn't take too long to isolate the cause of Professor Bradbury's death; a syringe and five empty glass injection phials stuffed in a wastepaper basket. He delivered his verdict promising a full autopsy and report within the week. 'It appears the Professor was given a lethal injection of Immobilon, a powerful equine anaesthetic in conjunction with phenobarbital, a massive overdose it looks like. God, enough to knock over a herd of elephants. The good news for him is he went to sleep pretty quickly, no pain.'

Stopping for a few moments to draw breath Nick added, 'The professor obviously knew he was in danger, but I very much doubt he realised to what extent. He must have thought he could have that meeting with you, not knowing his life would end so abruptly.'

'It doesn't bear thinking about,' Katie remarked. 'Whoever did this, carried out a cold calculated murder and I'm almost certain the Professor is not their first victim and possibly not the last.'

As Nick and his team continued with their work James put in a call to Doctor Rogers. After explaining what had just taken place Rogers assured him he would come straight over.

'Terrible business,' Allan Rogers said, shaking his head. 'Who would do such a thing?'

'That's what we intend to find out,' James replied, taking a seat over by the window and waving for Doctor Rogers to do the same. 'I'd like to start by asking you about Abigail Cartwright. I believe Abby was still a patient of Professor Bradbury's?'

'Yes, that's correct. I don't have much information to hand. From what I was told he'd continued treating her over the years as she was responding well to treatment. Quite remarkable after all she's been through.'

'Did Professor Bradbury ever feel threatened by Abigail?' James asked. 'I need you to think carefully and give me honest answers.'

'No not by Abigail but...'

He hesitated, wavering, unsure he should divulge the next bit of information.

James looked at him keenly. 'If you know anything, Doctor Rogers, which can be of help to us, I urge you to say.'

Doctor Rogers reached forward to grab a thick manila file from the top of an Edwardian chest of drawers. He passed it across to James without saying a word.

James opened the file and began reading. He kept reading for about twenty minutes before looking at the Doctor who was watching him with interest.

'This woman is so complex,' James remarked, putting down the file on the desk. 'At first she appears quite normal but then as you read on you begin to question her sanity.'

'Yes, indeed. I stumbled across this file when I was looking for some lost petty cash receipts. It was tucked behind one of the old filing cabinets.'

'Did you discuss this woman with Professor Bradbury?'

'I tried to but he just shrugged and refused to tell me anything. However, I came to my own conclusion that she was also a patient of his, and in my opinion, a very dangerous one.'

Katie almost ready to burst grabbed the file and avidly scanned the contents. She looked up in disbelief. 'Wow this is a turn up for the books.'

James turned back to Doctor Rogers. 'I need to ask you something and I expect a professional answer. In your expert opinion is this woman capable of murder?'

'Oh yes, without a doubt I would say yes, she *is* capable of murder.'

***

'James it's Matt, I've finally cracked the codes of White Rose. You'll be interested to know I have identified Ted's daughter.'

James gathered his siblings together and put Matt on speaker phone. After a brief silence, Matt delivered the crucial information they'd been waiting to hear. 'Abigail Cartwright changed her name to Deirdre Mulligan.'

***

'So Liz was right to be concerned about Deirdre,' Katie voiced to her siblings. 'We now need to discover what's happened to her.'

287

'That won't be easy,' Fiona protested. 'Devon's a large county, she could be anywhere. In fact, she may be in a neighbouring county by now.'

'Not necessarily,' Katie replied. 'If Deirdre *is* in trouble I believe the one place we're likely to find her is at Heather Lea.'

James clapped his sister on the back. 'Makes sense, let's go.'

The three sat in silence, James piloting the Land Rover at a maniacal rate of knots across the moor to the deserted property. There had been so much taking place over the last few days they felt drained and exhausted. If they did find Deirdre, there was no guarantee she would still be alive.

The house loomed up ahead dark and sinister in the pale moonlight. Not an inviting proposition.

James switched off the car head lights parking behind some large oak trees a hundred metres from the front of the house.

'Stay here,' Katie instructed James and Fiona as they approached the front of the old property. 'I think it would be best if I go in alone.'

'I don't think so,' James protested, stepping forward and pulling his sister back, 'you'd be crazy to go in there by yourself.'

Katie gently shook off her brother's protective arm. 'If I'm not out in fifteen minutes come and find me,' she informed him. 'I suggest you two keep out of sight. She'll be more receptive if she thinks I'm by myself.'

James grimaced but nodded in agreement as he and Fiona made themselves invisible behind a large holly bush.

Katie, feeling a certain amount of trepidation moved towards the front door and knocked loudly. A few minutes later the door opened and Jessica Cartwright stood staring blankly back at her.

'What are you doing here?' she enquired softly.

'Just a social call,' Katie replied trying to steady her nerves. 'I was surprised to hear you were at Heather Lea Jessica, I thought you lived in Bristol.'

'No. That's where I work,' Jessica explained. 'I clean for old Mrs. Potter remember but I live here at Heather Lea with my daughter Abigail.'

'You mean Deirdre?'

Jessica looked annoyed. 'Her name is Abigail. Silly name Deirdre, that's not the name Ted and I gave her. Why she needed to change her name I don't know.'

'Can I see Abigail?' Katie pressed.

'No, that's not possible, she's sleeping and I don't want to wake her. Why don't you come in and I'll make us some tea? I've set myself up nicely in the old scullery.'

Katie ceased the opportunity to gain access into the house following Jessica into the vast Edwardian kitchen.

'Tea with milk and sugar?'

Katie nodded, seating herself at the large oak table whilst Jessica busied herself around the kettle.

'You know it really was a shame Professor Bradbury had to die,' Jessica said, heaping tea leaves into a pot before filling it with boiling water.

Jessica gave a shallow laugh. 'He was a nice man but in the end he discovered my secret. Do you know my secret Ms Sinclair?'

Katie shook her head. 'No, are you going to tell me?'

'I can't do that,' Jessica scoffed. 'You have to guess like he did, but before you do we'll have some tea.'

Katie shifted uncomfortably in her seat watching as Jessica brought two mugs of tea over to the table.

'Do you make a habit of coming in to other people's houses when they're not at home?' Jessica asked, her eyes boring directly into Katie's bright blue ones. She looked angry.

'I err…' Katie stammered trying to find a suitable answer.

'Come now, I am aware of what's going on,' Jessica said, sipping from her mug. 'That pesky real estate agent thinks it's clever to try and sell this house from under me. I won't have anyone selling the house I grew up in. Now try and guess my secret.'

Before Katie could open her mouth to speak a loud knock sounded at the door. Katie felt relieved knowing it was James and Fiona coming to her rescue.

Jessica jumped violently. 'Friends of yours I presume?'

Katie nodded as Jessica stood up to answer the door. 'Do come in,' she beamed. 'I'm afraid Ted's out in the orchard but he shouldn't be long.'

Katie tried not to look shocked realising Jessica was jumping from present to past all in a matter of seconds. A bizarre fact clearly documented in the file produced by Doctor Rogers. One minute Jessica would appear quite normal, the next she was reliving the past, at times not being able to differentiate between the two.

'We're happy to wait,' James instructed Jessica, taking a seat next to Katie at the table. 'Nice place you've got here Mrs. Cartwright.'

'Yes, but it's hard to keep clean with a teenager around.' Jessica smiled, playing with a strand of her long blonde hair. 'My daughter loves to leave a trail of destruction wherever she goes.'

'Can we meet your daughter?' Katie asked.

Jessica rubbed a hand over tired eyes. 'Can I get you some tea?' she enquired of James and Fiona. They both shook their heads.

'We were hoping to meet your daughter,' Fiona said, speaking for the first time.

'That's not possible she's sleeping,' Jessica replied. 'Go on Katie guess my secret.' She stood up and danced around the room in a jovial fashion. 'The wicked witch is dead. Did you not guess?'

'Who's dead?' James enquired. When Jessica deliberately turned her back on James he retrieved his mobile phone from an inside coat pocket sending a quick text message. It was obvious Jessica Cartwright was totally insane and dangerous.

'Can we see Abigail?' Katie persisted. 'We just want to know she's okay.'

'She's sleeping,' Jessica replied. 'At least I hope she's sleeping and not dead.'

Katie sprung up from the table in alarm. 'Please Jessica, take us to see Abby.'

'All in good time, you know I wouldn't deliberately harm my daughter, don't you?'

Katie slowly nodded, trying to remain calm although inside her stomach was in knots.

Jessica moved slowly towards the door. 'Come. Let's go and see Abigail. She's down in the basement. All bad people go there.'

Katie followed Jessica down the cellar steps. James and Fiona weren't far behind.

As expected it was dark and cold under the house. A small bedside lamp stood on the floor in the far corner enabling Katie to make out a dark figure slumped along the back wall. Katie recognised Deirdre at once.

'She needs medical assistance Jessica,' Katie informed her briskly, 'your daughter is very sick.'

'My god, I must get Ted. He'll know what to do.' Jessica uttered these words but remained standing at the bottom of the steps.

Fiona and James engaged a swift glance before rushing towards the figure lying on the ground. Her breathing was shallow, her skin almost transparent.

Jessica didn't seem to notice they were attending to her daughter. She seemed to drift off into another place and time.

Fiona and James somehow managed to drag Deirdre up the cellar steps and outside into the cool night. An ambulance had been called and was waiting in the driveway. The paramedics immediately gave Deirdre the medical attention she required.

Katie looked at Jessica, trying to work out what was running through her mind. As if sensing this happening Jessica jolted back to the present not noticing her daughter had suddenly vanished.

'Why did you kill Muriel Jennings?' Katie asked softly.

Jessica smiled triumphantly. 'You guessed my secret. I am very proud of you Ms Sinclair.'

Katie began to feel sick. She longed for James to return to the cellar and get her out of the godforsaken place. She felt uncomfortable standing only inches from a killer with little means of escape.

'I hated doing it,' Jessica confessed, seeming to choose her words carefully, 'but I couldn't bear the fact Muriel and Ted had a daughter together, it was soul destroying.'

'How *did* you find out?' Katie asked, watching Jessica carefully, afraid she might suddenly lash out.

'One evening I was cleaning the surgery for Doctor Ashcroft and happened to stumble across medical records bound together with old ribbon. Curiosity getting the better of me I read the file from cover to cover. Oh was I angry. I wanted to kill her there and then but how could I? These things need careful planning.'

'So how did you plan such a horrible crime?'

Jessica let out a sardonic laugh. 'They say practise makes perfect and Muriel was putty in my hands. I was her cleaning lady for years. I took my time to commit the crime. I quite liked her once I got to know her, a real shame she had to die, but such is life.'

Katie felt her cheeks burning up, her mind confused by what she was hearing. Jessica appeared to be a cold calculating killer showing no remorse for the crime she'd committed.

Jessica continued with her story, seeming proud to relay every little detail. 'I gave Ted everything I could or at least I thought I did. The problem was Ted always wanted a son. It was unfortunate Muriel and I were only able to bear him daughters. This made me begin to hate all women. All women deserve to be punished for their sins.'

Katie shivered from fear more than cold, trying to understand exactly what Jessica was saying.

'I wept tears of joy when I read Lillian Webster's novel *The Sinner's Daughter,*' Jessica smirked. 'How wonderful she should put down on paper what I already knew. The story of five women killed on Dartmoor, in this very house, the exact place where we stand now.'

Katie's throat was dry. What was Jessica trying to tell her? Was she confessing to the murders of those five innocent women all those years ago? Katie's mind told her to run but her feet were lead weighs above the hard concrete floor. From the corner of her eye she saw James creeping down the stone steps closely followed by Mick Rose and three uniformed police officers. Relieved, she wanted to let out a sigh but remained focused on Jessica Cartwright and the story unfolding.

'Poor Ted. He was such a gentle man. He wouldn't hurt a fly, but I guess you know that already.'

The police officers were now within arm's reach of Jessica, yet she remained oblivious to the fact.

'So many people had to suffer for their sins Ms Sinclair. Muriel and Ted for their sordid affair and the others for...' Jessica stopped for a moment before continuing, 'you know, I don't really know why they had to die. I guess they were just unlucky. One important aspect you need to remember is Abigail played a major part in all of this. After all, she was *The Sinner's Daughter.'*

CONCLUSION

Katie made her way towards the Exeter Crown and County Court House fighting her way through the crowds. TV cameras and journalists swarmed everywhere like bees around a large pot of honey.

One journalist called out as Katie attempted to make progress up the court house steps, shoving a microphone in her face.

'Ms. Sinclair, can you confirm that Jessica Cartwright is insane?'

Katie spoke clearly into the microphone. 'I'll be making a recommendation today whether the defendant is competent to proceed to trial.'

'Do you feel sorry for Jessica knowing what she has been through?'

'It's not my job to be emphatic,' Katie answered softly. She deliberately kept walking edging nearer to the court house entrance in a bid to escape the machine gun-like questions.

'Will you be swayed by her vulnerability? Being married to Ted Cartwright must have been a living hell.'

Katie stopped in her tracks fixing both eyes directly on the television cameras. 'I can assure you my primary focus is on accuracy; my client's viewpoint is secondary.'

'What did you base your evidence on?' Katie bit down hard on her lower lip as she realised this latest question had been fired by Tom Markham.

Finding an inner strength and new confidence she took a deep breath before replying. 'From gathering factual information across multiple sources. Now if that's all I'd like to end this press conference. Thank you.'

Finally, she forced her way into the court complex breathing a sigh of relief already surmising tomorrow's headline.

***

Deirdre looked nervous as she was about to give her statement to the media. It was well rehearsed but it didn't stop her feeling numb; her eyes stared beseechingly beyond the media throng. There was to be one question, which would allow for one answer.

'Deirdre, what statement do you want to give in relation to your mother being found guilty of murder?'

Almost sick with nerves her mouth opened, willing the words not to become one mass of despair.

'Within us all is the capability of murder. For the majority of us it lies dormant yet for others it reaches the surface and explodes like a firecracker. Not everyone can comprehend how it would be to become that Sinner, perhaps even less of us The Sinner's Daughter.'